Max brush

"You're pretty remarkable. Most people would have crumbled under the pressure. But you keep working angles. Determined to get us to the finish line." Their lips were inches apart.

Desire blossomed within her. She could no longer deny that this man made her feel things she'd never felt before. Her life was on the line, and regardless of how much attention to detail she'd put into the plan, it was still fifty-fifty that she'd make it out of this unscathed. Why not enjoy this thing between them?

Max leaned in even closer. When his lips touched hers, she closed her eyes and sighed. But within seconds, they both froze.

"That noise. That's the elevator," Max whispered.

Jordan glanced at the digital clock on the copier. "It's four in the morning," she whispered. "Who could be coming here at this hour?"

Max turned down the corridor, Jordan fast on his heels. She came to an abrupt stop behind him and realized they were at his office. He turned the knob and threw open the door.

Max said, *"What the hell?"*

Dear Reader,

I've been married for many years and have learned a few things about relationships. Chief among them is that love cannot exist without trust. That's the basis for this love story.

Hardworking, fun-loving cybersecurity expert Max Ramirez likes his life just as it is. He plans to retire early and live on an island sipping ice-cold drinks. But his plans change when his world collides with genius hacker Jordan Logan.

Initially at odds, they must find a way to work together and take down the company for which they both worked before a global transportation collapse is unleashed. It's not an easy task when she trusts no one and he doesn't trust her.

There are many twists, a few surprises and a heavy dose of suspense. But most of all, this is a story about overcoming one's past, learning to trust and finding true love.

So, welcome back to Hollow Lake! The entire Ramirez family is here, including Max's brothers, Rafe and Zack, the Judge, and Tía Ellie. I'll let you in on a little secret: Tía Ellie is modeled after my kindhearted, loving real-life Tía Ellie.

These characters are dear to my heart, and I hope you enjoy reading about their lives as much as I enjoyed writing them.

I love connecting with readers. Find me at marialokken.com.

Happy reading!

Maria

OPERATION BLACKOUT

MARIA LOKKEN

ROMANTIC SUSPENSE

Harlequin®
ROMANTIC SUSPENSE™

ISBN-13: 978-1-335-47166-6

Operation Blackout

Harlequin Enterprises ULC
22 Adelaide St. West, 41st Floor
Toronto, Ontario M5H 4E3, Canada
www.Harlequin.com

Printed in Lithuania

MIX
Paper | Supporting
responsible forestry
FSC® C021394

A cozy reading chair and a romance novel are all
Maria Lokken needs to have the perfect afternoon.
The perfect evenings are spent with her husband—
her real-life romance hero. Both her husband and
her large family are inspirations for many of her
stories. Besides being an avid reader, she loves
popcorn, movies and walking around museums.
You can find her at marialokken.com or on Instagram,
@maria_writer_lokken.

Books by Maria Lokken

Harlequin Romantic Suspense

Breaking the Code
Operation Blackout

Visit the Author Profile page at Harlequin.com.

To Carly M. Duncan, a wonderful writer and my
critique partner, for her continued support and
always giving me great notes and advice.

To my husband, who checks my grammar
and always has interesting and often better
word choices and astute comments,
and for reading too many drafts to admit to.

To Rissy, the penultimate romance reader,
who always lets me know if I'm making sense.

And to Emma Cole and my editor, Allison Lyons,
for digging me out of the slush pile and
making my dream of becoming a Harlequin author
come true. For all you writers out there
working toward publication—don't ever give up.
Dreams do come true. Keep writing.

Chapter 1

Jordan Logan sat back and smiled. After working many nights until the sun rose, she'd finally hacked into Sintinex Corporation's mainframe computer. This had been her toughest assignment yet, requiring all of her expertise. But that was why they'd hired her—she had a reputation for being the best.

At last, she could take a breath. The pressure to hack into the system had been intense. She wasn't sure why they'd pushed for such a tight deadline, but at this point, it no longer mattered. In a few hours, her bank account would be that much richer.

Jordan arched her back and stretched her long, toned arms over her head. She scanned the room and frowned at the dozens of boxes stacked against the foot of her unmade bed. "Well, Buck. Looks like I have no more excuses. I'm going to have to unpack all this stuff and put it away."

Her black Lab sat up, tilted his head, and let out one short bark.

She smiled. "You know something, you're right. Before we unpack, let's take a nice long walk, get some fresh air, and get to know our new neighborhood." She reached down and rubbed Buck's head. "Maybe this will be the place. What do you think, boy? Will Brooklyn be it?"

Jordan hoped she might make New York her home. This city was big enough that she could get lost among the millions. Over the years, whenever she'd thought she might be able to settle in one place, there was always some nosy neighbor who wanted to get to know her. Have a coffee, join them for a yoga class, or come to dinner to be set up with one of their friends. She'd declined all invitations. It wasn't that she had anything to hide. She simply wasn't a big fan of people. Ultimately, she knew they would only disappoint her—like the mother who abandoned her. So she kept moving. Besides, with a laptop and Wi-Fi, she could work from anywhere, live where she wanted, and keep to herself. She hoped no one would notice her in a city like New York.

"Okay, Buck, give me a minute. I need to copy this ridiculously brilliant code I've created and then send it off to Sintinex." Jordan pulled up the company's mail program and began to type.

Hi, Sam,
Mission accomplished. Here's the code. Taking a break. Call me if you have any questions.

After hitting send, she dug inside her desk drawer for a flash drive, copied the code onto it, and dropped the drive into her oversize shoulder bag.

Jordan knelt and scratched Buck behind the ear. "You're such a good boy," she cooed. He licked her face, and she wiped her cheek with the back of her hand. "No need to get sloppy." She rubbed his head one more time. "Let me get a few things, and then we're off."

Grabbing her bag, she dropped in a bottle of water, her

wallet, and the latest paperback she'd been dying to read. "I think we've got everything we need." Buck's tail thumped on the hardwood floor in anticipation. "Oh, shoot. Hold on, let me find my cap."

Her gaze scanned the bedroom. "Now, where did I pack it?" She stepped into the living room and searched a few boxes on the coffee table. Buck trotted toward the front hall closet and let out two quick barks. Jordan put her hands on her hips. "You trying to tell me something?" Buck barked again. "Okay, I'll check the closet, but only 'cause you asked nicely."

On the top shelf, above the coat rack, sat several caps. "Buck, you have such a good memory," she murmured. "I forgot I unpacked these." She reached for her favorite navy blue baseball cap and jammed it on her head. "Well, I think we're ready."

A soft whooshing sound came from the bedroom, signaling an incoming email. She continued moving toward the front door but stopped mid-step, turned, and marched back into the bedroom. She couldn't help herself. Jordan was compulsive about checking email. After any job, it took days before she could relax and not continually check her phone. Leaning over her computer, she clicked the envelope icon and quickly read the message.

"For real?" she said to the screen.

The request was odd, and she wondered why Archer Kelly, Sintinex's CEO, would ask her to add a line of code to the program she'd created. Until now, they'd never even communicated. All work orders had come from his chief technology officer, Sam Morris—and she'd emailed him the code a few minutes ago.

Sintinex had hired her to hack into their system. The

whole point was to test the strength of their firewall, and she'd proven the firewall wasn't all that. There was no reason to mess around with her code. What they needed was to fix their computer security. But she was not the CEO, and she wasn't the one making dumb decisions.

Jordan sat and crossed her arms over her chest. "Well, guess what, Mr. Archer Kelly, I've been at Sintinex's beck and call for four straight weeks. Me and Buck are taking some well-deserved time off." She huffed out a breath and turned to Buck. "Isn't that right? He got what he paid for. He can wait another day for any additions. And it's gonna cost him." She dug the flash drive out of her bag, copied the new snippet of code, and powered off her computer.

The chime of an incoming text had her reaching into her jacket pocket. "What now?" She checked her phone and found a message from Sam Morris.

Don't email new combined code. Meet tomorrow. Breakfast. 8am. Olson's 55th and Lex. Then I'm off to DC.

Jordan sighed heavily. "Whatever." With her thumbs, she typed:

C u there.

This job had been all-consuming, and now it was getting silly. First, the CEO emailed her, and then the CTO texted her. Jordan wanted nothing to do with their office politics.

Once again, her phone pinged, and Jordan huffed in annoyance. When she checked the screen, it was an alert from her news app. Apparently, the L train was out of service.

Some transformer was down or something. She shook her head and pocketed her phone.

"Okay, Buck, enough of this craziness. Let's go." She hooked his leash onto his collar, locked her door, and stepped out of her brownstone apartment building into the sunshine of a glorious May afternoon.

They walked several blocks before entering the south side of Prospect Park near the lake. Despite the beautiful spring day, there was a heaviness in her step. This was the hardest part of completing a job. The free time. Because there was nothing to consume her mind. No puzzle to figure out. No code to create. Only her dim thoughts. Unhappy childhood memories always lurked in the background, threatening to consume her if she didn't keep busy.

For that reason, the animal shelter had been Jordan's first stop when she'd arrived in the city. She didn't much like people or trust them, but animals were different. She'd never been allowed to have a pet, but some of her favorite books had beloved dogs as characters, and she wanted to feel the closeness described in those stories. The right dog would keep her company the way people never could.

Buck had been deserted by his owner and left to roam the streets. The moment she spotted him at the shelter, his nose pressed against the cage, she sensed they were kindred spirits. And she'd been right. With Buck, she'd been able to drop her defenses. They'd instantly become attached as if they'd been together for years.

"Okay, boy. Let's get some exercise." They took off at a quick pace and walked inside the park for almost an hour before Jordan's mind began to clear, and Buck had the exercise he'd needed for the past week.

The constant pressure she put on herself whenever she

had a new client began to float away like the white puffy clouds dotting the sky. For the first time in days, the tightness in her chest began to ease, and she took a long, deep breath. Buck barked at a man zipping by on an electric scooter, and she had to hold him back as he tugged on his leash. A young girl across the lake laughed as she launched a miniature sailboat into the water. "This seems like a perfect spot. That bench over there has my name on it. Let's park it." Buck trotted toward the nearby tree and settled in the shade under its branches.

Jordan sat, got comfortable, and flipped open the latest Nora Roberts romantic suspense. For the first time in forever, she happily lost herself between the pages of a book. It wasn't until her stomach grumbled that she looked up. She had no idea how much time had passed, but the sun was lower in the sky, and the air seemed cooler. Buck, she noticed, hadn't moved and was gently snoring.

"Okay, buddy." She knelt next to him and petted his back. He opened one eye. "You had a nice nap, didn't you? You ready to eat? Because I'm starving." Buck licked her face. "Hey there, I'm not on the menu. We'll walk over to Joe's Joint and get some burgers to go. If you're lucky, we may even watch a movie."

It took some time for them to wind their way out of the park and walk the six blocks back to their neighborhood. On the corner was the burger restaurant she had frequently called for delivery since she'd moved into her apartment. The tables set up outside were already filling with people out for an early dinner.

Jordan tied Buck's leash to the bike rack at the corner. "I'll be right back. I'm going to pick us up something delicious." She rubbed Buck's head and entered the restaurant.

Jordan gave her to-go order to a server with spiked purple hair and a dozen earrings in her left lobe. Handing over her credit card, she leaned on the host station and turned to look out the window and check on Buck.

"Excuse me," the spike-haired girl said. "Your card isn't going through."

It took Jordan a few seconds to understand what she was saying. She shook her head. "Not possible. Try it again," she said unapologetically.

Jordan watched as the server swiped her card through the card reader again and waited for the machine to do its thing.

Spiked-hair's eyebrows narrowed. "Sorry. It's not going through."

"Oh, for goodness sake," Jordan huffed. "Here, try this." She handed over her debit card.

The server swiped the card and turned the machine toward Jordan to enter her PIN number. Jordan's eyes widened when the word *DECLINED* flashed on the screen. This wasn't possible. She was nowhere near her credit limit, which was high, and she had plenty of money in the bank. "Listen, I don't have time for this." Her tone was sharp. "There must be something wrong with your machine." She held out her hand. "Give me back my cards. I'll pay in cash." As a matter of habit, Jordan kept a sizable amount of money in her purse at all times. At an early age, she'd learned to be nimble and resourceful, and that didn't happen without cash.

The restaurant was filling up, and her order took longer than expected. When the hostess finally handed her a brown paper bag with her food, Jordan barely said thanks and rushed out. She was anxious to get home, call the bank and credit card company, and sort out the problem.

She climbed the front steps of her brownstone, shifted the bag of food to one arm, dug out her keys, and went inside. Her first-floor apartment was the second door on the left. She managed to hold on to her food and Buck's leash while putting her key in the door. As she crossed the threshold, Jordan dropped the leash and stared in disbelief. *What the—*

She stepped back and checked the apartment number on the door. This was her place. But how could it be? The boxes were gone, the furniture was gone, everything was gone. Her entire apartment was empty. With her mouth open, she walked from room to room. The only thing left was a white venetian blind hanging askew in the bedroom.

Buck's half whine, half bark, got her attention. "Hey, boy, where are you?" Jordan called out, but he didn't come. Instead, his barking became more insistent. She found him in the bathroom, growling at the closed shower curtain. "Hey, buddy, come here." She patted her thighs several times, but Buck wouldn't move. "What are you barking at?" The combination of nerves and the general creep factor of her empty apartment freaked her out. "You come out of there right this minute!" Jordan yelled, and that was when she noticed several dark-colored footprints around the tub. "What's that?" she said under her breath. Cautiously, she inched her way into the room. "Man, I should not be doing this." She squeezed her eyes shut, took a deep breath, and yanked back the shower curtain. When she opened her eyes, her immediate confusion turned to revulsion. Buck went wild, barking and circling her. Blood dripped from the shower wall, and a body lay face down in the tub with half its head blown away. She bolted from the room into the kitchen and vomited into the sink. Wiping her mouth with the back of her hand, she knew she had to call the police. Shaking, she pulled out her phone from her jacket. Before she could place the call, her news alert app pinged with an image on the screen.

Breaking News: Wanted for stealing classified government documents.

She didn't have the mental bandwidth for this. Jordan was about to click off the alert and dial 911 when an image of a woman's face filled her screen. She shook her head and blinked. *Wait. Is that me?* Could she be looking at a photo of herself? It didn't make sense. None of this made any sense.

While Buck howled and frantically jumped around the apartment, Jordan was paralyzed, unsure what to do. Her furniture was gone. A dead man was in her tub. And if the alert on her phone could be trusted, she was wanted for stealing government documents. The sound of sirens coming down the block freed her from her paralysis. Without thinking, she grabbed hold of the leash. "Buck. Come on. We gotta get out of here."

Chapter 2

Max Ramirez sat at his desk at RMZ Digital, the cyberse-curity company he owned with his two brothers. He hardly noticed the vibrant hues of orange and purple spreading across the sky as twilight descended on Hollow Lake's Main Street. Instead, his attention was laser-focused on the job he and his team were working on for the Sintinex Corporation.

"Yo! Max. What are you doing here this late? This is five nights in a row." Zack, the youngest of the Ramirez brothers, leaned against the door jamb. "I thought you had a date with Caroline."

"Not Caroline." Max gave a sideways glance. "Beth. And I canceled."

Zack shook his head and let out a low whistle. He entered the spacious office, threw his backpack on a chair, and sat facing his brother.

Max raised an eyebrow. "Yeah, sure. Come right in. Make yourself comfortable. I'm not busy."

"*Cálmate*, bro. I'm only going to stay long enough to annoy you. What do you mean you canceled on Beth?" He snapped his fingers. "Oh, silly me. This would have been the third date. Am I right?"

Reluctantly, Max nodded.

"Bro, you are too much. You never let a woman get close. What is up with that? Were you adopted?"

"It's not what I want right now. We have the business and a short window of time to make us a global force in cybersecurity. I need to stay locked in on the target. And that doesn't include a relationship." Max loved his brothers, but they were always in each other's business. And where his love life was concerned, he didn't need anyone's opinion.

As a former quantitative analyst on Wall Street, Max was accustomed to analyzing a situation from every angle. And he'd done a deep dive on the viability of long-term relationships—statistically, they rarely lasted. "Being with someone for the long haul takes too much work. Maybe one day, when I have enough to retire with no worries, I'll think about settling down." Max gave Zack a pointed look. "Although, I cannot even imagine being with one woman forever. You know how long forever is?"

"I got a general sense."

Max shrugged. "Well, there you go. Not now. Maybe not even ever."

"You know what Rafe says?"

"No, I don't." Max rubbed his hand over his eyes, wondering how they even got on this topic. "Is there a dollar amount I can give you that will stop you from telling me what our brother thinks about *my* love life?"

Zack put his feet up on Max's desk. "You got it wrong. It's not about forever. Rafe says once you find the one, you'll be helpless to do anything but want to be with that person for the rest of your life. And I agree with him."

"Really?" Max held out both hands, palms up, moving them up and down like a scale. "Gee. Rest of your life *or* forever. Seems about the same. So. No. Thanks. And get your feet off my desk."

Max knew his brothers only wanted what was best for him. And while he was genuinely happy that Rafe had finally been reunited with the love of his life and that Zack seemed to be in a serious relationship, it wasn't what he wanted. Max wasn't a romantic in any way. He would chart his own course in his own time. For now, he was all about the business.

"Listen, there's no sense in being alone this evening," Zack said. "I'm on my way over to Pop's house for dinner. Why don't you join?"

"Where's Taylor tonight?"

"She's on an assignment for the next couple of weeks. I'm on my own." Zack leaned forward. "Come with me to Pop's. We'll have fun."

"I love you and Pop, but that's a hard pass. I'd rather spend the night watching telenovelas than listen to the two of you try and orchestrate my love life." While Spanish soap operas were Zack's guilty pleasure, Max wasn't into them. "Raincheck? Anyway, I'm in the middle of a second proposal to Sintinex. Looks like the hacker they hired can't get through our Impenetrable Wall program. It's still holding up. And that's a good thing. By the end of the week, we should be able to close the deal and sell our program to all their subsidiaries. Then I'm taking the weekend off and heading to my apartment in the city for some fun."

Zack grinned. "*Chévere*, bro. Nice go—"

Max raised his hand. "Hold up. Let me get this." He pressed the speaker icon on his desk phone. "Max Ramirez."

"Mr. Ramirez." The tone was cold and authoritative. "This is Archer Kelly."

Zack mouthed the words, "Sintinex CEO?"

Max nodded and checked the time on his mobile. It was past seven. "Hello, Mr. Kelly. How can I help you?"

"Help me?" Archer Kelly gave a short, cold laugh. "Clearly, you're unaware that our system has been breached."

Zack sat at the edge of his chair while Max looked out into the empty bullpen area—his tech team had left for the evening.

"Mr. Ramirez, have I lost you?"

"Sorry, I'm still here, sir. I'm checking that right now." Max pulled up the program that connected him to the Sintinex mainframe and hit several keystrokes. There wasn't any sign of a breach. "I'm sorry, Mr. Kelly. It all looks secure from this end." Tiny beads of sweat formed on his upper lip.

"Mr. Ramirez, I'm extremely disappointed. You knew I pitted you against Jordan Logan, one of the best hackers in the world, because I wanted to make sure you brought your A game and would create an impenetrable firewall. You do understand the meaning of that word— *impenetrable*. Don't you? I chose your company out of dozens because I thought you had what it took to deliver a product that worked. You've failed."

It came as a surprise to Max that their firewall had been hacked. He knew Jordan Logan had been tasked with breaking through his firewall, but he truly thought that never would happen. What he'd built was impenetrable. For the last four weeks, he'd texted daily with Jordan, and not once had there been an indication that a breach was imminent.

Zack walked around the desk and stood over Max's shoulder as he continued to peck at the keyboard, looking for anything remotely resembling a breach in the Sintinex system. Max turned and looked up at Zack and shrugged his shoulders.

"Still can't find anything?" Archer asked.

"I'm not sure what you're seeing, Mr. Kelly, but we've got nothing on this end."

"Jordan emailed Sam Morris, our CTO, letting him know our firewall had been penetrated."

"And how is an email proof because, like I said, I'm not seeing the breach on this end," Max said.

"The only way that email could have been sent is if someone was actually in the system. The email was sent from our secure server."

Max sensed an odd gleefulness in Archer's tone, as though he were somehow delighted with the turn of events. It unnerved Max. But the truly distressing part of this conversation was that the firewall he and his brothers created and believed was impenetrable had not only been breached, but also no one from his team had detected it, and stranger than that, the breach wasn't even visible from his end. He tried to work out how this was possible.

"Let's move on to the next problem," Archer said.

Max gripped the arm of his chair, wondering what more could be wrong.

"It seems not only has our mainframe been breached, but also confidential government documents are missing from our files. Do you know anything about this?" Archer's sinister tone gave Max a prickly sensation in his chest, and he absently rubbed the spot.

"I'm afraid I don't know what you're talking about." Max exchanged confused looks with Zack.

"No matter. I'll take care of that myself," Archer said. "Now, about the breach. It needs to be handled. I'll give you until the end of the week to create a firewall that can't be hacked, or our contract with RMZ Digital will be revoked."

Chapter 3

Jordan stood on the subway platform and tried to blend in with the other New Yorkers. It had been an hour since she'd fled her apartment, and the image of a dead man with his head half blown off played like a never-ending loop in her mind. Her hands shook, making it difficult to hold on to Buck's leash.

The L train lurched into the station, and passengers on either side of her crowded closer to the platform's edge. When the car doors opened, Jordan stepped in, sat at a two-seater in the corner, and pulled Buck close. She kept an eye on her surroundings from beneath the bill of her baseball cap.

She'd already switched trains five times, walking up and down stairs and moving from platform to platform, in case she was being followed. But staying underground wasn't going to give her the answers she needed. And using her phone's Wi-Fi would be like shooting a flare into the sky, telegraphing her location. She needed a legit internet connection, one that couldn't be traced.

The moment the train pulled out of the station, her mind raced to formulate a plan. Twenty minutes later, when they crossed the Williamsburg Bridge into Lower Manhattan, Jordan knew exactly what her next steps had to be.

She held on to Buck's leash as they climbed the stairs

and emerged from the 14th Street subway station. The evening was balmy, and the streets were filled with tourists casually strolling about and taking in the sights of Greenwich Village. Jordan stepped aside and looked around, trying to determine which way was south. It took a minute, but she finally got her bearings. "Come on, Buck, let's go."

Dodging between pedestrians, Jordan walked south for two blocks to West 12th Street. This was the place she remembered. When she first moved to New York, the internet in her building was out for a day, and she'd had no choice but to use a public place. The store's signage glowed across its glass front in graffiti-like lettering. With her shoulder-length auburn hair shoved under her cap, she pulled the bill lower and stepped inside the Wayfront Internet Café.

Several customers sat casually at round tables, drinking coffee. The smell of freshly ground beans hit her with the stark reality that these people were living normal lives, but her world had imploded, and she had no idea why. She clenched a fist, fear turning to anger. Her life wasn't supposed to be like this. Not after spending years pulling herself out of the chaos and uncertainty of her childhood.

An acne-faced kid behind the coffee bar looked up. "You know we don't allow dogs in here," he said, then returned to wiping the counter.

Jordan bit back a scream. She was not in the mood for some skinny-necked teenager, who didn't look old enough to be out this late, to tell her what she could and could not do. She was tired, hungry, scared, and could give a crap about any rules. "He's an emotional support dog," she snarled. "Wanna see his cert?" Jordan knew the expression on her face dared him to question her.

The kid shuffled back a foot or two. "Well, okay," he

said, his eyes lowered. "But if anyone complains, you'll have to leave."

Jordan reached into her bag. "How much for an hour?"

"Five dollars."

She handed over the cash. The kid pressed some buttons behind the counter. "You can use terminal number ten."

At the back of the café, past the tables where several people sat having coffee, a dozen computers were separated by half partitions. Jordan slowly walked toward her terminal, sneaking sideways glances at the other customers. A few stations were filled with kids playing video games. A man appeared to be typing a résumé, and a woman sat hunched over, searching through apartment listings.

Jordan sat at number ten, rubbed Buck's head, and whispered in his ear. "You be a good boy. We won't be in here long." She placed her bag on the table next to the computer screen.

The first order of business was to check her accounts. If she had to stay out of sight for a while, she would need more than the two hundred dollars in her purse.

She pulled up her bank's website and entered her username and password. The swirling ball twirled for several seconds before the words *No Such Username* appeared. She blew out a heavy breath and retyped her information. The same error message popped up. She took out her phone and checked her notes app, where she kept all her passwords. The information she'd entered was correct. Determined to get into her account and find out what was happening, she typed in her username and password with slow, deliberate keystrokes. Again, the same result.

The sense of panic that she'd somehow managed to hold off until now ratcheted up to full-blown terror stomach. Perspiration formed under her arms, and her heart raced. With shaky hands, she closed out that tab, opened a new one, and pulled up the website for her credit card company. Again, her credentials weren't recognized. A similar outcome occurred when she tried to access her investment portfolio.

None of this made any sense. Dozens of thoughts came at her like scraps of paper caught in a strong wind, and she let out a string of curse words under her breath. *How could all of my accounts just vanish?*

Jordan didn't have an answer to that question and wasn't sure how she would find one. But she was smart enough to know that it definitely had something to do with her empty apartment, the dead body, and the news alert that had appeared on her phone before she fled. She sat straighter, uncrossed her legs, and tried to shake the feeling that her world was collapsing. *Time to find out what that news alert was all about.*

Her fingers hovered over the keyboard, and she closed her eyes. *Come on. Don't be a wimp.* She snapped open her eyes and typed an address into the web browser. The news page was slow to populate, but when it did, she gasped and put a hand over her mouth to stop the scream lodged in the back of her throat. Shocked to see her image on the front page, she blinked and read the words under her picture.

Lauren Chambers is wanted for hacking into Sintinex Corporation's mainframe and stealing confidential government documents. Although never convicted, Chambers has previously stood trial for intellectual property theft.

She sat back as the room began to spin. *Who in the hell is Lauren Chambers? And why is my face attached to her name?* Jordan slumped in the chair and rested her forehead in her hand. Buck nudged her thigh and placed his chin in her lap. Absently, she patted his head.

It was several minutes before she took a deep breath and lifted her head. With gritted teeth and a morbid curiosity, she decided to pull up other news sites. She needed to know exactly how much trouble she was in. Each site contained the same information. She felt unbearably exposed. *Who would do this?*

Jordan forced herself to mentally scroll through the last few weeks, looking for any explanation for why this madness was happening. She'd been paid to hack into Sintinex, but she never took anything, let alone government documents.

This had to be the work of another hacker. It was the only explanation she could come up with that made sense. There wasn't any time to try and sort it out. Instinct told her she had to find out how deeply her identity had been infiltrated. She pulled up the Department of Motor Vehicles website. From the drop-down menu, she chose the option *How to Get a Duplicate.* When she entered her driver's license number and last name, an error message popped up—*Name does not match the license number provided. Please check your entry and try again.*

Without drawing too much attention, her gaze scanned the room, and when she was certain no one was paying attention, she got to work surreptitiously hacking into the DMV to find out why the information she'd provided was no longer valid. When the page with her information populated, she nearly lost it. The name associated with her driver's license number was Lauren Chambers.

Swamped with fear, her breathing became labored, and she prayed she wouldn't pass out. Over the years, she'd found herself in tough spots, but never anything like this. *Think, damnit. Think.*

Finding out who had stolen and changed her identity would require sophisticated hacking skills, but couldn't be done without the proper equipment. The internet café didn't have what she needed. The only way out of this was with expert help.

Except for a few forgettable interactions, the only person Jordan knew in New York was Sam Morris, CTO of Sintinex. With the insanity of the last few hours, she'd forgotten she was scheduled to meet him in the morning. But this couldn't wait. She needed to speak with him now. Maybe he could help. Her fingers flew across her phone's keypad as she texted him. She waited for the three-dot bubble response to appear but saw nothing. A minute passed. Still nothing. Then, the word *Undelivered* appeared under her message. She blew out a frustrated breath and resent the text. Again, she waited. No three dots. Nothing. Seconds later, *Undelivered* popped up on her screen.

From the corner of her eye, she noticed a man with a black hoodie over his head sitting in the next computer carrel. There were at least four empty stations. Where had he come from? Was he looking over her shoulder at her screen? Her street smarts kicked in, and she shifted in her seat, obstructing his view. When she looked back at her computer screen, the web page had changed to the Wayfront Café's homepage, indicating her time was up. Had it been an hour already?

Spending too much time in one place wasn't wise, but Jordan needed to find Sam Morris. She grabbed Buck's leash and returned to the front counter, where she purchased another hour and asked for a different station.

"Number three in the corner is free." This time, the skinny-neck kid behind the counter didn't even look up.

Jordan wedged herself into the corner console and had Buck sit under the table by her feet. "Sorry, boy," she whispered, "we'll be out of here soon."

Over the years, Jordan had created dozens of email accounts, and sending a message from one that didn't have her name attached wasn't a problem. But that wasn't enough to protect her location. It took twenty minutes to set up a virtual private network. The VPN she created consisted of several relay points, allowing her email to bounce from one IP address to another before it hit Sam's inbox without a trace of where the sender was located. Once that was done, she kept the message short.

Need to see you. Tonight. IMPERATIVE. Meet same as first meeting in March.

Jordan rarely, if ever, met her prospective employers in person. For one, well, people weren't her thing. For another, she didn't always work in the same city as her clients. With a computer and an internet connection, in-person meetings weren't really necessary anymore. But Sintinex had been different. Sam had said Sintinex didn't hire people they hadn't personally met. Under normal circumstances, Jordan would have passed on the job. But, at the time, the idea of going up against a well-known cybersecurity firm, like RMZ Digital, and beating them at their own game by hacking past their firewall undetected had the promise of too much fun to pass up.

She was certain Sam would remember their first meeting because although he'd been the one to suggest lunch, she'd chosen the place. He'd had to trek all the way from his Upper East Side office down to the Broadway Diner on West 23rd Street. At the time, she was living in Chicago, and the inconvenience of taking a flight to New York for an in-person lunch, which could have easily been done on video, gave her all the reason she needed to pick where they ate. When it came to juicy burgers, apparently, Broadway Diner was the place. And there was no way she'd come all the way to the Big Apple and not experience it.

While she waited for Sam to respond to her email, she checked the time on her phone. She'd already been in the cybercafe too long. She crossed her legs and jiggled her foot nervously. More time passed, and she turned her attention to the people around her. The man in the black hoodie was gone. But a couple of kids who'd been playing computer games when she first arrived hadn't moved. Their eyes seemed to be permanently glued to the screen. The ding of an incoming email got her attention.

Sam Morris is no longer employed at Sintinex. If you need immediate assistance, please contact our HR department.

The hell. Am I being ghosted? She immediately dismissed the thought. Something more sinister was at work—that much she instinctively knew. A palpable fear shot through her, and blood pumped to her heart like she was running the hundred-yard dash.

As if he could sense what she was feeling, Buck began barking. Customers turned to look.

"Hey, I told you. If you can't control your dog, you gotta leave," Skinny-neck yelled from the counter.

Jordan scratched Buck behind the ears. "Come on,

buddy," she whispered, "I need a little more time. Please pull it together." Her soothing voice seemed to calm him, and he resumed his position on the floor near her chair. She turned back to the console. Max Ramirez was the only other person she'd worked with on this project. She thought about texting him and stopped, not wanting to take the chance that he, too, would somehow ghost her, disappear, or otherwise be unavailable. She pulled up the website of his company, RMZ Digital, and copied their address on the back of a flyer featuring the café's latest smoothie offerings.

"Looks like we're taking a trip," she said to Buck under her breath.

When Jordan finished checking Google Maps and the bus schedule from New York's Port Authority Bus Terminal to Hollow Lake in upstate New York, her phone pinged with an incoming text. She fished it out of her pocket, and her insides tightened as she read the words.

TRUST NO ONE

She didn't recognize the phone number and couldn't waste another minute to trace it. She had to leave now. She closed all the open tabs on the computer and erased her browsing history. With her heart knocking against her chest, she grabbed Buck's leash and, keeping her head down, walked out the door. Glancing around, she ripped the SIM card out of her phone, threw it under a passing bus, dropped her phone into the trash can on the corner, and she and Buck headed down the steps into the subway.

Chapter 4

The sun had barely peaked over the horizon, and one of Hollow Lake's favorite eateries, Fritz & Dean's Diner, was already doing a brisk business. Jordan Logan sat at the counter, nursing a cup of coffee, trying not to be noticed.

Each time the bell above the front door jingled and a customer entered, they were met with a smile. The regulars were greeted by name. Jordan had never lived in a small town, but she supposed there were diners like this all across the country, where you got to know your neighbors, and people greeted each other with warmth. For her, it was a strange concept.

A few customers got special treatment from Fritz, the wiry gray-haired owner, who stopped and chatted even while he manned the register, took orders from customers at the counter, and poured coffee. Most of the dozen tables down the center of the diner were full, as were several booths along the far wall. A steady clatter of plates being served and cleared battled with the Muzak pumping through the invisible sound system. The smell of bacon frying hung heavy in the air, and Jordan's stomach growled.

The early morning newscast was on the large flat-screen in the upper corner behind the register. Closed captions ran along the bottom of the screen. For the last ten minutes,

Jordan had sipped her coffee, watched the television from beneath the bill of her baseball cap, and occasionally peeked out the large glass front window to check on Buck, where he was securely attached to a tree and sleeping soundly. Her heart stuttered when a news alert filled the screen with her photo. The image lasted several seconds before being replaced by a smiling female anchor in a cobalt blue low-cut cocktail dress. A new image of a fender bender on the interstate appeared over the anchor's shoulder, and Jordan let out a breath.

As casually as she could, she looked around. Most regulars had their heads buried in their phones and didn't seem to be paying attention to the constant images flashing on the television screen. Two couples dressed in hiking gear sat in a booth animatedly discussing something she couldn't quite make out. At the counter, two stools down, a distinguished gentleman with eyeglasses resting halfway down his patrician nose stared at the screen while he ate a bowl of hot oatmeal. Dressed in a dark gray tracksuit, he looked like he'd come in from an early morning run.

"More coffee, Judge?"

"No thanks, Fritz. One's my limit, doctor's orders. Just the check, please."

Jordan turned away and checked the time on the clock behind the counter. Two more hours before RMZ Digital opened its offices. Knowing that Max Ramirez was a night owl, she had no idea if he would be in this early. But she was prepared to wait the entire day if it came to that.

Before putting the coffeepot back on the warming station, Fritz lifted it toward Jordan. "Ready for a refill?"

Jordan looked down and shook her head, hoping she wasn't being rude to the point that he might remember her.

She needed to stay unremarkable. Invisible. Zero. She spent the next five minutes pretending to read the paper the previous customer had left on the counter.

When the bell over the front door jingled again, Fritz waved, and Jordan turned. A tall, extremely attractive man dressed in blue jeans and a white button-down shirt nodded.

"Hey, Max. You just missed your father."

"Nah, I caught him outside."

"I don't know how he does it. Every morning, running at the crack of dawn," Fritz smiled.

"Me either. That's too much morning for me."

"Speaking of," Fritz said, "what brings you here this time of day?"

"Got a project that needs my attention. I already put my order in online, so it should be ready."

"To go?"

"Nah, I'll eat it here. Catch my breath before the day starts."

"Good deal. Sit anywhere. I'll send Penny over with coffee."

Max took a booth by the far wall. He was well over six feet and cut an imposing figure with his dark brown hair and chiseled features. A young, freckle-faced server walked over, her high ponytail swinging as she went. She placed a mug on the table and poured the coffee.

When Max was settled, Jordan eased off her stool, crossed the room, appeared to head toward the ladies' room in the rear, and instead slid into Max's booth opposite him.

Max looked up from his phone and furrowed his brow. "Do I know you?"

"Yes, you do. I'm Jordan Logan."

For a moment, Max stared in silence, then pursed his

lips and frowned. "Look, I don't know what game you're playing, but you are not Jordan Logan."

She leaned forward, her voice low but insistent. "I am."

Max chuckled. "Not possible. The only Jordan I know is a man. And you—" he waved a hand toward her "—are clearly not."

"Max. It's me. Jordan." She paused and looked around. "I'm here because I need your help."

"Here you go, Max." Penny placed his breakfast plate on the table. "More coffee?"

He put a hand over his cup. "I'm good."

"And for you?" Penny turned to Jordan.

Max looked up. "Oh, she's not—"

"I'll have a bacon, egg, and cheese on an English muffin. Extra bacon on the side." The words rushed out of her mouth before Max could finish his objection.

"Coming right up." Penny strode back through the double doors that led into the kitchen.

"That was presumptuous," Max said. "I don't even know who you are."

"I told you. I'm Jordan Logan." She sat forward, lowering her voice so that Max had to lean in. "Listen, I spent the night in Port Authority, took a bus at the ass crack of dawn. I've been waiting here a couple of hours, and I'm starving. Until you arrived, I was too jittery to eat. The least you can do is let me have a meal while I prove to you who I am."

Jordan began to think her lifelong desire to be a loner and avoid people was backfiring. She'd never spoken on the phone or had a video chat with Max or anyone from his company. Her name could easily be mistaken for that of a man. And since their only means of communication had been texting over a chat program, she could almost understand his reluctance to believe her.

"Here. Let me show you." Jordan reached into her purse for her wallet and pulled out her driver's license and credit cards. He didn't need to know they were now worthless. She slid the cards across the table.

Without touching them, Max looked them over.

"I know you have two brothers who run RMZ with you," she offered.

"Pfftt." Max tilted his head and gave her a who-are-you-kidding look. "Anyone can find that information on our website. For that matter, your identification could be fake."

The look of disbelief on his face stunned her. She hadn't thought he would give her such a hard time. "Wait. Listen. You and I worked together for four weeks on the Sintinex project," Jordan's voice rose impatiently. "We spent every night text chatting while I waited for my codes to build. I even told you I'd only recently moved to New York and was waiting for the job to be over so I could finally unpack my boxes. You typed back, 'LOL.'" She made air quotes. "Then you wrote that I would live with those boxes for the rest of my life because I would never hack past the firewall you created for Sintinex." Jordan stopped talking when Max slid her cards back to her side of the table, showing no signs he believed her.

"Why are you being difficult?" Jordan pushed up the bill of her cap. "Okay, look," she said, and began ticking items she remembered from their text messages. "You fancy yourself a wanna-be chef, and you unwind by cooking. But your favorite meal is a good steak. Last week, you played in a pickup game at the courts behind your old high school because a buddy named Cliff was in town. You like animals, but you have no pets. One day, you hope to get a dog and name him Spot. Your brother, Rafe, is newly married, but you're a commitment phobe. Since we started this job, you've been out with three different women—"

Max held up a hand. "Let's take a beat. If you are who you say you are, then why didn't you stick to our arrangement?"

Jordan's mind went blank, not sure what arrangement he was talking about.

"Well?"

"I… I…" She glanced up at the ceiling. "Help me out here. I got a lot going on."

"We had an arrangement when you completed your end of the job." Max glared.

A few seconds passed before Jordan remembered what the heck he was talking about. "I didn't text you when I broke through the firewall because Sam Morris asked me not to alert your company."

"We had an agreement. You were supposed to give me a heads-up. And why would Sam ask you to do that?"

Jordan shrugged. "I don't know. I guess to see how long it would take for you to discover the breach. Besides, that doesn't matter—"

"Like hell. Of course, it matters," he said, leaning forward, his voice low and menacing. "Archer Kelly has threatened to take away his business if we don't fix the breach. You must have known my company would take a big hit. If you are who you say you are, the least you could have or should have done is warn me *like we agreed*." He punctuated the last three words with a tap of his index finger on the table. "I had to find out from Archer Kelly."

Max scoffed and sat back. "Archer wasn't pleased. He

wants the firewall fixed, and I'm under a lot of pressure to make that happen. But there's something else. Do you want to know what that is?"

Jordan remained silent. Her lips pressed together. She couldn't believe he was acting like the injured party when she was the one in a dangerous situation.

"I'll tell you anyway. Archer seemed particularly pissed off about some missing government documents. You wouldn't happen to know anything about those? Would you?"

Jordan felt heat rise from the back of her neck to her cheeks. She glanced around the diner.

"What aren't you saying?"

Before she could respond, Penny approached their table and placed Jordan's order in front of her. "Max, you haven't touched your breakfast. Something wrong?"

Max looked up and gave Penny a tight smile. "Everything's fine. Thanks."

When Penny was out of earshot, Jordan leaned forward. "The situation is complicated. Ever since I hacked into that damn system—" she put her fists on either side of her head and then flicked open her fingers "—my life has exploded."

Max scrunched his forehead and gave her a questioning look.

"Is there a word you didn't understand? 'Cause I thought I was being very clear."

Max continued to stare without saying a word.

"Look. When I finished the hack, as instructed by the people who were paying me, I emailed Sam Morris, Sintinex's chief tec—"

"I know who Sam is."

"All right." She arched a brow. "I let him know I'd completed the job. Then, out of nowhere, I get an email from Archer Kelly asking me to add a line of code. I never met the guy. Never spoke to him. My sole contact has been with Sam. So, a few minutes later, when a text pops up on my phone from Sam asking me to bring him the combined code and not to email it back to Archer, I'm curious, but I—"

"What has this got to do with the stolen documents?"

"I'm getting to that. Let me finish." Jordan blew out an exasperated breath. "I figured I had time to add the code after I met with Sam, and he'd tell me what was happening."

"And did he?"

"No. We were supposed to meet this morning for breakfast."

"But you're here."

"Aren't you observant?"

"Do you always have such an attitude when you're trying to get someone to help you?"

There was no mistaking Max's clenched jaw, and as difficult as it might be, she thought maybe she should take it down a notch. Squeezing her eyes shut, she took a moment to collect herself. "Okay. So, after I got Sam's text, I left my apartment to take a much needed break, and when I came back—my apartment was empty."

"I don't understand."

"Oh, my god. I'm speaking English. Are you pretending to be thick?" The words spilled out. She couldn't help herself. Lashing out had always been one of her defense mechanisms.

"Lady, I haven't done anything to you. But you roll up in here uninvited, with an attitude as thick as the maple syrup on my plate. And I asked you a question, and it feels to me like you're stalling." Max gave her a pointed look.

Jordan couldn't afford to burn this one contact. "I'm getting to the stolen documents. Let's see if I can explain. When I got to my apartment, every single thing I owned, from furniture to toilet paper, was gone. Nothing was left. Not so much as a dust bunny. It looked as if no one had ever lived there. Except for the one thing they left in the bathroom—"

"Wait. Be quiet." Max leaned forward, looked over her shoulder, and squinted.

Jordan turned to see what caught his attention. She nearly fell out of the booth when her face stared back at her from the television screen in the corner.

Max turned his gaze back to Jordan. His look could have cut glass. "Is that you? It says you're someone named Lauren Chambers."

"I was getting to that."

"Too late. We're done here." Max was halfway out of the booth when Jordan quickly stood and stepped in front of him.

"Please," she said. Her voice was low and urgent. "I don't want to make a scene. It's not what it looks like. Please." It was unlike her to plead, but she was desperate. She couldn't afford for him to walk away.

Reluctantly, Max lowered himself back onto the bench. "You got two minutes. Go."

Jordan slid back into the booth opposite him. "That was a photo of me on the screen. But the name Lauren Chambers—that's not me. I'm Jordan Logan. I'm being set up." She shook her head. "Wait. I'm not explaining this correctly. What I think is really going on is that I've been erased. My bank account, investment accounts, credit cards—they've all vanished. As far as the world is concerned, Jordan Logan never existed. My face, my driver's license, and, by now, probably my social security number have all been assigned to someone named Lauren Chambers, and she is the one wanted for government theft."

"Erased? Wait a minute. Who would do that?"

"Isn't that the million-dollar question? And I do not have the answer." Jordan put her hand to her chest. "I was erased, and this Lauren Chambers person was put in my place, and I don't know why." Tears formed at the corners of her eyes. She never cried, and she wasn't about to start now. Jordan gritted her teeth and willed them not to spill. "I need to get my life back. And I'm asking you for help."

Max folded his arms across his chest. "Why me?"

"Because I believe this all has to do with the job we did for Sintinex. And there's no one else. I have no family. No friends." She looked down at her hands. "The only person I've met at Sintinex was Sam, and I haven't been able to reach him."

"This whole thing barely makes sense. Archer tells me documents are missing from his mainframe. The news is filled with your image identified as Lauren Chambers, who's wanted for that crime." Max sat back. "You can see how this might look incriminating."

"Someone is doing this to me. I'm Jordan Logan. Not Lauren Chambers. And I haven't stolen anything!" Her words were rapid fire. As she slammed her hand on the table, the bell above the entrance jingled, and two New York State troopers walked into the diner.

Chapter 5

The shorter of the two troopers lowered his mirrored aviator sunglasses and scanned the diner. "Who belongs to the dog outside?" he called out over the din.

Max turned to Jordan and recognized the fear in her eyes before she pulled the bill of her cap down and sank further in her seat. He mouthed the question, *Yours?* And she nodded. At that moment, he instinctively decided to give her some help. "He's mine."

"He's looking a bit thirsty," the trooper said.

"Thanks. Just wrapping up." Max raised a hand, and Penny came over with the check. He dropped a twenty on the table and stood. "Come on," he said. "Let's get out of here." But Jordan didn't move. She seemed frozen in her seat. "Time to go." He spoke without moving his lips, his tone insistent.

Max followed Jordan's gaze as she watched the troopers walk to the counter. Once they were seated with their backs turned to them, she grabbed a few paper napkins from the dispenser and wrapped the bacon.

"What are you doing?"

"It's for my dog. I know he's hungry and thirsty." Jordan scooted out of the booth and stood.

"Walk like you got no issues," he said under his breath.

"Hey, Fritz. See ya." He waved as he ushered Jordan toward the door.

"Enjoy the day." Fritz went back to pouring coffee for the troopers.

Max was barely two feet outside the diner when a black Lab jumped at him, planting its paws on his chest, nearly knocking Max over. "Hey, there, boy," he said, tilting his head back to avoid sloppy dog kisses as he worked to maintain his balance. "You're a friendly one, aren't you?"

"Buck. Get down." Jordan tugged on his collar, but Buck seemed immovable. She untied his leash from the lamppost. "Come here, boy." She pulled him off Max but had difficulty restraining him.

"It's okay." He rubbed Buck's head. "Nice to meet you."

"Buck, this is Max. And he's going to help us."

Max held up both hands. "Whoa. I didn't say that."

Jordan narrowed her eyes. "But you just did. You could have turned me in."

"I'm not saying I believe you or don't believe you, but something about this entire situation doesn't add up. I'm willing to give you some time and a little assistance to get to the bottom of it."

There was no doubt Max was conflicted. His rational mind told him to be cautious, but his instinct said to trust her. Not because she'd accurately quoted their text messages—because any computer nerd could have hacked into those. No, it was the look in her eyes when she pleaded with him to sit back down after her image flashed on the TV screen. A few years earlier, his brother Rafe had had the same look when he'd been accused of a crime he hadn't committed. Either way, Max hoped he wasn't making a mistake by bringing her to the office.

"If I find out you're lying, I won't have any problem calling Archer and the authorities. Understood?"

Jordan raised a brow.

"Understood?" Max repeated a bit more forcefully.

She huffed out an annoyed breath and shifted her stance to one hip. "I don't like being backed into a corner. Never did. But here we are, and you clearly have the upper hand since I'm the one who needs the help." Jordan looked down at her sneakers. "All I need is access to a computer and a secure internet connection to find out *who* is doing this and why."

"And I have no idea why *I'm* doing this. But okay." Max nodded reluctantly. "We're across the street."

RMZ Digital was housed in the old post office building on Main Street across from Fritz & Dean's Diner. They entered through the double glass doors and walked across the polished granite floor to the elevator. "We're on the second floor."

The reception desk was empty, and the large antique railway clock on the wall read seven thirty-five. When the company took over, they redesigned the entire floor. The whitewashed brick walls, exposed-beam ceilings, and massive arched windows along the south wall held the brothers' offices enclosed in glass, allowing natural light to pour into the bullpen area. The concrete floors and open architecture gave it a modern look.

In today's world, most clients never came to the office, preferring video chats. So, the space was made comfortable for the firm's employees. In addition to the low sofas and plush chairs, there were cutting-edge tech stations with high-resolution monitors, ergonomic keyboards, and noise-canceling headphones. The rec room at the far end of the floor was a combination coffee bar and adult playroom. When the office personnel weren't staring at their computer monitors, they could grab a snack or relax with a game of ping-pong, foosball, or air hockey.

"This way," Max said, leading Jordan down the hall to his office.

Brittany, the receptionist, stopped them. "Hey, Max. I didn't expect to see you here this early. You here for the call to Barcelona? If I'd known, I could have connected you at home."

"No, that call is all Zack. I'm working on Sintinex."

"Oh. Okay." Brittany looked at Buck. "Who's this precious fellow? Huh?" She rubbed under his chin. Buck barked, wagged his tail excitedly, and seemed to enjoy the attention.

"We'll be in my office. No calls, please." He continued walking. "Wait." Max stopped short. "Do we have some sort of bowl to put water in for the dog?"

Brittany crouched in front of Buck. "You thirsty? Is that right, fella?"

Max felt his patience waning. He wanted to get to his office quickly and avoid as many people as possible. "Yes. I told you he needed water." His tone was sharp.

Brittany straightened and stepped back, her gaze lowered to the floor. "Stan sometimes brings his Chihuahua. He'll have a bowl. I'll get it."

Damn, Max hadn't meant to upset her. The pressure he felt to sort out this Jordan Logan-Lauren Chambers thing and get back to fixing the problem with the Sintinex firewall was making him short-tempered. "Sorry. Didn't mean to snap."

Brittany didn't look up. "No problem." With brisk, determined steps, she walked away.

Max opened his office door and ushered in Jordan and Buck. The room was spacious, with a floor-to-ceiling arched window that nearly spanned the width of the entire wall and looked out onto Main Street. To the left stood a dark, sleek desk. Opposite it were two rust-colored leather chairs with thin gold legs. At the far end of the room sat a mid-century modern green velvet couch.

Buck went straight to the couch. "No, Buck." Jordan tugged on his collar. "Come sit by me. I've got a treat for you."

Brittany knocked on the glass door. "Here's the water." She set a dog bowl by the chair, and Buck lapped it up greedily. "Is there anything else you need?"

"No. Thanks. Please close the door on your way out." Before saying a word, he pressed a button on the underside of his desk, and the glass walls turned opaque. "There. Some privacy."

Jordan took the napkin from her pocket and fed Buck the bacon she'd taken from the diner. Once he was settled, she stood in front of Max's desk. "I'm ready to get started. Do you have a laptop I can use?"

When Jordan removed her baseball cap, her thick, deep auburn hair spilled down, framing her face, and Max found himself staring. The first word that came to mind was *elegance*. Yes, he thought, she had a tough exterior, but there was also a quiet elegance about her. Maybe it was her statuesque build. If he had to guess, he'd say she was about five eight. Her jeans accentuated her lean, tight muscles. The photo of her on the news didn't begin to do her justice. Up close and in person, she was stunning. His gaze traveled from her deep green eyes to her full, sensual mouth. He wasn't sure if he'd ever seen a woman as beautiful as Jordan Logan.

"Why are you staring?"

Her words broke the momentary spell. This wasn't the time to be infatuated with a woman's looks. Shoving his hair from his forehead, he straightened. "Sorry, I was thinking," he lied. "I really would like to give you the benefit of the doubt, but much of what you're saying doesn't make sense."

"Yeah. Yeah. I know." Jordan scoffed. "But this all has to do with Sintinex."

"How?"

"That's what I need to find out if I have any hope of getting my life back." She reached into her purse and pulled out the flash drive. "This has the code I wrote, plus the code Archer sent me. I didn't have a chance to look at his, but maybe the answer is in here."

Max held his hand out for the drive, but Jordan didn't move. He wriggled his fingers in a give-it-here motion. When she placed it in his hand, her fingers grazed his palm, and electricity shot through him. It felt good, but he quickly chastised himself. This woman was either in trouble or a very good con artist. Either way, being attracted to her was a bad idea.

Max cleared his throat and placed the drive on his desk. "Before we do anything, I'm going to contact Sam Morris."

"Yeah. Good luck with that." Jordan rolled her eyes and sat back in the chair.

"I'm going to go out on a limb here and guess sarcasm is how you get people on your side. Right?"

Jordan closed her eyes and, in a whisper, said, "Sorry."

"Why are you wishing me luck anyway?"

"Don't you think I already tried to reach Sam?"

"And?"

"And I sent him a text that bounced back. I emailed his office and got a response that said he no longer worked for the company."

"Seriously?"

"Yes. Seriously."

"Man. Another thing that doesn't make sense," Max muttered. "Let me try." Max scrolled through his phone and pulled up Sam's number.

"There is one more thing that happened before I left my apartment." Jordan cleared her throat. "You're not going to like it, but I need to tell you—"

A quick knock on the door, and Brittany walked in. "Sorry to interrupt. Zack wants to see you in the conference room. Says it's urgent."

"I thought he was on the Barcelona call?"

"It was rescheduled."

Max shrugged. "I'll be there in a minute."

Brittany didn't move. "Sorry, Max. He said he needs you right away."

Max hesitated. He looked at Jordan and then at the drive. It appeared Brittany wasn't going anywhere until he followed her. "All right." He pointed a finger at Jordan. "Stay here. We'll finish this when I get back."

With Brittany leading the way, Max marched down the corridor to the conference room. "Britt, what's so urgent?"

She shrugged.

After last night, Max figured Zack wanted to know what was happening with the Sintinex firewall. Little did his brother know that since the call with Archer, there was more to that story—a whole lot more.

The office was beginning to fill up with techies and admins. Their quiet conversations, the rhythmic click of fingers on keyboards, and the aroma of fresh coffee being brewed settled Max. This was how his day was supposed to start. This was normal.

"You need anything?" Brittany asked as she stood in front of the glass-walled conference room.

"Nah, I'm good. Thanks." Max went in, surprised to see not only Zack but also his brother, Rafe. "Hey, bro. I didn't expect to see you. Has it been two weeks already?" He hugged Rafe. "Geez. I lost track of the time." Max took a step back. "And look at you, all tan. Even your eyes look rested. Must have been sweet." He patted Rafe on the shoulders.

"The honeymoon was everything and more," Rafe said. "Didn't want to come back."

"Que chévere," Max said. "How's Mallory?"

"Enough with the reunion." Zack crossed his arms over his chest. "Rafe can fill you in on his honeymoon later."

Rafe let out a laugh. "What's with him? Since I walked in, he's been buzzing like he went past the legal limit on *café con leches*. Will one of you tell me what's going on?"

"We may lose the Sintinex contract," Zack began, "if we can't fix the firewall that was breached yesterday, and—"

"Wait, what?" Rafe interrupted.

"Yeah. It ain't good. But hold up, there's one other thing bothering me right now."

"Worse than losing a big client?" Rafe asked.

Zack shrugged. "Maybe. I'll let Max tell us. Who's the woman with the dog in your office, and why is it blacked out?"

"Your office is blacked out?" Rafe asked. "What are

you hiding? We don't black out our windows unless we're in conference with each other. *¿Qué pasó?*"

Max shoved his hands in his pockets and shifted from one foot to the other, wondering where to begin. He'd hoped to have more information before involving his brothers. They were his closest confidants, and he'd never kept anything from them. No matter how difficult the situation, they'd always discussed everything, even when Rafe had been falsely imprisoned a few years earlier for cryptocurrency theft. They'd worked together to get him exonerated. It was the reason he and Zack had joined the firm Rafe had created.

Max let out a long, slow breath and walked over to the conference table. Pressing a button on the sleek silver box, he spoke to their AI digital assistant. "Rudy, black out the room and pull up a web browser." In an instant, the wall of glass facing the bullpen area was opaque. The shades rolled down over the three large arched windows facing Main Street, and the large screen at the far end of the room came to life.

"What are you doing?" Zack asked.

Max pointed to the screen. "Hang on." He typed the URL for The Union News into the browser. The page loaded in a few seconds. Below the masthead was the picture of the woman now in his office claiming to be Jordan Logan but identified as Lauren Chambers, wanted for stealing government documents from Sintinex.

"What's this got to do with the woman in your off—" Zack took a step back as the realization of what was really happening dawned on him. "Oh, man!" He put his hands on his hips and lifted his face to the ceiling. "You cannot be serious!"

"What am I missing here?" Rafe asked.

"You tell him, Max."

"Let's all take a seat. Okay?" Max said.

"I'm good," Zack said. "Stop stalling."

"All right, the woman on the screen is in my office." Max waited for a verbal explosion, but there was utter quiet. Rafe stared, and Zack finally sat in one of the conference chairs lining the table.

"I feel like I've walked in on the middle of a movie," Rafe said. "You're going to have to catch me up before I lose the nice Zen-like quality I developed over the last two weeks relaxing on a beach, enjoying tropical drinks garnished with pretty little colorful umbrellas."

"I don't have all the details or any answers yet." Max rubbed the back of his neck. He needed more time to determine if he was harboring a real criminal. "I think I need to get back to her."

"I think whoever you got in your office can wait," Zack said. "I mean, like, where is she going to go when her face is plastered all over the news and social media? Like Rafe said, start at the beginning. And don't skip the good parts. Give us *all* the details."

Max and Rafe sat in their usual seats, with Rafe at the head of the long table.

Max began by describing how he and Jordan Logan started working on the Sintinex project four weeks ago. "We were tasked with opposing goals. We build the wall. She tries to break it down."

"I always thought that was strange," Rafe said. "But whatever, it's the client's money."

"Not so strange. Archer Kelly is a bit eccentric. But I'm

guessing he wanted to make sure whatever we delivered was in fact impenetrable," Max said.

"Like I said, whatever, just get on with the story."

Max brought Rafe up to speed on the call with Archer Kelly the night before. He told his brothers about the bizarre breakfast meeting at Fritz's diner. When Max got to the part where her identity had been stolen and everything she owned had disappeared, Zack laid his forehead on the table. For several seconds, no one said anything.

Rafe broke the silence. "You realize what you said sounds whacked. You know that, right?"

Max stiffened, then let out a long sigh. "Yes. It sounds crazy. But before you dismiss her altogether, let's approach this analytically."

"Why? Why do we even need to touch this?" Zack said. "Man. You may be the oldest, but that sure don't make you the smartest."

"Hear me out." Max pulled out his phone. "Look at these messages." He slid his phone across the table toward Rafe. Zack got up and looked over his shoulder. "I think the woman who I've been texting with on the Sintinex project—Jordan Logan—is the one who's in my office. And I don't believe she stole any documents."

"How do you know?" Rafe asked.

"Tengo un instinto." Max pointed to his nose. "I've never been wrong when it comes to my instincts. And my gut is telling me she's telling the truth."

"Tell me how," Zack demanded.

Max took a deep breath. "Okay. First, Archer Kelly calls to tell us Jordan Logan hacked into his system."

"Nothing strange about that. He paid us to create an impenetrable firewall. I understand if the man wants to call us out for delivering an apparently faulty product," Rafe said.

"Okay. But in that same conversation, he wants to know if we know anything about missing documents," Max said.

"Again. Doesn't seem strange. He's trying to handle a problem," Rafe said.

"Until now, we have never spoken with Archer," Max said. "Throughout this entire project, we've only dealt with Sam Morris. Why didn't he call last night? Something isn't right. I feel it in my bones."

Rafe rubbed at his eyes. "I am *so* not following. You're talking straight-up crazy."

"Nah, bro. It's not crazy," Zack said. "It's bordering on unhinged. The door is off the submarine."

"Well, despite what you both think, I'm ready to go back in there and figure this out with her," Max said.

"You ain't going in there alone. We're in this together."

Max headed for the door. "She's not great with people. Let me handle this."

"Hang on," Rafe said. "Let's be smart. I want to see if there's any new news." Rafe pressed a button on the remote to an all-news broadcast. The lower third crawl continued in a loop of the latest stories, and every third item was about Lauren Chambers and the stolen documents. Rafe stared at the screen. "Whatever we do, we need to do it fast 'cause it looks like we are harboring a criminal. And I have no intention of going back to prison."

The image on the screen changed. "Holy crap!" Zack leaned forward and pointed. Max's gaze followed, and he couldn't believe what he saw. It felt like he'd been punched in the gut and needed an oxygen mask.

"Turn up the sound. Now!" Zack demanded.

Rafe pressed the volume button on the remote, and a photo of Lauren Chambers/Jordan Logan appeared in the upper third of the screen behind the female anchor.

"Lauren Chambers is now wanted for murder. The police have released this statement: Sam Morris, chief technology officer for the Sintinex Corporation, was found shot late last night in the Brooklyn apartment of Lauren Chambers."

Chapter 6

Jordan sat at Max's desk studying the combined program code she'd uploaded to the laptop and couldn't believe what she saw. Leaning in closer, she squinted at the screen. "How can this be?" Before she could answer her own question, the glass door swung open, and Max burst in, followed by two men she recognized as his brothers from their photos on their RMZ website.

Buck sprang up, barking furiously. She grabbed his collar, but he fought against her restraint.

With his hands on his hips, Max stood in the middle of the room, grinding his teeth so hard she could see his jaw muscles move.

"Hey, Rafe. Shut the door," he said.

"Sure thing." With a flick of his foot, the door closed, and Rafe leaned against it.

Buck growled.

"You want to tell us what's going on?" Max clenched his fists.

Jordan hesitated. There were so many things going on in her life that she wasn't sure which situation he was referring to or if it was something new. She thought it best not to say anything and to get him to talk. "How about we start with introductions?"

"Really?" Max arched a brow. "Are you serious with this?"

Jordan shifted in her seat. She didn't like feeling cornered, and while it wasn't an altogether unfamiliar situation given her upbringing, she couldn't rely on old attack patterns. First, she needed to find out what caused their over-the-top reaction. So she kept her expression neutral and nodded. "Yes. I'm serious."

Max huffed out a breath. "These are my brothers. That's Rafe with his foot on the door." He hooked a thumb over his shoulder. "And that's Zack, standing next to him. Now your turn. What the hell is going on?"

His brothers glared at her, and she inwardly shuddered. Both were well over six feet tall and had olive complexions. They looked almost identical with deep brown hair, chocolate eyes, and a dimple in the center of their chins. But where Rafe wore his hair long, Zack's was neat and trim.

"I'm waiting." Max crossed his arms over his chest.

"You all seem upset."

"Upset? That's rich," Zack scoffed. "Lady, where you're concerned, we sailed right past upset and straight into a wave of fury." He stepped forward, but Max held out an arm, stopping him from getting closer.

Buck snarled.

"Hey there, boy. Take it easy. Their aggression is just a bit misplaced." She pulled on his collar and spoke in gentle tones, easing him into a sitting position next to her chair.

"They found a dead body in your apartment. Did you know about it?"

"There's an explanation for that." Jordan swallowed hard. "And I did try and tell you."

"Really, when?" Max looked around. "Was I there? Because if I was, I think I'd remember that."

Jordan's glance darted from brother to brother. "How did you find out?"

"See, now that's *not* the question you should be asking," Rafe said. "Because it makes me think you had something to do with it."

Zack leaned against the glass. "Yeah, kinda does, doesn't it?"

Reason demanded she remain calm in this situation. But Zack's last remark pushed her past the tipping point, and now she was the one who was pissed off. "Oh, get real—" she slammed a hand on the desk "—do I look like I could put a bullet in someone's head?"

"Well, now. That's pretty specific," Zack said.

"It's specific because I was there! Because when I came home from what I thought was a lovely afternoon, my entire apartment was empty except for one thing—a dead body in my bathtub with half its skull blown off." With no way to stop it, the image flashed through her mind. Jordan pressed her lips together, focused on a paper with a coffee stain on Max's desk, and took a deep breath, praying she wouldn't be sick.

"Well, now we know why you couldn't reach Sam Morris," Max said.

"What?" Jordan stood. "What are you talking about?"

"The body in your tub was Sam Morris."

Jordan slumped back in her seat and wiped a hand over her face.

"What do you have to say for yourself?" Max asked.

What was there to say? This new revelation shook her to her core, and she wasn't sure how much more of this nightmare she could take. She didn't understand any of it.

"Jordan… Lauren…whatever your name is," Max said. "It's all over the news. That's how we found out."

"I had nothing to do with it! I'm sorry he's dead. But I… I only met him once. After that, it was all texts and emails. I didn't really know him, let alone kill him." She looked up at Max and then turned to his brothers, hoping to find something other than disbelief on their faces. "What's wrong with you people?" she shouted. "Are you thick? Don't you get it? I'm being set up. I don't even own a gun!"

Zack pushed off the wall and stepped forward, and Buck challenged him with a low growl.

Jordan stood. "Hey, you need to stop right there. You're crowding me, and Buck doesn't like it."

Zack huffed and looked at Max. "I can see what you meant when you said she's not very good with people."

"I'm being accused of something I did not do. How would you react?" Jordan sneered. She couldn't quite wrap her mind around what was happening. The entire situation was one sucker punch after the next. She needed to stay strong, but her body wasn't cooperating. Her throat was dry, she was having difficulty focusing, and the slight tremble in her hand was a dead giveaway that she was not in control of her emotions.

Jordan hadn't reacted like this since her days in a group home. Back then, she was always suspected of one thing or another, like when she was accused of stealing another girl's sweater but had nothing to do with it. She'd taken a beating despite her innocence. She was innocent now, but she'd hidden the part about the dead body from Max, and that made her look guilty.

"Let's all sit," Jordan said. She knew it was a lame attempt to give herself time to explain, but she didn't have another suggestion for releasing the tension that filled the room.

Zack seemed to lean harder against the wall, arms crossed against his chest. "I'm fine right here." Rafe sat in one of the chairs, and Max leaned against the edge of his desk, facing her.

Jordan felt cornered.

"Before we go any further, just tell me how, in all the time we spent together this morning, it somehow managed to slip your mind that there was a dead body in your bathtub," Max said.

Jordan pulled Buck closer. She slowly petted his head, more for her comfort than his. "Look, I tried to tell you twice."

"You tried?" Max's tone was snide.

"Yes. You interrupted me the first time in the diner because you saw my face on the television screen."

Max snorted. "Oh yeah, when you tried to convince me you were Jordan Logan, but your picture came up on the news as Lauren Chambers. I remember that."

"Exactly. I did try to tell you. And then, when we came into your office, I tried to tell you again, but you were called away urgently and left."

"You should have tried again and again. That was a vital piece of information," Max said.

"How did that body end up in your bathtub?" Rafe asked.

"I don't have a clue. I told you. It was just there."

"Now that's where I'm having trouble with your story. How does a body just get there?" Rafe asked.

"You know what?" Jordan threw up her hand. "I give up. The body in my bathtub freaked me out. There was blood and brains. I ran. My identity was stolen. And here I am.

And given all that—" she held her arms out to the side "—if you can believe it, I think we've got even bigger problems."

Rafe let out a belly laugh. "Oh, that's a good one. Bigger problems. How?"

"While you were all conferring about what to do with me, Brittany said I could use your laptop."

"She what?" Max asked.

"I needed to find out what would happen when I combined my program with the snippet of code Archer emailed me. The same snippet Sam Morris told me not to marry with my code." She blew out a breath. "To do that, I had to upload both to a laptop."

"You what?" Max leaned toward her, and Buck snarled once again.

"It's okay, Buck. Max and his brothers are in a mood. Ignore them."

"Lady, we're more than in a mood," Zack said.

"Would you stop calling me *lady*."

"*Lady* works for now because we don't know who you are—Jordan or Lauren," Zack answered.

"I'm Jordan. Always have been. Always will be. And you can sit around and attack me all you want. You can even call the cops. In fact—" she waved a dismissive hand "—go ahead. I don't even care anymore. But hear me out. Archer Kelly is behind this, and there is something way more sinister at work besides who I really am and the dead body they think I killed."

"How is that even possible?" Max asked. "How?"

"That is what I'm trying to tell you." Jordan pulled the chair closer to the laptop on the desk. "I wasn't sure what adding Archer's code would do. So I disconnected this laptop from RMZ's system and the internet. That way, if

it were going to do any damage, it would be localized."
Jordan looked up to see Max and Zack exchange glances.
"I'm not an idiot. I'm good at what I do. And I always pro-
tect the client."

"Keep going," Max said.

"When I added Archer's snippet of code to mine, the
combined program began doing something very strange,
and I couldn't stop it."

"Strange how?" Max asked.

"It has a wormlike quality. It went through every file
without so much as a keystroke from me. It actually dug
up deleted files."

"Deleted files? How is that even possible?" Zack asked.

"Yeah. Good question," Jordan said. "That's what we
need to find out. The code is designed to do this for a reason, but I don't know what that is. The other odd phenom-
enon has to do with the fact that most people would never
detect this worm. I was looking for unusual activity. That's
why I found it."

"What are you talking about?" Max asked.

"Usually, something like this enters a system, the antivi-
rus software sends up a warning, or there's a power drain,
or the computer slows down. None of that happened. This
worm virus gets in, and it's undetectable."

"What's the point?" Zack asked.

"I need more time to figure out the end game. What I do
know, what I feel in my bones, is that Archer needed my
code and was able to modify it to serve his purpose." Jordan glanced from one brother to the next and saw skepticism written on their faces. "Dang, you people are clones
of one another with your disbelief."

"Maybe that's because I'm still grappling with the dead body found in your bathtub," Zack said.

Jordan felt unbearably exposed and wasn't certain she could talk her way out of this. "Look. I don't own a gun. All I know is I was supposed to meet Sam Morris for breakfast this morning. When I tried to reach him last night, the text bounced back. His company email said he no longer worked there. And then he's found dead in my apartment. What reason would I have to kill him? None! I don't kill people. But Archer is powerful enough to do that."

"Hang on," Rafe said. "It sounds like you're grasping at conspiracy theories."

"No. I'm not. But I think Sam wanted to meet with me to tell me about this. He was the one who told me not to email the new code. He must've known something."

"Now, we'll never know," Max said.

"The answer is in this code," Jordan said.

"Max," Rafe said. *"Vamos. Quiero hablar ahora mismo."*

"I took high school Spanish. You wanna talk to your brother? I'll leave the room."

"You stay right there." Max pointed to where she was seated. "We'll be right back."

Max stepped into the corridor with Rafe, whose fury was palpable. Before Rafe spoke, Max tilted his head toward Rafe's office, silently indicating they needed to have this conversation in private, away from the rest of the staff. There was no need to involve anyone else.

Rafe huffed and headed into his office.

"Before you say anything, I believe her." Max closed the door. "Kind of."

"I'm miles away from 'kind of.' I totally don't believe her. Something isn't right. Her entire story is convoluted. Even Zack couldn't make this up in those manuscripts he keeps writing. A telenovela isn't this jangled."

Max gave a look. "Oh, come on, they are that complicated and twisty."

Rafe waved his hands. "We're getting off-topic. Let's stick to the immediate problem, and brother, we have an immediate problem." Rafe pointed at the far wall, indicating Max's office on the other side. "That woman is trouble. I don't believe Archer Kelly has anything to do with this. And I think we should call the sheriff. Let the law take care of this. We're cybersecurity experts. We do not deal with this kind of stuff."

"We're already involved," Max countered. "Sintinex is a client. We built them a firewall, and now they want us to fix the breach they hired that woman to create. So, whatever else, we're involved. And like I said, I kind of believe her."

Rafe paced. Max sat in the chair. They eyed each other for a few minutes. Neither said a word.

Max couldn't help but feel that there was a lot of hurt beyond that hard exterior Jordan Logan wore like a coat of armor. Her tough facade cracked enough to expose some vulnerability when he told her Sam Morris was the one found dead in her apartment. The look on her face was too real. He was certain she had nothing to do with his murder.

Max stood. "We're getting nowhere. And I don't like the feeling of being in a standoff with you. So let's make a decision. I know what I want to do. I want to give her a chance to prove herself and help her get her identity back."

"You would." Rafe stopped pacing. "Hold up. You're not

attracted to her, are you? I mean, is that why you're willing to give her the benefit of the doubt?"

Max stared at his brother. "For real? That's what you think?" He knew he had a reputation, and his brothers were constantly ribbing him about it, but now was not the time to even go there.

"Yeah. For real. Sorry, bro. You're a player." Rafe waved a hand. "Don't even try to object. You like dating and don't want to settle down, but I want to make sure that in this instance, where there is so much on the line, the fact that she's a beautiful woman isn't clouding your judgment."

"I'll admit, I like to date. But I don't take advantage of women, and you know that. She's vulnerable, and she needs our help. Nothing more. So whatever you were thinking, pluck that thought out of your head right now." Max headed for the door.

Rafe grabbed him by the elbow. "Sorry. We can't be too careful. We have a business and employees. I've got a wife and a child. I don't want to take chances."

Despite the fact that he was insulted by Rafe's insinuations, he understood. Rafe had already had trouble with the law and now had a family to protect. Max let out a breath. "I get it. But I still want to give her a chance."

Rafe dug his hands in his back pockets. "I'm willing to give her twenty-four hours to prove she is who she says she is. If she can, then we'll help her."

Max raised his eyebrows.

"Listen, if she's as good a hacker as she claims to be, she should be able to make headway in finding out a thing or two. We don't have the luxury of time. Twenty-four hours. Take it or leave it. Otherwise, I'm going to the sheriff now."

Max paused before nodding his reluctant agreement. He

only hoped Jordan could prove herself because there was no doubt Rafe would call in the authorities. "Okay. I'll let her know we're giving her twenty-four hours to—"

Zack stomped into the room. "What are you guys doing? Negotiating the Treaty of Versailles?"

"Get out of my way," Max said. "We can't leave her alone."

"Where's she going to go? Huh? She's a wanted felon. Fe-lon." Zack emphasized each syllable. "One thing's for sure—she can't stay in the office. Her face is plastered all over social media and comes up on a news cycle every ten minutes."

Zack was right. Having Jordan in the office was putting the employees in jeopardy.

"Okay," Max said. "I'll get her out of here and take her to my place."

"Say what?" Rafe put his hands on his hips.

The look on his brothers' faces was a cross between surprise and disbelief.

"Calm down. I have a guest room. Remember? And we all agree she can't stay here—unless you're willing to take her to your place, Zack."

Zack shook his head. "Hell to the no."

"And there's no way you're sending her home with me," Rafe said. "None of us knows this woman, and I'm a little concerned about you taking her to your place." He paused and eyed Max. "Man, I just hope you're not feeling like you need to ride in on a white horse and protect her 'cause we need the truth, but if she feels you're going to make it easy for her to con us—"

Max threw up his hands. "Can we please focus on what's important? Shoot." He huffed. "No white horse. No saving.

I know this is serious, and I also know we need answers. Get your heads on straight."

Zack stepped forward. "Forgive us, but we're in uncharted territory."

"Yes, we are. And I'm open to suggestions," Max said. He waited, but his brothers remained silent. Max figured they'd come to the same conclusion he had. There wasn't another option. They each wanted to know if there was any validity to what Jordan/Lauren was saying. Because if there was truth to her story, and Archer Kelly was behind all of this, they had bigger problems than fixing the breach into the Sintinex mainframe.

"Now, if that's settled, I'll take her back to my place, where she'll be out of sight," Max said, regaining his composure. "And for the sake of full disclosure, I'll stop at the store on the way. She probably needs some clothes. She came here with nothing. And the dog needs some food."

"Whoa. Whoa. Are you nuts?" Rafe said. "You are not going shopping for women's clothes. People around this county know you. They'll wonder what the heck you're doing. Gossip is practically an Olympic sport in Hollow Lake. Let's keep this as quiet as possible." He shook his head and thought for a moment. "I'll ask Mallory for some things and drop them off at your house later."

"Thanks, bro." Max turned and headed back to his office.

Jordan looked up the moment he walked in. She was sitting on the couch, petting Buck on the head.

"Well?" she said.

"Well, looks like you're coming with me."

"Where to?"

"My place."

Jordan raised a brow. "What for?"

"You'll work from there. It's too risky having you in the office." Max walked to the window. A black SUV was parked across the street, outside the diner, and he wondered if Jordan had been followed. "How'd you say you got here again?" He didn't bother to turn around, keeping his eyes on the car.

"I took a Greyhound bus."

"Do you think you were followed?"

"No. But I can't be one-hundred-percent positive."

The front door of the diner swung open. A man and woman dressed in hiking gear exited, followed by two teenagers carrying backpacks. The beep-beep sound of a car's key fob flashed the lights on the black SUV, and the family hauled themselves into the vehicle. Within seconds, they took off. *Tourists.* "Okay then." Max walked behind his desk and shoved folders and thumb drives into his backpack. "Let's go. First order of business is to prove to us you are Jordan Logan. From there, if there's enough time, you can work on getting your identity back."

"What do you mean if there's enough time?"

Max placed his palms on the desk and leaned forward. "My brothers and I are giving you twenty-four hours to prove who you are."

"That's generous." She stood. "What happens after twenty-four hours?"

"If you can't prove you're Jordan Logan, we'll call the sheriff and turn you in."

Chapter 7

Jordan put on her cap, carefully tucking her hair underneath. "Come on, Buck. We're leaving." She picked up Max's laptop and slung her bag over her shoulder.

"Leave that computer here. It has all my business files, and I need to wipe out that worm program you uploaded," Max said. "I'll get a fresh one you can use. Be right back."

Her hand felt clammy as she held on to Buck's leash and waited. She'd thought somehow there'd be a way out of this, but right now, it wasn't looking good. If she were being completely honest with herself, she'd have to admit that she was officially worried. Could she prove who she was within twenty-four hours? Max seemed to be willing to give her the benefit of the doubt. But his brothers were clearly gunning for her. From the little she'd seen, this was a close-knit family. If push came to shove, as it often did, she knew he'd damn well choose his brothers over a total stranger.

"This is a laptop used by our last intern," Max said, entering the room. "Not too much on it. It should be fine." He handed it to her. "You ready?"

Jordan nodded and followed him to a parking lot at the rear of the building. Max stopped at a shiny silver-blue four-door BMW with beige leather seats. Jordan looked through the rear windows at a spotless interior. "Hey, do you have a blanket or something?"

Max shot her a puzzled look over the hood of the car.

"For the dog hair."

"Don't worry about it." He waved her off and pressed the key fob. "Let's just go."

Once Buck was settled in the back seat, Jordan strapped herself in, and Max pulled out of the space. In a matter of minutes, they were on the outskirts of town. If Jordan hadn't been mentally immersed in her problems, she might have enjoyed the scenery.

The leaves were bright green, the forsythia bloomed, and dozens of shrubs with clusters of brightly colored flowers lined either side of the road. The landscape was in full-on spring mode, but she barely noticed.

They drove in silence, and Jordan stared out the window, absently pulling at her lower lip, trying to focus. One question continued to circle around in her mind—how would she prove her identity? "Uh…listen." Jordan cleared her throat. "This time frame of twenty-four hours—" she sucked in a breath "—it's tight."

Max spared her a look then turned to face the road. "In the diner, you told me you had no family or friends. But I find that almost impossible to believe. Isn't there anyone who can vouch for you?"

Jordan swallowed hard. Unable to answer that question without revealing her life story, she chose to remain silent.

"Hello? You got anything to say?"

"I'm not sure what to say."

They drove for a few more miles. This time, the silence was filled with unanswered questions.

Max flipped the blinker. "I don't understand. But we're

here. So, for now, let's get settled, then we'll talk." He pulled onto a tree-lined drive, came to a stop, and put the car in Park.

"This is *your* house?"

"That's what the mortgage papers say."

She wasn't sure what she expected, but it wasn't a pale gray one-story modern farmhouse nestled among a group of pine and birch trees. The wide front porch featured a tall, burgundy door flanked by two large windows. In her mind, it was postcard idyllic.

Max opened the back passenger door for Buck, who leaped out and immediately began chasing a squirrel. A couple of minutes passed while Jordan watched Buck through the driver's side window as he dove behind trees, his tail wagging furiously.

Jordan jumped in her seat when Max knocked on the window. "Shoot. You scared me." She put a hand on her chest.

"You planning on staying in the car, or you gonna get out any time soon?"

"I'm coming. I'm coming." She gave him what she hoped was an icy stare while she tried to settle her racing heart and unhook her seat belt.

Max opened her door. "This is home for the next twenty-four hours."

Jordan looked around. The secluded location put her on edge. "How far from civilization are we?"

"Not that far. I have neighbors on the other side of those trees." He pointed to a densely wooded area to the left of the house.

"Hey, I don't see Buck."

"He'll be fine. He's probably behind the house chasing something."

This was more space than Buck had ever been in without a leash since she adopted him. She couldn't lose him now. He was her only lifeline to sanity. The only one who knew she was the real Jordan Logan. She put her forefinger and pinky in her mouth and let out a piercing whistle, which seemed to startle Max.

"Where did you learn that?"

Jordan ignored the question. "Buck, come!" she called out and waited. When she heard the familiar sound of his bark, she let her shoulders drop. He charged toward her, panting and wagging his tail. She crouched down, hugged his neck, and gave him a good rub. "You like all this space. Don't you, buddy?" He licked her face.

"I hate to break up a good thing, but you have work to do, and I still have questions," Max said.

Jordan gave Buck a final pat and stood. "Lead the way."

She followed him onto the porch and through the front door. Her first impression was that the house was…clean. No, she thought…it was more than that. It gave off a peaceful vibe, and she unclenched her jaw.

The left half of the house had an open floor plan that merged a large living room with a modern kitchen and dining area overlooking a spectacular lake view.

A large glass vase filled with asters stood on the coffee table in the living room. The deep purple blossoms were eye-catching against the light woods and stark white fireplace. Like his office, the furniture had the low, sleek lines of the mid-century modern period.

In contrast to what could only be described as an *Architectural Digest* magazine spread, Jordan felt grungy and was suddenly acutely aware that it had been a while since she'd bathed, and she now probably smelled rank.

She held on to Buck's leash and stepped a foot away from Max. "Uh, I don't suppose I could take a shower. It's been a while since I—" Jordan stopped herself. "Forget it." She shook her head. "I don't have anything to change into, and I can't put these back on." She looked down at her jeans, which felt heavy with dirt and wear. Her white short-sleeved T-shirt was now a dingy gray, and her jean jacket needed to be thrown straight into the wash.

"Don't worry. Rafe's going to get some things from his wife, Mallory, and bring them over. We figured you'd need something."

"She didn't have to do that."

He held up a hand. "It's not a big deal. They're also bringing over some dog food for Buck."

Jordan put a strand of hair behind her ears and looked down at the floor. "Okay. Thanks."

"In the meantime, I have some sweatpants and a T-shirt you can wear after you shower. I'll put you in the guest room. It's on the other side of the kitchen wall. First door on your right. It has its own bath and everything you'll need."

Being dependent on anyone was killing her, but she had no choice. She swallowed hard and looked up at Max. "Thanks. I appreciate it."

"I'll be right back."

While she waited, she let Buck walk around the house, sniffing every piece of furniture before coming back to stand by her side.

"Here you go," Max said as he entered the room.

She took the offered T-shirt and sweatpants but immediately felt awkward. The idea of taking a shower in his house and wearing his clothes gave her an odd sensation. It felt intimate. Regardless of how much she needed his help, he was still a stranger. She held the clothes to her chest and took a step back.

Max must have sensed her discomfort because he said, "Look, maybe we all need a minute to figure out next steps. Why don't I take Buck for a walk while you're getting cleaned up?"

Yes, Jordan thought, that would help put her at ease.

"My neighbor lives about a mile from here. It's a chance for Buck to get some exercise, and she has a dog. Maybe she's got a treat for him till his food gets here."

"That would be nice." Jordan knelt on one knee, taking Buck's face in her hands. "Hey, boy, Max is going to take you for a walk. You be good. You hear?" She kissed him on the nose, rose, and started walking toward the guest room. Buck barked and followed her. "No, come on, boy. This is your chance to be in the great outdoors. You'll love it. Now go." She spoke the last words like a command and pointed at Max. Buck turned toward Max and then back to her and didn't move. Jordan continued to hold her arm out, pointing to Max. Buck seemed to be considering his options and finally turned and went to Max, allowing him to put his leash on.

"I'll leave my cell phone number on the pad on the kitchen island in case you need me."

"I don't have a phone."

Max gave her a questioning look.

She sighed. "Long story."

He furrowed his brow, and she knew he didn't consider her explanation adequate. She rolled her eyes. "Short story. I had to dump it."

Max closed his eyes for a brief second. "We'll get into

that later. There's a wall phone in the kitchen. You can use that if you need to."

"I'm sure I'll be fine." Her words came out clipped. Jordan was in a hurry for them to take their damn walk. She desperately wanted to wash the stink off. "Now go," she said with the same commanding voice she'd used on Buck.

"Close up behind us. I've got the key." They walked past the dining room and out through the French doors. Jordan locked them and watched as Buck and Max headed toward the woods. When she could no longer see them, she turned and headed for the other side of the kitchen.

While she knew she was the only one in the house, the last twenty-four hours had been unlike any she'd ever experienced, putting her off her game and making her more wary than usual. She'd listened to enough true-crime podcasts to make her proceed cautiously as she slowly turned the doorknob to the guest room. With the door open a crack, Jordan peeked in to make sure no one was hiding inside before crossing the threshold.

The large room was light and airy, with a high ceiling and large windows. The queen-size bed with its dozens of throw pillows looked so inviting that she spent a moment mentally debating whether to jump into it, pull the covers over her head, and stay there for the rest of her life.

Instead, she sighed, made an about-face, and headed straight for the bathroom. Getting cleaned up was a priority, and then she could concentrate on the rest of her problems. Although her money was on Archer as the culprit behind this entire nefarious operation, it didn't appear the Ramirez brothers were on board with her hypothesis. She'd work on that after she proved to them she was Jordan Logan.

The well-appointed en suite bathroom was as lovely as

the rest of the house. One shelf held an assortment of shampoos, conditioners, and bath lotions, all with floral scents. In the drawers, under the wide sink, were women's razors, extra toothbrushes, and toothpaste. The room was stocked like a private spa for women, and since he had no sisters, these had to be for whichever woman he happened to be dating at any given time. She shook her head. *None of my business.*

Jordan peeled off her clothes and turned on the faucets. She stepped under the large rain showerhead and, for several minutes, stood with her head tilted back and her eyes closed, allowing the luxury of the hot water to pour over her, almost forgetting where she was. Even knowing that time was running out, she opted to steal a few more minutes of bliss before finally forcing herself to turn off the faucets and get out of the shower.

After toweling dry, she poured body lotion into her palm. A sweet springtime aroma filled the air. The scent was subtle, as if someone had opened a window and the fragrance from a nearby lilac bush was carried in by the wind. "Max doesn't play around. This is the good stuff," she said and looked up to see her smiling reflection in the mirror. It stopped her dead. *Girl, what are you doing? This isn't a spa, and you're not on vacation. Skip the pampering and get dressed!* She let out a bitter laugh, left the lotion on the edge of the sink, and walked out of the bathroom.

She put on the overly large T-shirt that reached midthigh. The sweatpants needed several roll-ups around the waist before she was sure they wouldn't fall off or she wouldn't trip on them. Finally, she blew her hair dry, and only then did she feel marginally better.

Stepping out into the long corridor, she noticed for the

first time a rogue's gallery of sorts with dozens and dozens of framed family photos. When she pressed the light switch, recessed spotlights illuminated the wall. The first photo she studied was of Max standing in a crouch, baseball bat in hand, ready to swing. If she had to guess, she'd say he looked about ten years old. Must have been a Little League game. She followed the images all along the wall, glancing at each one. It appeared to be a chronology of the Ramirez family, from the birth of each brother to the more recent photos of Rafe's wedding. She noticed their mother missing from the pictures about halfway down the hall. She wondered what had happened, and a heaviness closed in on her.

These photos represented everything she'd never had—a family. It wasn't that she was jealous. She was sad—sad that life had cheated her. And now she didn't even have her own name.

Jordan looked away from the photos. She was exhausted. It was nearly impossible for her to think anymore. All she wanted was to lie down and sleep, but that would be irresponsible. Not to mention dangerous. The clock was ticking.

In the kitchen, she checked the time on the microwave. She had no idea how long Max had been gone, and it didn't matter. It was time to get to work. Jordan picked up her purse and the laptop he'd left on the kitchen island and carried them into the living room. She sat cross-legged on the sofa and opened the computer.

Max opened the French doors and unclipped Buck's leash. He watched as Buck padded straight for the sofa where Jordan slept. With her eyes closed and her face relaxed, she looked quite beautiful and oddly peaceful.

Apparently, Buck wasn't content to let her sleep and nudged her hand with his nose. An unfamiliar sensation tugged at Max. Was it empathy? He didn't know, and for a moment, he wrestled with the idea of pulling Buck back and letting her sleep before quickly changing his mind. Rafe had been serious about the timeline, and too many questions needed answers that only this woman could provide. He stood back and let Buck do his job.

It didn't take long before Jordan opened her eyes and smiled. For an instant, she seemed genuinely happy.

"Hey there, boy." Jordan sat up and looked around before her gaze locked with Max's.

He hadn't meant to stare, but he couldn't help it. He was attracted to her. "Hi," he said.

"Were you watching me sleep?" Jordan wiped the side of her mouth with the back of her hand.

She caught him off guard with the question. Max shoved his hands in his pockets and leaned against the kitchen island. "Don't worry. You weren't drooling."

Wiping her mouth again, Jordan stood, and when she ran a hand through her thick hair, he felt a tightening in his gut. She looked sexy as hell in his baggy T-shirt and sweats, maybe because she wasn't trying to be anything but herself. He needed to shut down any thoughts other than solving the problem of her identity and how Sam Morris ended up in her bathtub. He cleared his throat. "So, did you make any progress?"

"What time is it?" she asked, not answering his question.

"It's almost one o'clock. Did you make progress?"

"Honestly, I didn't get far."

He pointed at his watch. "We're a little short on time." As a cybersecurity expert, there were things he could do to help her, but he'd discussed with Rafe that he would let her begin the search on her own to see what she could find. Behind the scenes, Rafe and Zack were working on their own investigation into the Jordan/Lauren situation.

"Let's back up," Jordan said. "I know I need to prove to you who I am. But I truly believe the code Archer asked me to add to what I created is the key to what this is all about. And I needed to find out. I turned the laptop's Wi-Fi off and uploaded the combined code. I did as much work as I could before I fell asleep."

"I'm having a hard time understanding why you would sleep when so much is on the line?"

"Let me explain." She walked into the kitchen area and opened the refrigerator. She pulled out a glass jug of water with a filter top. "Mind if I have some? I'm really thirsty."

"Help yourself."

She looked at him over the rim of the glass and appeared to be stalling for time. He tapped his finger on the counter while she took several healthy gulps and seemed to collect herself. At last, Jordan put the glass on the counter.

"Okay. So. Once the combined program was on the laptop, not much happened," Jordan said. "I mean, you gave me a clean laptop. The only thing on it was a Word program and a couple of files. There wasn't much that could happen. But, yes, it did behave like a worm, exactly as it did when I uploaded it to the computer in your office. I haven't figured out what it's supposed to do after that." She shrugged. "Like I told you and your brothers, I don't know Archer's end game."

"If he has an end game."

"Would you allow me the benefit of the doubt? For one

second, could you see my side, that I am being set up, and this worm has something to do with it?"

"It's difficult. You were supposed to be proving your identity, but I come back, you're sleeping, and all you've managed to do was find out that you don't know what the program does." Max made a tsking sound. "That's about where we left off in my office. Essentially, you're saying there's been no progress."

His phone buzzed. "Wait a second." He pulled the phone out of his back pocket and found a lengthy text from Rafe. He held up a finger. "I need to answer this."

Max quickly typed back a response. When he finished, he walked into the living room, sat in a chair, and put his phone on the coffee table. "Have a seat." He held out a hand, indicating the couch opposite him. "That was a text from Rafe, and it involves you. He won't be able to drop off any clothes for you tonight."

"That's okay." She folded her arms across her chest.

"Rafe and his wife, Mallory, came back from their honeymoon last night." Max continued. "Our aunt, Ellie, took care of Mallory's seven-year-old while they were gone, and she's staying over tonight. Rafe doesn't want to rush out while she's still there. She'll ask too many questions."

"The clothes aren't the problem." She waved a hand over what she was wearing. "I can wait. But I need to get some food for Buck."

"We're all set. My neighbor gave me some dog treats, a bowl, and some food as backup."

"That was lucky."

"Not so lucky. When she met Buck, she said he looked a little malnourished. Said she swore he was eating nothing but processed food. She was horrified and immediately packed a doggie bag with her special homemade organic dog food. She's a little overprotective."

"Did you say homemade and organic in the same sentence as dog food?" She pursed her lips. "I don't think I can find any words to say what I think about that."

"I bet that's a first." Max coughed to cover his laugh. "In the meantime, let's get back on track. The part about you proving your identity? What's your plan?"

"That's the problem. In order to prove who I am, I need Wi-Fi."

"So?"

"I would have connected back to the internet and begun a search for Lauren Chambers or done a further search into my own records, but with this computer already infected with the worm, I didn't want to take a chance that what I was doing was traceable."

Max gave her a pointed look. "You really think Archer Kelly is tracking you? For a minute, back in the office, I thought you might be on to something. But while I was walking with Buck, I had time to think. He's a well-respected billionaire businessman. Why would he do that?"

A short laugh was her only response.

Max stared at her. "Come on. That's not an answer. What are you thinking?"

"You have no idea what it's like to discover everything you've worked for is gone. The person who did that to me, who erased my identity and framed me for murder, I believe is capable of anything. I believe that person is Archer, and, yes, I believe he could track me now that I've put the program on the laptop you gave me." She stopped for a moment and looked around the room. "I'm surprised. You're the cybersecurity expert. This should all be obvious to you."

Max gave a slight shake of the head. "Like I said. I don't buy that it's Archer. He's our client."

"Do you have a computer that I can hook up to the internet?"

"What for?"

"Part of getting my identity back starts with checking my social security number. I didn't get a chance to do that last night. I have to find out if by some miracle it's still assigned to me, or it's been *reassigned*—" she made air quotes "—to someone else."

"You really believe your social security number could be reassigned?"

"Yes. And if it is, I'll dig around to find out who it's been, quote, unquote, 'reassigned' to because that's what I think happened. From there, I'll do some more digging until I get answers that prove who I am."

"Are you talking about hacking into a federal government website on a computer I own? Sorry, but I'm not cool with that."

"Look." Jordan stood and stared down at him. "You're the one who gave me this ridiculous deadline. And I'm at a disadvantage because the laptop you gave me from the office is now infected with the combined program, and I don't believe it's safe. I need a laptop and a Wi-Fi connection. Are you going to help me out here? Because I'm running out of ideas."

Something in her eyes said she was telling the truth, and something inside him wanted to help. "Hang on." Max went to his bedroom, retrieved his personal laptop from his bedside table, and brought it over. "I fully expect you to bounce a signal off every overseas IP address and that nothing gets traced back to my computer or this house."

Jordan didn't say anything, and Max held on to his laptop. "Is that understood?"

"Yes. Yes. I get it." She held out her hand for the laptop. "What's your password?"

Max sat next to her on the couch, gave her the information she needed, and watched as she created a virtual private network and several relay signals to establish an untraceable Wi-Fi connection.

"Happy?" Jordan asked. "VPN in place. Can I continue?"

"Go ahead."

Jordan typed in the URL for the Social Security Administration. When the site loaded, she put in her information, and in seconds, a prompt appeared indicating it was the wrong username or password. She put in her information, which she knew to be correct, a second time, but the identical prompt came up. The third time, she was locked out.

Jordan pressed her lips together and stared at the screen. "Well, that tells me my number isn't mine anymore. Or at least it's not connected to the email address and password that I set up." She turned to face Max. "I have no choice. I need to find out who has my number. I'm going to have to hack in."

"Do what you gotta do. I don't want to know. And whatever you do, don't let it trace back here." Max sprang up from the couch and held up his hands. "I'll be in my study. I'm going to check on the office and see if Archer's called or if there's any other news on the firewall fix."

"But I have your computer."

"I work in cybersecurity. I have several laptops. That's my personal computer, which I use for gaming and watching Netflix. My work unit is in the study. So all good." He stopped. "Well, not all good. But you know what I mean." He shook his head and walked away, hoping this wasn't going to be the biggest mistake of his life.

At five o'clock, he walked back into the living room and found Jordan hunched over the laptop, squinting at the screen. "You've been at this for hours. Did you find out anything?" She looked up at him with an expression he could only describe as grim. "Tell me."

"My social security number, the one I've had memorized since I was fifteen years old and got working papers, is now under the name Lauren Chambers." She held up a hand. "Don't worry, I covered my tracks. That's the one thing I'm an expert at. Anyway, I discovered that my social security number had been assigned to the name Chambers about twenty minutes after I sent word to Sintinex that I'd hacked past the firewall you created for them. For all intents and purposes, according to the world, I'm now Lauren Chambers."

Chapter 8

For several minutes, Jordan stared blankly at the far wall, practically despondent. She didn't care about anything anymore. She'd worked hard to build a life. How had it all been snatched away in the blink of an eye?

"I think maybe it's time for a drink," Max said.

Jordan didn't acknowledge him.

"Hello? Anyone home?" Max waved a hand in the air.

She let out a heavy breath. "I'm trying to think, but my mind's fried. I've run out of solutions. I'm tired and irritable, and I haven't eaten anything since breakfast." She rested her head in her hands. "If I have a drink, I'll pass out."

Max checked his watch. "Come over to the kitchen. I'll fix us something to eat." His voice was gentle. "Together, maybe we can come up with plan B."

Jordan eyed him and wondered why he was suddenly being so…accommodating. Understanding people and their motives had always been a mystery to her. That was one of the reasons she kept to herself. "I'm going to be honest with you," she said. "I know I asked for your help. But I don't typically trust people." She hesitated. "I have to ask. Why are you being so nice? Since we met, you've been a bit of a hard ass much of the time."

Max frowned.

The question wasn't meant to antagonize. She genuinely wanted to know. Again, the trust factor. She wanted to be sure he wasn't playing with her because, right now, he was the only thing standing between her and Archer or maybe even the law. She purposefully kept her tone even and non-confrontational. Her habit of giving attitude as a defense mechanism always got her in trouble. Tonight, she was painfully aware she needed to play it cool. She needed him.

Max rubbed at his jaw. "It's a fair question. I wasn't very nice to you this morning. My brothers and I have put you on the defensive—"

"Ya think?" She put a hand on her hip and quickly took it off, realizing her attitude was showing.

"I see how difficult this is for you." Max leaned on the kitchen counter. "First things first. You're running on empty. Let's eat. Then we can work out where we go from here. I'm the cybersecurity guy. You're the hacker. Between us, we should be able to come up with something."

Jordan nodded. She was more than ready for even a short respite where she didn't have to think or worry.

"I'll make something simple so we can eat sooner rather than later."

"Works for me. And where is the dog food for Buck?"

"In a bag near the back doors. If you look to the right, you'll see an alcove with a washer and dryer. You can set him up in there. There's plenty of room."

Jordan walked to the French doors and looked into a shopping bag that contained a cooler. Inside was a Tupper-ware filled with meat and vegetables, along with ice packs and two dog bowls. "What's all this?"

Buck came rushing over, barking and jumping to reach

for the container. "Hold up, boy. I'm getting to you." Jordan held the container higher. "Man, you weren't exaggerating when you said your neighbor fed her dog people food."

Buck barked and circled Jordan.

"Hang tight, Buck." Jordan filled one bowl with water and grabbed the scooper from the bag. Before she could portion out food into the other bowl, Buck was practically climbing up her leg to get to the container.

"Let me finish." Jordan barely got the last scoop out before Buck put his face in the bowl and lapped up the food.

"That'll keep him busy for about a minute."

"Oh, and the rest goes in the fridge," Max said. "Can't have him eating spoiled food, now can we?"

"It's your fridge." She shrugged. "But I hope he doesn't get used to this."

Max laughed. "Have a seat while I cook."

Jordan washed her hands and then sat on a stool at the kitchen island facing the cooktop, watching Max prepare their dinner.

He'd said he was making something simple, but from the looks of it, it was anything but. The cutting board held onions, green peppers, cilantro, and garlic, and he wielded his knife in a series of slices and dices that reminded her of the cooking shows she'd seen over the years. The muscles in his forearms seemed to dance as he chopped. It wasn't that he was trying to be sexy. He simply was. Naturally. When a lock of dark hair fell over his forehead, she had the urge to reach over and brush it away. She leaned forward but caught herself and quickly settled against the back of the stool.

Her life was in total shambles, but she wasn't dead. Anyone with half a beating heart would notice literally everything about him. But she also wasn't falling for it. This whole let-me-cook-for-you-while-you-just-relax dance was probably something he did at least once a week with a different woman. He'd told her as much in their text chats. He was a serial dater. And his seduction technique was pretty good. She could see women falling for it. Maybe that was why his guest bathroom had all the products of an expensive spa. She might even be into it if she were in the market to be seduced and not in the market to save her life.

Jordan cleared her throat and tried to focus on the preparation rather than on Max. "Where did you learn to prep like that? Your knife technique is impressive."

"You know good knife technique, do you?"

"Don't be a smart ass. I watch cooking shows on television."

Max laughed. "My mother taught me. Actually, all my brothers cook. But I guess I loved it more than they did. Both my parents were lawyers. And they had busy schedules. My mother taught us not to expect that she would work all day, come home, cook, and clean up after us while we sat around watching TV or playing video games."

"Smart woman."

"Oh, she was that all right." Max smiled. "She taught us each how to make different things, and we had a routine. Except Friday night. That was pizza night. And then on Sunday, we had big dinners after church."

"What kind of big dinners?"

"My mother's sisters lived in the area," Max explained as he put the vegetables into a blender. "Aunts, uncles, cousins, all gathered on Sunday at someone's house. We're what you could call a tribe."

While he poured olive oil into the blender, he spoke

about his cousins, Carlos, Marisa, Javier, Jack, and Andres. Where they lived now, and what they did.

Jordan pictured it. She could almost put faces to the people he described. "Are those the people in the photos in your family gallery?"

Max looked up and smiled. "Yes. That's the tribe."

She nodded. "I noticed that your mother isn't in the later photos." As soon as the words were out, she knew she'd overstepped. His back stiffened. His face appeared neutral, but she thought she detected him swallowing harder than usual.

"She died a few years ago. Breast cancer." Max went back to prepping the dinner.

Jordan wondered if losing a mother was worse than never having had one. Now, it was her turn to swallow hard.

"Since we're both starving, I'm keeping it simple. A salad and skirt steak with a cilantro sauce. It so happens I bought steak yesterday. It's in the fridge and needs to be cooked."

He was changing the subject, and that was fine with her. "Sounds amazing." She was so hungry that fried cardboard would do the trick.

"When I worked on Wall Street, we—"

"You worked on Wall Street? You mean you weren't always a computer nerd?"

Max laughed. "Nope. My heart has always been about making money. Retiring early and lying on a beach somewhere. Sounds shallow to some, but to me, it's my slice of heaven."

"But what did you do on Wall Street?"

"I was still a nerd. I was a quantitative analyst."

"Whoa. Nerd with a capital *N*."

"Yeah. You could say that. For a long time, I liked what I did, and then, one day, I stopped liking it." He lifted one shoulder. "Don't get me wrong. I was good at it, but I was tired of making money for other people. Then my brother, Rafe, had some trouble, and me and Zack needed to be there for him. One thing led to another, and we joined his company and became a partnership."

"What kind of trouble?"

"Long story. Let's say the main reason I'm giving you the benefit of the doubt is because I've seen what happens to innocent people when they don't have anyone in their corner."

Jordan studied her hands on the counter. "I appreciate it."

"You're welcome." Max took the steaks out of the refrigerator. "We have about twenty minutes for them to come to room temperature. I'll get the salad going, and we'll eat soon." Max took plates from the glass-front cabinet, two wine glasses, silverware, and cloth napkins. He pushed them over the kitchen island toward Jordan. "Why don't you set the table?"

The dining room table was situated in front of the French doors. The sun was setting, and the lights from the houses across the lake flickered. The setting was peaceful, and Jordan could almost forget she had anything to worry about. The terror stomach that had plagued her all day was easing, and her muscles weren't as rigid. *Hey now. Don't get too comfy. Nice sunset, beautiful view, dinner. It may look like a picture-perfect postcard, but this is not real.* She turned her attention to setting the table. The fortress she'd built around her emotions was there for a reason. It was that trust thing again. The proverbial rug had been pulled out from under her too many times.

She turned when she heard the sizzle of the steaks as they hit the stovetop grill. The aroma was heavenly, and her stomach growled. She thought, first eat. Then she could worry. She needed to keep her strength up because she literally had no idea what was coming around the corner.

Max made a salad and brought the food to the table in serving dishes.

"This looks good," Jordan said. "Thank you."

He uncorked a bottle of cabernet. "Can I offer you some?"

"One glass." She held up an index finger.

He poured them each a glass and then sat, determined to let her eat before he launched into the many questions he had. From the opposite end of the table, he watched her devour her dinner. He waited for her to take a breath. "So, how is it?"

"Looking for compliments?" she asked between mouthfuls.

"Nope. I know my food is good. Just wondering if you're satisfied with it."

She chewed and nodded.

Max took a sip of his wine. He thought she seemed less tense than she'd been since he met her this morning. Now would be the time to find out more about her and get some answers. He put his glass down. "Back to my question from this afternoon."

"Hmmm." Jordan continued to eat.

"How is it that there isn't anyone who can vouch for who you are?" He speared a tomato with his fork. "Like, there's no one who can say you're Jordan Logan?"

Jordan took the napkin from her lap and wiped the corners of her mouth. Swallowed. Looked up. "No."

They stared at each other for several moments before Max spoke again. "How's that even possible?"

Jordan picked up her knife and fork. "I don't have any family. Well…none that I know of."

Max heard what she said but was having trouble digesting that piece of news. Since she'd cornered him at the diner, she seemed to have one on-and-off switch, either tough or defensive. But now, he thought he recognized sadness in her eyes. This was new. "How about friends?" he asked, deciding to tread lightly.

"Nope. Don't have any of those." She sat back in her chair, her gaze directly on him.

Max thought she looked resigned. Ready for an interrogation. And if that was the case, then he'd bring it. "You're saying you have no family and no friends. Sorry, but I don't get it." Given how Max was raised, with a family member never more than a few feet away whether he was at home, in school, at work, or sometimes even on a date, it didn't compute. He pushed his plate away, leaned forward, and folded his arms onto the table.

Jordan sighed heavily. "I don't know why it's hard to believe. I was abandoned by a mother I never knew. My father, whoever he was, was apparently nowhere in the picture, not even on my birth certificate. Dear old Mom was a heroin addict. As a baby, I had to go through withdrawal."

Max tried to keep his expression neutral so she'd keep talking.

Jordan pressed her lips together. "Thanks to my addict mother, most of the time I was sick with one infection after another. Kids with lots of illnesses aren't high on the list for adoption." She scoffed. "Hell, no one even wanted to foster me. I was placed in group homes that were crowded and offered no privacy, and I spent most of my time on the streets where I learned to defend myself in order to survive."

Jordan picked up her wineglass and took a swallow. "I got stronger, of course. Physically and mentally. Most of the time, I was angry, except when I was in school." She let out a harsh laugh. "Go figure. Turns out I was freakishly smart, especially in math. I was able to solve the problem before the teacher could finish writing it on the board. When I started high school, there was this one teacher. Elaine Loeb—she was different. She could see my potential and had me tested. Turned out my IQ was off the charts."

"I can see that," Max said.

Jordan shrugged. "Anyway, Mrs. Loeb helped me. She helped me a lot. For four years, she personally tutored me after school in advanced calculus. It also turned out that there was this guy on her block, Kit Larson, who once taught at MIT. She got him to tutor me in computer science. I got really good with computers. I could practically build one." Jordan closed her eyes. "I guess you could say Mrs. Loeb was my only friend. Anyway, she and Kit helped me get into MIT on a full ride. I got lucky. For the first time in my life. I guess it made up for how I started in this world."

"Doesn't sound like you had it easy."

She tilted her head down and stared at him through her lashes. It was a hard look.

"Yeah. Sorry. I stated the obvious. But why not call this teacher? What was her name… Loeb?"

"I can't." Jordan looked away. "She died two years ago."

"I'm sorry to hear that."

"Me, too. She was special."

"Then what about the guy who taught at MIT?"

"Kit? He was already in his mid-eighties when I met him. He passed away soon after I got into MIT."

Jordan's story explained a lot. It shifted Max's viewpoint, and now, he sincerely wanted to help her. "Listen. You're one of the best hackers I've worked with. I mean, you got past our Impenetrable Wall program. Something our company tested for a year before we presented it to Sintinex. I have to believe there's a way out of this for you."

She leaned forward. "You know what I think. Archer Kelly's behind this—whatever *this* is. And you're not going to get me off that train of thought. It all begins and ends with the program I created to get past your firewall, plus the code he gave me to add to it. I believe he had Sam killed. I believe he wants to get rid of me because I know too much."

"Too much of what?" Max asked.

"I don't know yet. If I knew that, I'd know how to solve this." She blew out a breath. "I need to start with the program." She stood. "Thanks for dinner. I'll clean up and then get back to work. I'll use the infected laptop. Okay?"

Max nodded.

"There's an answer in there somewhere. And I'm running out of time." She picked up her plate and wineglass.

"I'll help you with that."

"You cooked. I got this," she said.

Max ignored her protest and picked up his plate and a serving bowl. "You don't know where anything goes."

"It's a kitchen. And it's not that big. I'll figure it out. Go do whatever you do in the evening."

Max paused and stared at her.

"What?"

"I'm wondering where your clothes are?"

She gave him a quizzical look. "What?"

"The clothes you wore today. I'll throw them in the wash."

"You don't have to do that."

Max shook his head. "On a night like this, without a date, I'd be doing laundry."

Jordan smirked. "Yeah. Right."

"Where are they?"

"Your choice. They're in the bedroom."

"I'll get them, and I'll let Buck out."

Jordan frowned. "Is it safe?"

"He's a smart dog, he's been around the property, and he knows where the house is. He'll do his business and come back." Max opened the French doors, and Buck raced out. Max chuckled. "I had a feeling he had to go. I'll get your clothes. Be right back."

Jordan found containers in the pantry and put away the leftover salad. She scraped the dishes and began loading the dishwasher. Her mind drifted over their dinner conversation. Apart from Mrs. Loeb and the mandatory social workers, she'd never told anyone about her childhood. Or her mother's addiction. Or any of the rest of it. The people who ran the group homes knew. They had her file. And that file contained every infraction, real or created, that had followed her to many different homes.

The last home had been the worst and the best. The worst—because her roommate stole from her. The couple who ran the home fed them poorly and had the bad habit of threatening them with corporal punishment. And in a system too crowded to care, there was no one to complain to.

The silver lining of those dreadful four years was that she landed in Mrs. Elaine Loeb's homeroom class. She'd quickly become the closest thing to family Jordan had ever known. Tonight, spending time with Max, making dinner, and cleaning up made her almost forget her situation. Tonight, something inside Jordan shifted, and it surprised the hell out of her that she found she enjoyed Max's company.

Jordan dried the big glass bowl she'd hand-washed and was on the tips of her toes as she reached to put it back in the overhead cabinet when Max came up behind her to help. His breath on the back of her neck and the touch of his hand, as it grazed hers when he grabbed for the bowl, had her heart rate accelerating and desire blooming from inside. It was a heady feeling. Of all the things to be thinking about. She must be out of her mind. Her life was down the tubes. She was under a deadline. Sex should be the last thing she was thinking about. And yet...

Jordan stepped back and wiped her hands on a dish towel. "I think I'm done here. I'm going back on the computer. But fair warning, I'm going to use the intern's laptop that already has the program on it, and I'm going to connect it to the Wi-Fi."

"Is that wise?"

"It's the only way to really know what this thing does. And the key to proving who I am."

Max opened his mouth, about to say something. But he stopped and scratched the back of his head.

"What?"

"Earlier, you were afraid that by putting the computer online, it would be traceable. What's different now?"

"Nothing." Jordan shifted her weight to one hip. "But we're running out of time. While I was doing the dishes, I thought about it, and my hacker's instinct tells me the only way to get answers is to open up the Wi-Fi and find out what this thing really does."

"I'm not sure about that."

"Twice, I've tried to figure out what this worm does—at your office and this afternoon. Both times, the computer was offline. Maybe its real capability turns on when it's connected to Wi-Fi."

"That makes me nervous. Why don't we discuss it further over a nightcap?"

She took a step back. The invitation seemed to come out of left field. Having a drink with Max had "bad idea" written all over it in indelible ink, but she found that she was tempted, and her body was definitely reacting in the affirmative. Buck's barking startled her. Her mind had been so focused on Max she'd forgotten all about Buck.

Max opened the French doors, and Buck rushed in and circled Jordan. The interruption gave her enough time to come to her senses. "I think this is the only way. I'm going to be super careful, use a VPN, bounce signals, the whole nine yards." She waited for his response, but he looked like he was still mulling it over. "Besides, that laptop belonged to one of your interns. There's nothing on there but a couple of Word documents. It's the safest bet."

She grabbed the laptop. "Thanks for dinner. I'm going to work in my room. I'll say good night. Come on, Buck." As Jordan headed toward the bedroom, she forced herself not to turn around, because if she did, she might lose her resolve.

The coffee brewed while Max cracked a few eggs in a bowl and chopped basil and Italian parsley. He picked up the remote and pointed it at the TV sitting on the corner of the counter. The weather report came up on the morning newscast.

When Jordan walked into the kitchen area, he turned and stopped whisking the eggs. Her shoulder-length auburn hair framed her face in a sexy, sleep-tousled way. She'd ditched the sweatpants and only wore his T-shirt that ended right above mid-thigh. She had long, lean, muscular legs, and he wondered if her skin was as soft as it looked. Max turned away, facing the television, and whisked harder, wishing he hadn't seen so much of her. "Good morning," he croaked. "Did you sleep well?"

"Actually, I didn't sleep much. Last night, I found something on the program. It's important, and we need to talk about it."

"I'm anxious to hear what you found. Let me finish making breakfast, and then I'm all ears. You like scrambled?"

Jordan nodded. "Is there coffee?"

"Yes. It's ready. Help yourself. The mugs are in the first cabinet."

"Where's Buck?"

"I fed him and let him out. He should be back soon."

"Thanks for taking care of him." Jordan looked up at Max. "Coffee first, and then I need to tell you what I discovered."

"And your clothes are washed and folded. There, on the chair."

"That was nice." She walked to the chair and picked them up. "Thank you."

Max couldn't help but take another look at her long legs. He forced himself to turn back to the television to avoid being caught ogling. He stared at the screen, pretending to listen, when a story caught his attention. He put the bowl down, grabbed the remote, and turned up the volume.

A news anchor in a dark gray suit and blue tie, an image of a construction site over his shoulder, spoke directly into the camera. "Axis Industries, one of the largest global companies supplying materials for transportation and infrastructure, came under fire today for using substandard materials. They were recently awarded the contract to construct the new tunnel from New Jersey to Philadelphia, but all work has stopped as an investigation gets underway. Since the announcement this morning, Axis stock is in a free fall."

"Isn't Axis Industries the chief competition for Sintinex?" Jordan asked.

Max slowly nodded. "I believe you're right."

"That's a strange coincidence," Jordan said. "Don't you think? I mean—"

Max held up his hand. "Shhh. Listen."

"In other news—" the anchor continued, now full screen "—Archer Kelly, chief operating officer of Sintinex, appeared on *Early Morning with Stan and Ollie*, along with his newly hired chief computer analyst, Jordan Logan, to discuss the allegations leveled at their fiercest competition."

The camera cut away to the *Early Morning* set. Four high chairs sat in a semicircle. The hosts, Stan Francelli, an ex-Marine sporting a dark crew cut, and Ollie Smith, giant slalom gold medalist in the '22 Beijing Olympics, sat opposite an odd-looking man with a long nose and white-blond hair. The lower third of the screen read Archer Kelly, CEO Sintinex Corp. Sitting to his left was a woman with a wide forehead, thin lips, and a short, dark bob—identified as Jordan Logan, his chief computer analyst.

Rage surged through Max. He turned to Jordan, his face set in a snarl. "If that's Jordan Logan—" he pointed to the screen "—who the hell are you?"

Chapter 9

"You want to tell me what the hell is going on?"

Jordan fisted her hands on her hips. "I'm Jordan." She pointed to the television. "Not that imposter. Whatever is happening, Archer is behind it. Can't you see that?"

"All I see is Archer Kelly, a respected global leader on a morning talk show, with a woman named Jordan Logan, who he has apparently hired to be his chief computer analyst. That's all I see."

"It's a lie! Why won't you believe me?" She put her hand on her chest. "I am Jordan! I told you last night that Archer is trying to destroy me because he doesn't want anyone to know what I created for him, a piece of something more powerful than we could imagine. And I think I've almost found out what it is."

"Do not try to distract me from what's really going on here. How could the woman on television not be Jordan Logan?"

"Because I'm telling you for the last time—I. Am. Jordan. Logan." She spat out the words. "The question you should be asking is, what's Archer's next move? Because if it doesn't seem coincidental that Axis, their biggest competition, is suddenly on the chopping block after decades of good, honest work, then you're not paying attention. And

Archer has you and the rest of the world exactly where he wants. Stupid and looking the other way."

Before Max had time to react, his phone chimed with an incoming text, and he quickly looked at his screen.

NOTHING IS AS IT SEEMS

Max's nostrils flared, and he tossed his phone onto the kitchen island. "Give me your phone. Now," he hissed.

"I don't have one." Jordan crossed her arms over her chest.

"I don't believe you." He marched into the guest bedroom. Jordan followed close behind. Max picked up her leather satchel and dumped it on the unmade bed.

"What word didn't you understand? I told you I don't have a phone. I had to toss it in New York because I thought I was being tracked."

Ignoring her, Max went through each of her things. And came up empty. There was no phone. He scanned the room, not totally convinced she wasn't hiding one. Abruptly, he turned and checked the drawer in the bedside table. Nothing.

"What the hell?" Jordan said.

Ignoring her protests, he stomped into the bathroom and checked inside the drawers and cabinets, surprised to find nothing but toiletries.

Jordan stood in the middle of the room. "What do you want with my nonexistent phone anyway?"

Max gave her a pointed look. "I've been getting these strange text messages from an unknown number. This one said NOTHING IS AS IT SEEMS. I thought maybe you were sending them to force me to believe the story you've been selling, that you're Jordan Logan."

"I *am* Jordan Logan," she screamed. "And I didn't send you any texts. How could I? I was standing right there when you got it. But those messages are the same reason I dumped my phone before I came here. I got an anonymous text that said to trust no one. It was a redundant warning since I naturally don't trust anyone. And this—" she waved a hand at him "—is a perfect example of why."

"Really?"

"Yeah, really. I lost count of the number of times I was accused of stealing some girl's shit and had my things searched, only to be found innocent. Or when I arrived as a newbie in a house, and a girl decided she didn't like me for no good reason, she'd plant stolen stuff in my room, and then I'd be the one in trouble." Jordan grabbed her clean clothes, stomped into the bathroom, and slammed the door shut. "You know what?" she yelled through the closed door. "Forget it. I'm over you and over trying to prove to you who I am. You don't believe me, and your brothers don't trust me. I'm so very tired of fighting people. I've spent a lifetime doing that. No more." She opened the door fully dressed and looked around the room, her gaze searching for something. She blew out a breath. "I'm leaving." She began stuffing everything back into her bag. She threw on her jacket and glanced around the room. "Oh, hell. Where's Buck?" She glared at Max. "I'm going out to look for my dog. Then I'm out of here."

Jordan stormed out of the room. Within seconds, she was on the other side of the French doors and stepping onto the patio, unconsciously clenching and unclenching her fists. Why couldn't he believe her? His distrust stung deeper than it should have, and she recognized it was because she'd let herself become drawn to him. Let herself trust him. She shook her head. Such a foolish mistake.

She stamped her foot. "Buck! Buck!" She blew a piercing whistle and waited for Buck, but he didn't come. Jordan whistled several more times and called Buck's name again and again, to no avail. "Damn, you're going to make me go look for you?" She took in her surroundings. Fifty yards in front of her were dense woods. To her right was the lake. To the left was a road. Jordan suspected Buck went exploring the woods, and she made a beeline for the trees.

She walked on a carpet of fallen leaves from the previous fall, still damp from the morning air. Her mind raced. She thought she was onto something with what she'd found on the laptop last night. She thought Max trusted her. She thought they'd go over it this morning and maybe get some answers. But no, he was still too busy not believing a word she'd said.

"Buck, where are you? Come here, boy. It's time to go." Jordan stopped, hoping to hear his bark; instead, the only sound was her breathing. The canopy of trees overhead blocked the sun, and she bent under low branches as she continued down a nonexistent path. "Buck, come back now!" Jordan blew out a frustrated breath. "Last night, Max said not to worry—" she muttered under her breath "—you'd remember where the house was, and you'd come back. Ha! A lot he knows."

A few feet ahead, she spied a grassy open field. As she got closer, she thought she saw a flash of black dart through the grass. This time, when she whistled, she heard Buck's bark. "Hey, boy, come here." She ran through the knee-high grass but lost sight of him. When she realized he probably thought she was playing a game, she stopped running and waited for him to come to her.

Standing in the middle of the field, she patted the side of her leg. "Boy, I need you to come here now." Finally, he ran toward her and then circled her. "What are you doing, you crazy dog?" He barked several more times, turned, and ran toward the woods on the opposite end of the field. This time, Jordan was in hot pursuit. "Buck, you come back here. Where are you going? Come on, get out of those woods. Now!" Jordan followed him for several yards, all the while calling his name. She stopped when she heard what sounded like twigs breaking. When she turned, she could just make out a tall man coming toward her through the dense leaves. Her fight-or-flight instinct kicked in, and she took off running.

The blood rushing in her head nearly drowned out the barking sound. All she heard was the pounding in her ears, her footsteps as they fell on the ground, and her heavy breathing. She had no idea how far she'd run before she felt a hand on her shoulder, and she was forcibly turned around. Fisting her hand, she drew her arm back and threw a right cross into Max's face.

"Ow! What the hell?" Max covered his nose with his hand.

"Max?" Jordan couldn't quite grasp that she'd punched him.

"What did you do that for?" His voice came out nasally.

"I didn't know it was you." She rubbed the knuckles on her right hand. "Why did you sneak up on me like that?"

"I didn't sneak. I was calling your name."

Jordan shook her hand out. "After I started running, I

couldn't hear you. Between the barking and my breathing—I thought I was running for my life."

Still covering his nose and slightly bent over, Max looked at her sideways. "Where did you learn to swing like that?"

"I've had the opportunity to perfect it over the years. I had to." Jordan didn't want to apologize for learning to take care of herself. That was simply part of who she was and what she'd lived through. But she was sorry she'd hurt Max. "What do you want anyway? Why were you chasing me through the woods?"

Max stood upright.

"Looks like I only clipped you. With some ice, it shouldn't bruise."

"Don't worry about me, I'll ice it. It's not the first time I've been punched. Remember, I have brothers." He wiped his nose one last time.

"So?" Jordan put a hand on her hip.

"I came to find you. My brothers are at the house and want to talk to us."

She threw her hands up. "Oh, well, that's just perfect." Jordan walked past him then spun on her heel and stared at him. "I'm not really feeling like facing a firing squad this morning. I told you I'm leaving—"

"Oh, shut up. Please. Could you possibly be quiet for one minute? You think you can do that?"

This was a side of him she hadn't seen. He sounded frustrated and tired.

"Come with me. They have something to show us."

"What?"

"They wanted us both there, and I'm equally anxious to hear what they have to say."

"Oh, I doubt that." Jordan whistled for Buck, who came

running. Together, they followed Max back to the house. Her mind's eye pictured where she'd left her leather satchel, and she had every intention of grabbing it as soon as they entered his house and making a run for it. She didn't care what his brothers had to say. They'd already shown her who they were, and they weren't to be trusted.

Chapter 10

As soon as they entered the house, Buck rushed over to Zack and Rafe, who were sitting at the kitchen island.

Jordan shook her head. *Traitor.*

"Bro, what happened to your face? Run into a tree?" Zack asked.

Max raised an eyebrow. "Low-hanging branch."

Jordan ignored Max's brothers, walked into the bedroom, picked up her leather satchel, and slung it over her shoulder. She marched back into the kitchen area and stood on the opposite side of the island from Zack and Rafe. "Okay. You got a couple of minutes. What do you want to tell me?"

"Good morning to you, too," Rafe said, sliding a shopping bag across the counter.

"What's this?"

"Clothes," Rafe said. "From my wife. She picked up a few things for you. Hope they fit."

She peeked into the bag, surprised that the tags were still on the clothes. It immediately reminded her of all the times she'd arrived at a new group home and been given a bag of hand-me-downs. "Thanks," she mumbled.

"The dog food is in the pantry," Rafe said.

Jordan gave him a skeptical glance. She wasn't planning on staying and was done with pleasantries. "What is it you want to tell me?"

"Want some coffee first?" Zack asked.

Jordan wrinkled her brow, unable to wrap her mind around this one-eighty change in attitude. But since she hadn't had a chance for any caffeine this morning, she figured one cup wouldn't hurt, and then she was gone. "I know where it is. I'll get it."

"You get your coffee. I'll get Buck settled," Max said.

Why are they all being so solicitous? Yesterday, they couldn't wait to throw me in jail. From the corner of her eye, Jordan kept the brothers in sight while she grabbed the mug of her now cold coffee and tossed it in the sink. After pouring a fresh cup and swallowing a grateful mouthful, she looked up. "So, can we get on with this?"

Zack took a laptop from his backpack and turned it to face Max and Jordan. The screen featured a black-and-white newspaper photo of a group of twelve people dressed in jeans and T-shirts standing in front of a whiteboard.

"What do you see?" Zack asked. "I'll give you a hint. Check out the woman on the far right of the picture. The one who isn't smiling."

It took a few beats before anyone said a word.

"Is that you?" Max pointed at Jordan. "Your hair was so short."

"Yeah, that's her," Zack confirmed. "Now read the caption below."

The photo had been taken over ten years ago. Inwardly, Jordan smiled, remembering it as the best summer she'd ever had. She'd finally gained independence and was officially deemed an adult by the courts. That was the summer she did what she wanted when she wanted.

"Holy crap." Max turned to look at her. "That's you. For real. Your name is in the caption."

Jordan pursed her lips, knowing the expression on her face read—*Yeah, dumb butt, that's what I've been trying to tell you. I'm Jordan Logan.*

"Hang on there. This says you were working at a computer lab at Stamford. I thought you went to MIT?" Max asked.

Ever doubtful. Jordan blew out a breath. "It was a summer program working with underprivileged kids, developing computer games to teach math. At the time, MIT didn't offer anything like it. Since I wasn't officially a student at Stamford, I got Mrs. Loeb to get me in as a volunteer, and that's the reason I didn't appear in any official paperwork."

Max stared.

"What are you looking at? It was a chance to help the less fortunate. I knew what it was like to be disadvantaged. I wanted in. You know, a chance to give back."

"I thought every bit of the real Jordan was erased?" Rafe said. "How did you find this?"

"It's like Jordan said. She wasn't registered at Stamford. She was technically a volunteer and wouldn't be listed as part of the program. If there's nothing listed, there's nothing to find to erase," Zack explained.

"But that still doesn't answer how you found this article with this photo," Max said.

"Glad you asked," Zack smirked. "I used my new facial recognition program. The scary part is that every photo the program found came up as Lauren Chambers except for this one."

Max frowned. "I don't get what you're saying."

"Only one photo out of the dozens that were online indicated she was Jordan Logan. That one photo was an anomaly. And that made me curious. I did some more digging and discovered all the photos indicating she was Lauren Chambers had their metadata changed two days ago."

"You mean someone with technological know-how changed all of Jordan's online photos to appear with the name Lauren Chambers?"

Zack nodded. "It had to be a powerful program and someone who knew what they were doing to accomplish that change so quickly."

"Devious," Max said.

Jordan was flooded with a sense of relief. While she knew there was more work to do to get back her identity and figure out what Archer was planning, at least she no longer had to prove who she was to Max and his brothers.

Max reached over and squeezed her hand. Oddly, the resentment she felt toward him only moments before was gone. His touch and wide smile seem to release a thousand butterflies in her stomach. The fluttery sensation threw her off balance. Over the years, she'd met some men on dating apps. Being the expert hacker, she'd been able to separate the crazies from the lunatics and date the sane ones. But she'd never had a real relationship. Had never wanted one. And the rush of attraction she felt for Max was alien. Whatever this was, she needed to push it aside. Without her identity restored, she couldn't afford to be distracted. And from where she stood, Max was a definite distraction.

"But there's more." Zack turned the laptop back to face him and typed several keystrokes. "I thought I'd do some searching on the real Lauren Chambers since you—" he pointed at Jordan "—seem to have been given her identity." He hit more keystrokes. "Turns out, in addition to being accused of corporate espionage for stealing manufacturing secrets, it appears she has several aliases."

"What do you mean aliases?"

"Does the name Lauren Caine mean anything to you?" Zack asked.

"Sounds familiar," Max said. "Hang on. I'm pretty sure she's the one who invited us to bid on the Sintinex job. I know I have an email from her somewhere." He pulled out his phone and scrolled. "Yup. Here it is." Max showed Zack his phone screen. "This is the email from Lauren Caine, Sintinex, director of new projects."

"Jeez," Rafe said, pulling his hand through his hair. "Have we been set up?"

For a moment, no one said anything.

Jordan's mind was spinning like a windmill in a hurricane. Between this new revelation and what she uncovered last night, she was convinced they'd all somehow been duped into helping Archer.

Jordan cleared her throat. "Now that you've all agreed I am who I say I am, there's something you need to know."

"There's more?" Zack's voice was deadpan. "Please tell me you've found a way to get your identity back and, miraculously, despite everything we're discovering, that Sintinex had nothing to do with it, and we can all go back to living our lives."

Jordan didn't answer because it was an unrealistic hope. What she had to tell them wouldn't be well received. "Be right back." She hurried into the bedroom, grabbed the intern's laptop, and returned to the kitchen island. "This is what I was going to tell you about this morning before that woman appeared on TV pretending to be me, and *you* went crazy." She raised an eyebrow at Max.

"Yeah. Uh. Sorry about that."

"Last night, when I combined the program I wrote with the snippet of code Archer asked me to add and uploaded it to this computer, it did what I expected."

"Which is?" Rafe asked.

"Well, we know it goes through firewalls undetected. My part of the program was designed that way. What Archer's portion of the program would do was a little trickier to figure out because it acts like a worm—"

"The worm part has already been established," Max said, sounding slightly irritated.

"That's not the point I was trying to make," Jordan said.

"It's not?" Max exchanged glances with his brothers. "I'm not sure I'm ready for this."

"The combined program has the ability to access every file that ever existed on that hard drive. Even deleted ones." She looked at Max. "You gave me a laptop that belonged to an intern. We both thought there were only a few Word documents on it."

Max nodded.

"Turns out that laptop once belonged to your accountant, Randy Silver."

"How do you know Randy Silver?" Zack asked.

"I don't. That's the point. The combined program dug up all his old spreadsheets and financial projections, even though the files had once been encrypted and deleted and the trash emptied."

Max let out a low whistle. Zack moaned. And Rafe shook his head.

"This combined program is mind-blowing," Jordan continued. "It will find ghost files. You know what that means? Even if you use file-shredding software to destroy a file and think it's gone for good, once this program is in your system, that once deleted, destroyed, shredded file miraculously reappears."

She took a moment to let her words sink in. "It can even create new documents and write emails based on what is or what once was in the system."

"Is this for real?" Zack asked.

"'Fraid so." Jordan nodded. "But that's not the worst of it."

"I can't *even* with this," Rafe said. "What could be worse?"

"The reason I couldn't figure out what the worm was capable of when it *wasn't* connected to the Wi-Fi is because for it to function, it relies on instructions from a remote server. Once I discovered that, I was afraid to take it further. I shut it down and removed the program from your laptop."

The brothers' stunned looks said it all.

Max began pacing in a circle. "I don't even know what to say."

"This is probably what Archer used to bring Axis down. He infiltrated their system and planted false information. Why else would a global company like Axis, with a sterling reputation for decades, suddenly be found guilty of substandard materials?" Jordan said. "It makes no sense."

"She has a point," Rafe said.

"With this information—" Jordan looked at Max "—you could go to the authorities and have them start an investigation into Archer."

"Why don't *you* go to the authorities?" Zack asked.

Jordan cocked a brow. "Seriously? Did you forget you three are the only ones who know who I really am?"

"Uh. Excuse me, but I have proof with that news article you're Jordan Logan."

"Zack, that's one article, up against a driver's license, bank accounts, social security number, and God knows what else that says I'm Lauren Chambers."

"Yeah," Max said. "Let's think this through."

"Let me show you exactly what's what so you can present the case." Jordan opened the laptop and turned it on. She typed in Max's password and, within seconds, was on the home screen. "Okay, here's what—"

The screen turned to static.

"What the hell?" Max said. "I've never seen that before."

The static lasted for a few seconds, and then a green light appeared, indicating that the laptop's camera was activated. A moment later, Archer Kelly appeared on the screen. "Hello, Max. Hello, Jordan."

Chapter 11

The room was silent, and Max was dumbfounded. He was trying to work out if this was a recording or a live feed. Either way, it was distressing to see Archer Kelly on the screen, smiling broadly.

Max approached the counter, and Jordan, Zack, and Rafe crowded around him. "What the hell is going on?"

Archer let out a soft laugh. "Relax, Mr. Ramirez. No need to get into a huff." His long fingers brushed away a wisp of blond-white hair that fell across his forehead.

Max thought his eyes looked like pale blue marbles and were oddly familiar, but he couldn't quite place where he'd seen them before.

"I see in addition to Jordan, your brothers are with you. How very convenient for me."

"What are you talking about?" Max asked and grabbed hold of Jordan's hand. His instinct was to protect her. This creep had certainly put her through enough. Whatever doubts he'd had about Jordan's stolen identity were gone. He now knew this man was dangerous.

"The minute you uploaded my program onto your laptop, it pinged me—allowing me entrance into your hard drive. And poof—" Archer raised his arms in a heavenly motion "—here I am. It didn't matter that you removed the program because it's designed to leave traces on any hard drive it invades. You only *think* it's deleted, but it's still there, and I have total access. I own this computer now." He laughed again. "Don't you just love technology? And I have all of you to thank."

"What are you talking about?" Max sneered.

"RMZ Digital created a firewall I can use to protect Sintinex. Of course, I've added a few modifications. I had to in order to protect myself from you. Didn't I? Then there's the lovely Jordan Logan, or shall I say, Lauren Chambers. Her program was genius. All I had to do was have her add one little snippet of code, and it became a program that not only breaks barriers but also takes over any system it infiltrates, undetected."

Max could barely speak. The fact that Archer had used them all pissed him right off. He wanted to reach into the screen and smack the bastard around a few times. But Max didn't want him to know he believed him or cared. At this point, he needed to prevent him from using the program on anyone else. Because it was clear what Archer now controlled was a serious threat. "I'm going to stop you right there."

Archer laughed again. "Stop me? Ha." His expression hardened. "You have no clue who you're dealing with."

"Look, I'm going to cut to the chase. We have enough information to go to the authorities and get you put away. We know you were behind stealing Jordan's identity. We know Lauren Chambers is really Lauren Caine. We know you sabotaged Axis Industries, and we can prove it. So you can laugh all you want, you son of a bitch, but we're going to take you down."

"Silly man. You have no proof. I've made sure I'm coated

with digital Teflon. Nothing you come up with will stick to me. The only thing the authorities will find is the program that Jordan wrote. She combined her program with my snippet of code on this computer, and *voilà*, it's a whole new program with her digital fingerprints all over it, not mine. *She* is now the author of the program. After you've presented the evidence to the authorities, it will only prove the program was created by Ms. Logan, who by now is only known as Lauren Chambers, who already has a record as a thief and, wait for it, a murder charge. They'll have no choice but to arrest her."

"You piece of sh—"

Jordan placed her hand on his forearm. "Max, don't worry about me. I'll find a way out of it. You have to go to the authorities."

Archer leaned forward and smiled. "I don't suggest that, Ms. Logan. Listen to me carefully, I can and I will destroy you, Max, his family, and his business."

Max had had enough. The idea that Archer was video conferencing them uninvited and threatened Jordan with an arrest if they informed the authorities was bad enough. But now the bastard was going after his family and his business. He'd reached his limit of listening to crazy. Without warning, he slammed the laptop lid, picked it up, and, with all his might, threw it on the floor. He lifted his foot and stomped on it until he'd smashed it enough to free the hard drive from its casing.

The room fell silent as they all surrounded the murdered laptop. Max was breathing hard. He retrieved the hard drive and headed to the French doors and onto the back patio. On the way, he grabbed a hammer from a drawer in the kitchen. Buck followed him while the others watched from the kitchen area.

Max placed the hard drive on the patio floor. "Hey, boy, stand back." Buck tilted his head, clearly not understanding, but Max didn't want him to get hurt. He took Buck by the collar and walked him to the patio's edge. "Sit." Remarkably, Buck sat. "Now stay." Max turned and sensed Buck was right behind him. He turned and held up his hand. "Stay." When it appeared the dog would obey, he walked back to the center of the patio, lowered to one knee, raised his arm, and smashed the hammer down as hard as he could. He continued to hammer until only tiny shards of silver and black remained. And still, he wasn't finished. He stormed back into the kitchen and retrieved the broom and dustpan. His brothers and Jordan watched in silence. He swept up all the pieces and walked down to the lake. This time, he welcomed Buck's company. When he got to the water's edge, he heaved the debris as far out as he could.

When he returned to the house, there wasn't much to say about what he'd done. He'd had no choice but to destroy the laptop. For all intents, Archer had been in his house. He'd found a way to get into his computer. His techie mind thought it was remarkable. But as a human being, forgetting technology, it was scary as all get out. He wanted to burn incense or sage and do some sort of spiritual cleansing. Or at least fill a bucket with water and ammonia and wipe down his counters. He wasn't sure what his next move should be.

For a long time, no one spoke, and each of them seemed to be in their own world. Rafe sat on the couch, elbows on his knees, head in his hand. Zack was perched on a stool, staring off across the lake. Jordan leaned against the kitchen counter, arms crossed over her chest, eyes closed.

Finally, the silence was broken by the ringing of Max's phone. His heart quickened when he saw his father's number. "Pop's calling me." Max swiped open the call. "Hey, Pop. What's up?" Max nodded and listened with the occasional "Uh-huh" thrown in. Several minutes passed before he said, "I understand. Zack and Rafe are here. I'll fill them in, and we'll call you back." There was another pause. "Don't worry. We'll find out what's happening. Love you, too." The call ended. Perspiration gathered on his brow, and he ran a hand over his face. He couldn't believe what his father had told him. His stomach was crowded with the same jitters he experienced when Rafe was sent to prison, and he and Zack had tried to discover who had framed him.

"You going to tell us what that was all about? Or are you going to keep us in suspended animation?" Zack asked.

Max blew out a breath. "I don't even know where to start."

"Just spit it out!" Rafe demanded.

"Pop got a call from Chester Holly at the bank. He said a quarter of a million dollars was deposited into his savings account. Chester thought it was odd because Pop had never made a deposit that large, and the money he already had in his account put him over the FDIC limit. Pop told him it was a mistake."

"I'd say so," Rafe said.

"Chester said the money was definitely meant for Pop. He triple-checked his account number against the wire transfer."

"Who was the wire transfer from?" Jordan asked.

"It came from an offshore account," Max said.

Zack put up a hand. "Let me guess, the transfer's untraceable, right?"

"Bingo," Max said. "But wait. The money in Pop's account was there for maybe an hour before another transfer order was put through, allegedly by Pop, to one of *Tía* Ellie's accounts."

"I'm completely lost," Rafe said.

"Yeah," Max said. "Pop and Chester had similar confusions."

"Let me see if I'm tracking with you on this." Rafe stood and circled the coffee table while he talked. "A quarter of a million dollars from an offshore account goes into Pop's account. Then he supposedly transfers it to *Tía* Ellie. Have I got it straight?"

Max nodded.

"But why? How? Who?" Zack asked.

"All good questions, brother. But if I had to guess, I'd say this is Archer's attempt at messing with us," Max said.

"But how could he do that?" Jordan asked. "It's only been maybe ten minutes since you ended the call and smashed your laptop."

"He probably already had this in motion before he popped up on the computer," Max said. "It has to have something to do with that all-powerful combined program with the worm."

"That may be, but we don't know why the money was deposited and then transferred. So, what's our next move?" Zack asked.

"I think we should get Taylor involved. She has to be able to help," Max said.

"Who's Taylor?" Jordan asked.

"She's my girlfriend," Zack said, "and she'd be the perfect person. She's FBI."

Jordan's eyes widened.

"Unfortunately, that's a no-go. She's on assignment undercover, and there's absolutely no way for me to reach her."

"Come on. Family meeting time. Let's sit." Max walked to the dining room table and pulled out a chair. There was too much happening, and they needed a plan. Zack and Rafe followed, but Jordan stayed where she was. Her arms folded across her chest, leaning against the kitchen island. Max stared at her. "That means you, too."

Jordan didn't move.

"It's going to take all of us to get the hell out of this."

"Look, this is all happening because of me." She put a hand on her chest. "The best thing for me to do is pack up and leave. If I disappear, Archer will leave you alone."

Max tilted his head. "You done?"

Jordan didn't answer.

"'Cause no one at this table will let you do that. I don't want anything to happen to you."

"He's right," Rafe said. "Archer is dangerous. We're in this together."

"We're in this together," Zack repeated.

"Now that that's settled, we need to find out why Archer did this and devise a viable strategy to stop him." Max wrapped his foot around the leg of the chair beside him and swung it out. "Jordan, come sit next to me."

At first, Jordan didn't move, afraid her jellylike legs would give out and they'd see her tough exterior crumble. She'd never had anyone stand up for her like Max and his brothers. The idea that they would want to include her made her feel slightly fragile. For now, she'd stick with them. But only because she'd brought this hell to rain down on their family, and that had never been her intention.

Jordan pushed off the counter, walked to the dining table, and sat in the chair next to Max. "Where do we begin?"

Max's phone pinged, and he looked down at the screen. "Hang on. Looks like Archer isn't done with us yet."

"What is it?" Jordan frowned.

"A bank alert. They want me to call."

"Could be a scam," Zack said. "Call the number from your contacts. Don't press anything in the text. I trust none of that."

"I think I know how to avoid being scammed. Avoiding a crazed power-hungry maniac, not so much."

The call with the bank lasted several minutes before Max put his phone down and relayed the news. "A half a million dollars was transferred into my account from *Tía* Ellie's account." He looked at Jordan. "We all bank at the same place. It's the only game in town." He brushed his hair from his forehead. "But as soon as it hit my account, I allegedly authorized another transfer for fifty thousand to a man named Mario Fusi. Chester called to remind me anything over a ten-thousand-dollar deposit gets reported to the IRS. Also, he said, with these many transfers in such a short amount of time, it was all looking sketchy. He was worried and said there was sure to be an investigation." He let out a heavy sigh.

"Who the hell is Mario Fusi?" Jordan asked.

Max shrugged.

"On it," Zack said, heading to his laptop on the kitchen island. They all turned and watched him type on the keyboard. It took several minutes before he turned and faced them. "Well, well. Isn't this an inconvenient turn of events? Now I think I know the reason behind all these transfers."

"I almost don't want to know," Rafe said.

"Yeah, it would have been better, but we're in too deep now," Zack said. "Mario Fusi is an attorney. But not just any attorney. He's the state prosecutor assigned to the Rustokov case."

"Rustokov?" Jordan asked.

"The biggest Eastern European mafia family on the East Coast," Max said. "Now it's all beginning to make sense."

"How? I still don't get it," Jordan said.

"The head of that crime family is a man named Davide Rustokov. His son, Davide Jr., is currently out on a two-million-dollar bond awaiting trial for running the biggest meth lab syndicate on the Eastern seaboard."

"Oh, man, the hits keep on coming," Rafe sneered.

"I still don't get it," Jordan said.

"In this part of the state, it's a big case. Rustokov has been featured in the news every day." Max shook his head like he was trying to shake away a buzzing fly. "The trial starts in two weeks, and the presiding judge is none other than Emilio Ramirez, our father."

The room seemed to spin, and Jordan held on to the corner of the table. Archer had truly tied them all together into one big knot. "This is not good. All those money transfers. Does that mean—"

Max put up a hand. "The first transfer was into my father's account, and it came from an offshore source. The Rustokov family's holdings include numerous offshore accounts. It wouldn't take a big leap for an eager journalist to imply that there's a money trail and my father was taking a bribe."

"And the fact that the money left his account and went into yours and *Tia* Ellie's makes it look like money laundering," Rafe said. "Pop's reputation would be ruined."

"But the trial hasn't even begun. And what if this guy— what's his name—Rustu-whatever—ended up guilty in court? Your father would be okay."

"That's not how they're going to play this," Max said. "I bet Archer will leak this to the press before the trial even starts. And the evidence is damning. It would be grounds for disbarment."

"Not to mention the case would be thrown out," Zack said, "and you and *Tia* would be accused of money laundering."

"Wow. A complete train wreck with no survivors. Archer said he'd destroy us, and this is how he starts. We are so totally screwed." Max paused and looked at his brothers. "I'm at a loss for how to make this go away."

"Damn him!" Jordan smacked the table with her hand. "Archer is like ten steps ahead of us, ready to hit the destruct button at a moment's notice. I refuse to be on the losing end to this dirtbag." She stood so fast that she almost lost her balance. "I need a minute to think." Wrapping her arms tightly around her waist, she paced. Buck was soon at her heels.

Jordan made her way over to the French doors and looked out on the lake. The wind had picked up, and dozens of helicopter seeds from the nearby maple trees spun in the wind. She was nearly mesmerized watching them whirl around before they dropped onto the water's surface. "Hold on," she whipped around. "I got an idea. But you're probably not going to like it."

Chapter 12

"I think I know how to make this money disappear," Jordan said. "At least temporarily, until I figure out how to remove the program from the Sintinex mainframe. That's ultimately how to stop Archer," Jordan said.

"How exactly do you plan to make money disappear?" Max asked.

"I'll need the internet at the office because the Wi-Fi here might be compromised. Then I'm going to do some things that aren't one-hundred-percent straight up and *move* the money." Jordan read the skepticism from the creases in Max's brow. "Listen, until Archer came into my life, I'd never done anything illegal. But we're under attack and—"

All at once, Max and his brothers began to object.

"Stop. Please stop." Jordan waved her hands like she was ground control, landing a plane. "We aren't dealing with a sane person. He's unlawfully transferred money into your accounts to make it look like your father will take a bribe. Archer is trying to get him disbarred. If you think playing it by the book against someone as evil as Archer is better, then you're woefully underestimating what you're up against." She scanned their faces. "I don't know why he picked us, but we must stop him. And we need to move that money out of your accounts before he can leak this to the media."

Max nodded. "I don't like the idea of doing something illegal, but I don't see how we have a choice. Too much is on the line."

After a few more minutes of discussion, they agreed they would go to RMZ's offices. Zack and Rafe would work on what access they still had, if any, to the Sintinex system while Max and Jordan worked on moving the money.

On the way to RMZ, they dropped Buck off at Max's neighbor's house. Once they were in Max's office, he hit the blackout button, turning the glass wall opaque. "Okay. What do you need from me?" he asked.

Jordan made herself comfortable at Max's desk and turned on his computer. "I need the birth dates, social security numbers, and bank account information for you, your father, and your aunt. Any idea how I can get those, or should I—" she wiggled her fingers over the keyboard "—hack away?"

"Hold on, scooch over." He tapped her knee, and Jordan rolled away from the desk. Max squatted, pushed some buttons under the desk, and a hidden drawer opened. He rifled through several index cards, pulled two out, and handed them to her.

"What's this?"

"What you asked for. I'm the executor for the family. I have everyone's information."

"And you keep it on index cards hidden in a drawer under your desk?"

"I'm a cybersecurity expert. I know how easily someone's information can be compromised on the cloud. I opt

for storing personal information the old-fashioned way."
He shrugged. "It helps me sleep better."

Jordan rolled her eyes.

"How else can I help?"

"Uh…there is something. Considering we never got to
eat breakfast, and now it's lunchtime, maybe you could go
across the street to that nice diner and pick me up a fried
chicken sandwich with fries. I have a craving. And hold
the mayo—" she shuddered "—I hate mayo."

"I can do that. Rafe and Zack could probably use something to eat, too. I'll be right back."

"And a Coke."

Max nodded and headed out the door.

Jordan caught herself staring at how nicely his jeans fit
from behind. She sighed and turned her gaze back onto the
screen. *Stop being stupid. Get to work.*

Twenty minutes passed, and she had only just begun
working on moving the money.

"How's it going?" he asked as he set a brown paper bag
on the desk.

Her stomach grumbled. "Man, that smells so good." She
opened the bag and pulled out the sandwich, Coke, and
fries. "Oh, super cool. Bottles are the best. And it's ice
cold. Yum." She tore the aluminum foil off the sandwich
and took a huge bite. While she chewed, she used her nails
to tear open a ketchup packet and squeeze it onto a corner
of the foil, making a little puddle. She took a fry, dipped it
in, shoved it into her mouth, and chased it with a big gulp
of Coke. Jordan took a minute to chew and then swallowed.
"So good. Sorry, I was starving."

"I see that. Food seems to have a big presence in your life."

Jordan smirked. "It's from all the years I didn't get

enough to eat. Now, if you have nothing better to do, sit. Eat. And watch. But do not get in my way."

Max smiled. "Got it." He unwrapped his sandwich and reached for a fry. "Mind?"

"Help yourself," Jordan said and turned her attention to the screen. She needed to move quickly and be mindful of the clock. She had no idea if Archer had planted any minefields or if he had eyes on what she was doing.

"Can you at least tell me your plan?" He reached for a napkin. "I mean, since most of the money is in my account, I think I have a right to know what we're doing here."

Jordan sighed and turned to face him. "I'm almost done with step one. I'm taking the fifty thousand dollars that came from your account and was then deposited into Mario Fusi's account, and I'm putting it back into your account." She pressed several keys on the keyboard, stared at the screen, and waited for about two minutes. "There. Done. The money is back in your account, and there's no trace of it ever being in Mr. Fusi's account."

"How'd you do that?"

"Let's keep it short on the details." She reached for a french fry.

Max chuckled. "You're too much."

"Don't celebrate yet." Jordan took a few more minutes and typed in a string of code. She stopped, took a bite from her sandwich, and continued keying in code. She wiped her mouth and waited, staring at the blinking cursor.

"What are you waiti—"

"Shhh. Be patient." Jordan took another bite of her sandwich and chewed. Several seconds passed, and she pressed more keys and waited another several minutes.

"Okay. There is no trace of the money ever being in your aunt's or your father's account."

"I don't even want to know how you did it. But thanks."

She checked the time on the screen. "All the money is now in your account. Getting it out and putting it someplace else is going to take a bit more time."

While Jordan typed, she explained her plan to Max. "I'm creating a new identity with its own tax ID number in order to open several overseas accounts. I'll hack into the databases of those banks to make it look like they've been there for years. That's step two."

For the next thirty minutes, Jordan worked at the computer, scanning data spread over several open tabs. When all the accounts were finally active, she stretched her arms overhead and arched her back. "We're all set."

"What's next?"

"Max, you don't have to sit here and wait. I'll find you when I'm done. Why don't you check on Rafe and Zack?"

"Not a chance. I'm not leaving your side. In case you need me, I'm right here." He winked.

Apart from her high school teacher, Mrs. Loeb, she'd never known anyone who was there for her. Max was growing on her in ways she'd never thought possible. She smiled. "I'm going to start making small wire transfers from your account to these four overseas accounts. Each time I make the transfer, the account number will be slightly off. The receiving bank will see the error but will hold the money until they figure out where it belongs. It's a temporary solution. But with the money out of your account, it will buy us a few days to figure out how to destroy the program and take Archer down."

"Clever. I like your thinking."

Jordan began working. It took over an hour before she finished the transfer to the third bank. When she got to the fourth bank, located in Tokyo, she was feeling a little bleary-eyed and took the last swallow of Coke. When everything was set, she pressed the Enter button and watched as the last sixty thousand dollars was transferred into the Japanese account. Within a minute, she noticed an unusual spike in the bank's traffic. "Hey, Max. Come here."

Max rose and came around the desk.

"Take a look."

Max leaned over her shoulder and stared at the screen.

"Are you seeing what I'm seeing?"

"Yeah. Looks like you got a sniffer. The bank is checking that transfer, and it looks like they've alerted their cyber team. You need to get the hell out of there."

Jordan's hands flew over the keyboard as she worked to abort the transfer.

"You're not out yet," Max yelled.

"I know. I'm working on it."

"You need to move faster. That red light is flashing."

"Stop talking to me!"

"Get out of there!"

"They're blocking my abort."

"How?"

"I'm a little busy at the moment to give you a hacking lesson." Jordan's hands were sweating, and her mind raced as she wrote code to try and backpedal. If she simply powered off the computer, she'd leave a trace, and they could track it back to RMZ offices.

"Jordan, you have to get out now!"

"Give me a minute."

"You don't have a min—"

"There! Done." Jordan sat back and let out a long, slow breath. "That was too freaking close."

Max put his hands on her shoulders and squeezed. "You did it. Damn, you're cool under pressure."

The feel of his hands was the only thing keeping her from telling him she'd nearly had a coronary. His soothing touch gave her a warm sensation in the pit of her stomach. She curled her toes inside her sneakers to get a grip. As much as she would have liked to sit like this for a while, there wasn't any time. "Max, it's too soon to relax. That last transfer was obviously a bust. Give me thirty minutes, and I'll create a new one."

"I could use a walk around the office. Slow my heart rate. And I need to check with Rafe and Zack. Find out if they've made any progress getting into Sintinex."

"Okay." Jordan focused on the screen and got to work.

About forty minutes later, Max walked back into the office. She looked up and, with a tired smile, said, "It's done."

"Amazing. Takes some of the pressure off."

Jordan shook her head. "It's not party time yet. What I did is like plugging holes in a leaky dam with Scotch tape. I have to get to the source. I need to get back into the Sintinex mainframe and destroy that program. How's it going with getting access?"

"It was wishful thinking that we'd still be able to get in." Max exhaled sharply. "Zack and Rafe tried several ways based on our previous access. Nothing worked. We're cybersecurity, not genius hackers. It's over to you."

"All right, not to brag, but hopefully, this won't take long. I'll retrace the steps I used the first time to break in." Jordan interlaced her fingers and cracked her knuckles. "Go sit over there."

Max moved to the other side of the desk, sat in the chair across from her, and crossed one leg over the other. "I won't say a word."

"Good." She stretched her arms in front of her and moved her head from side to side. "Okay, here goes. I remember this like it was yesterday." She performed several keystrokes, paused, and then several more. She worked her way into the Sintinex system, but had several more layers to penetrate before she could get into the mainframe. She checked the time on the upper corner of the screen—her sense of urgency ratcheting up a few notches.

Jordan didn't yet know Archer's ultimate goal, but she was certain he was behind Axis Industries's problems and the attempt to ruin Judge Ramirez. Her instincts told her these were only warm-ups for something much bigger.

An hour passed with no luck. She rolled up her sleeves, more determined than ever to get in, but when the three-hour mark went by, she had to concede that Archer had changed the code to the firewall, making it nearly hack-proof. If she wanted to get in this way, it would take just as long as her original assignment. And they didn't have the luxury of time. "I don't know how he did it, but he's definitely souped up what you gave him."

"Any luck?" Rafe asked, stepping into the office.

Jordan shook her head. "I was telling Max that Archer has taken your program up a notch."

Rafe groaned. "But the accounts are okay? Right? The money was all transferred out of them."

"Yes, but don't get too excited. It's a temporary hold, and unless I can get into this mainframe, I won't be able to stop Archer from coming after your family again with a vengeance." Jordan looked out the window. "I'm so terribly sorry."

Max came around the desk, turned Jordan's chair to face him, and took her hands in his. "Hey. Stop. *We'll* solve this. This is not only on you. RMZ was involved the moment we accepted this job from Sintinex. You had nothing to do with that. Sadly, we were all pawns in this game of his, whatever the hell he's playing."

"Listen," Rafe said. "Our aunt is at my house. Well, technically, it's her house, but she doesn't live there anymore. She lives with her sister, our aunt Claudia, up in Saratoga Springs."

Jordan scrunched her forehead.

"Long story." Rafe waved a hand. "But she took care of my wife's daughter, Justine, while we were on our honeymoon, and she brought her back last night. We're having a dinner for her tonight with Pop. This was all planned before Archer decided to rain hell down on our lives. I suggest we all take a break, have something to eat, and come up with a new game plan."

Jordan pushed back in her chair. "Thanks. I'm good. I'll stay here and keep working on this."

"Jordan. That invitation wasn't giving you the option to say yes or no," Max said. "We all need a break. And you're coming with me."

"I don't think so."

Chapter 13

Jordan chewed on her bottom lip and didn't move from her perch on the edge of her seat.

"Hey, bro," Max said to Rafe, "give us a minute."

"Sure. Meet you at the house."

"What's the problem?" Max asked once his brother had left. Then he shook his head. "Considering the circumstances, that's probably a dumb question. But you look... I don't know...annoyed?"

"Did you bump your head when I wasn't looking and forget there's a crazy person after us? I'm annoyed because I want to stay and get into the Sintinex system. Taking a break is not only stupid—it's irresponsible." Jordan couldn't hide the sharp edge to her voice if she wanted to. It was part of a defense mechanism she'd carefully honed from too many years of being in a system that forced her to be around people she didn't know and didn't want to get to know.

"It's only for a couple of hours. Stepping away from things sometimes helps me gain a better perspective."

For a split second, she thought he might have a point. She'd become bleary-eyed from staring at the screen for so many hours, and she was hungry again. But people? Why did she need to be around people? In general, they made her uncomfortable. She'd only just gotten used to his brothers. "Just leave me here."

"No can do. We've sent everyone home, and I'm not leaving you here by yourself. There's no telling what Archer is up to. Besides, we need a break."

Jordan rolled her eyes. "You guys are pathetic."

"Look, we're in a tight situation. I know that." Max scoffed. "But that attitude you're wearing like a hat that's too tight is not helping. You might want to think about parking it, especially around my aunt and my father. They're good people. And I do not want them concerned. I know we're all dancing on tenterhooks, but that's no reason to add to the tension."

"Oh, please. Are you giving me lessons in manners? Because better people than you have tried. Being around family isn't my thing."

Max laughed.

"What's funny?"

"Better people than you have tried to resist my family. Let's see how you fare. Should be interesting." Max hoisted the backpack on his shoulders and put his hand out, showing Jordan the door.

Jordan huffed and pursed her lips. She hated giving in to this but didn't see a way out. She snatched up her satchel, gave him a look, and headed past him and out the door.

The company parking lot was empty except for Max's BMW. Shivering against the night chill, Jordan stomped toward the car, yanked open the door, and plopped into the passenger seat.

Max slid in and started the ignition. "There's a button for the seat warmer if you're cold." He pointed to the panel with a switch in the center console.

"I'm good," she lied. Jordan was still getting over the fact that she wasn't in the office with a boatload of french fries from the diner, working on breaking into the Sintinex mainframe. She let out a long sigh.

Max placed his hand over hers. "It's only for a couple of hours," he reminded her.

Jordan gave him a sideways glance, but he didn't notice. He focused on pulling out of the parking lot and onto Main Street. Normally, she'd be offended at the physical contact. It was as if he were trying to calm down a petulant child. But Max's touch gave her butterflies, the good kind, making it damn hard to stay pissed off.

If she ever had the chance to date again, which was a big if, considering she might not make it out of this madness alive, Max would definitely be someone she'd want to go out with. The thought made her smile.

"What are you thinking?" Max glanced at her.

"Nothing." Heat flooded her cheeks, and she sat straighter. Now was not the time to let her mind wander into areas that were better left unexplored.

"We're here," Max said, pulling up to a large yellow Victorian house sitting on a rise away from the street.

"That wasn't far," Jordan said.

"They live in town, close to the office." Max unclicked his seat belt, exited the car, walked around the front, and opened the door for Jordan.

She stared up at him, not moving.

"Come on. I promise my family isn't that scary. And this is only a small sampling of the clan." Max squinted at her. "Besides, I have no doubt you're hungry."

He got that right. She was always hungry, especially when she was stressed. In foster care, she'd either never had enough to eat, or whatever they were serving wasn't very good. State-run homes didn't have a lot of variety, and after a while, there was only so much boxed mac and cheese she could take.

Jordan took a breath, swung her legs out of the car, and reached for his hand.

They climbed the stairs to the front porch. Before they reached the door, it opened. A woman with a gray bob, kind eyes, and a wide smile stood in the doorway. *"¡Sobrino!"* She held her arms wide open. Max had to stoop to embrace her.

This must be his aunt Ellie, she thought.

"Tía, this is my friend Jordan."

"Con mucho gusto." Ellie stepped forward and embraced Jordan, taking her by surprise.

In all her years, she'd never had a woman hug her like this. It was a strange yet comforting feeling. Without warning, Jordan felt herself almost, but not quite, returning the gesture. Embarrassed, she quickly stepped back, combed her hair behind her ears, and studied the floor. "Hello," Jordan said, her voice quiet.

"Come in. Come in. It's chilly out there."

Jordan followed Ellie and Max into a bright, open foyer featuring a center staircase with a mahogany railing. To her left was a parlor with turn-of-the-century pocket doors and a baby grand piano in the corner between two tall windows.

Loud conversation came from the dining room on her right. Rafe and Zack were sitting at a long table with a man who had a shock of white hair and looked to be in his late sixties. This had to be their father, Emilio, the county judge. She remembered seeing him at the diner's counter the morning she arrived in Hollow Lake. The resemblance between him and Max was unmistakable.

The kitchen door swung open, and a tall woman with coal-black hair and deep blue eyes walked in, wiping her hands on the front of her jeans. Following her was one of the cutest kids Jordan had ever seen. Light brown curls framed her face, and she bounced up and down as she walked.

"Hello. You must be Jordan. I'm Mallory." The woman extended her hand, and they shook. "I see you've met *Tía* Ellie."

"What about me?" The little girl bounced on her toes.

"This is my daughter, Justine." Mallory smiled.

Justine waved. "Are you Uncle Max's girlfriend?"

The word *girlfriend* made Jordan blush, which was out of character. Not that she wanted to be his girlfriend or was even thinking about it, but a friends-with-benefits situation could work, at least for the time being.

"Justine," Max said, "as you can see, she's a girl. Right?"

Justine nodded.

"And she's my friend. So I guess she is my girl-friend. Get it?"

Justine tilted her head, and her forehead scrunched up in thought. "Oh, you mean, like Allison at school? She's a girl. And she's my friend. Is she that kind of girlfriend?" Justine pointed at Jordan. "Like you mean just friends?"

"Exactly." Max bent down and scooped her up. "Now give your uncle Max a hug."

Jordan wasn't sure she liked that explanation. Had she wanted him to say they were more than friends? *Oh, shut up. You met the guy like two minutes ago. Your identity was stolen. You're running from a ruthless psychopath, and you're worried about your girlfriend status?* Seeing this family was slowly making her aware of what she was missing in her life. Maybe that was where this ridiculous mind noise was coming from.

Jordan was ushered into the dining room and introduced to Emilio, who was sitting at the head of the table.

"I'm going to finish up in the kitchen," Mallory said. "Dinner will be ready in about fifteen minutes."

Quickly assessing the situation, Jordan realized she could be stuck in the dining room with Max and his family, who'd likely be asking all manner of questions she didn't really want to answer, or she could help Mallory in the kitchen. She instantly volunteered. "Hey, Mallory, let me help." Before anyone could object, she headed out of the room and into the kitchen.

The smell of garlic and rosemary filled the air, and Jordan dropped her shoulders. Food always made her feel more relaxed.

"Smart move," Mallory said. "I would have escaped, too. Being surrounded by the Ramirez clan can be intimidating." She picked up a potholder, opened the oven door, and basted the chickens. "Would you mind putting the salad together? The lettuce is in the fridge. You can wash and dry it. The spinner is on the counter."

"Easy enough." Jordan opened the refrigerator and took a head of lettuce from the crisper. It wasn't in a plastic bag like you buy from the grocery store. It was a huge head of red-leaf lettuce. "Did this come from a local farm?"

"Yes." Mallory smiled. "First of the season. Nothing like fresh."

"Want me to wash the entire head?"

"Uh-huh." Mallory checked the pan on the stove. "This family is big on eating and loves their fresh veggies. I've also got some tomatoes, cucumbers, and radishes already washed in that bowl on the counter. If you don't mind, you could put it all together."

"Sure thing," Jordan said. Whenever it was her turn for kitchen duty at a home, she typically had to prepare dinner for as many as ten girls. But they never had fresh vegetables from a farm. She washed the lettuce and placed the leaves in the salad spinner. Jordan wondered how much Mallory knew about the current situation between herself, RMZ Digital, and Archer. She didn't feel she could come right out and ask, so she settled for the circuitous route. "Um. I want to thank you for the clothes and the dog food."

"Don't think about it." Mallory turned to face Jordan. Her expression was serious. "Rafe filled me in. I know about your identity being stolen, and the dead man in your apartment, and Archer going after this family." She sucked in a breath. "I know it looks like we're all pretending nothing is happening. But this is a family that's used to ups and downs in life. Some pretty big swings in fact. I also know you're having trouble hacking back into the Sintinex mainframe. We've all been put into this impossible situation, and we're not ignoring it. But maybe spending a couple of hours with the family will help you recharge and come up with a solution, or at least figure out next moves. You know what I mean?"

Not sure how to respond, Jordan only nodded. She was out of her depth when it came to family caring about each other. She returned to spinning the salad and was lost in the movement of the lettuce going round and round in the plastic basket when she felt an arm around her shoulder. This time, she didn't jump. She was becoming accustomed to Max's touch and his subtle pine scent.

"You okay?" Max asked.

"Hmmm." Jordan didn't look up. His words had a concern to them—a kindness she hadn't expected and couldn't quite trust.

"Max," Mallory called out. "We got it all covered in here. Go back out there and stop hovering."

Max squeezed Jordan's shoulder and kissed her on the temple. "I'm in the next room if you need me," he said softly.

She turned toward him. Their faces were inches apart. He gave her a crooked smile, and something inside her softened. Her attraction to him amped up another notch. His unexpected affection had caught her off guard, and all she could do was stare up at him. There was no denying she liked the feeling.

"Max! Go." Mallory pointed to the kitchen door that led into the hallway. "Out."

"This family can be a little overbearing sometimes." Mallory sighed. "Well, that's not exactly what I mean. Let me put it this way. They care about each other, and when one of them is hurting, we all hurt. Being an only child, it took me a while to get used to how protective they are of one another. But I have to say, it's reassuring to know someone is there, always looking out for you." Mallory patted Jordan on the shoulder. "Looks to me like Max has taken to you. You're not alone. Max is here for you, and so is the rest of the family." She paused. "I think that lettuce is dry. Let's get that salad ready and feed those hungry people out there."

A lump formed in the back of Jordan's throat. She'd never been sentimental in her life. She didn't dare speak for giving herself away. Instead, she swallowed hard and blinked back the tears. She put the salad ingredients together in a bowl and carried it into the dining room, placing it on the table.

"That looks good," Max said.

"And it's colorful," Justine said. "We learned that in school. All the different colors of the vegetables. And now Mommy makes colorful salads. I like them."

"Rafe, come help me bring in the rest of the food," Mallory called from the kitchen.

Jordan began to follow him when Max touched her arm. "Sit. My brother's got this." He pulled out a chair next to him.

Jordan dropped into the chair, her eyes downcast, afraid they'd all be staring at her. But all eyes were on Justine as she talked about the things she and Ellie had done while her mother and Rafe were on their honeymoon.

Mallory waltzed her way into the dining room carrying a large bowl of rosemary-roasted potatoes. Rafe followed, holding a large platter with two roast chickens. As he placed them on the table, the family applauded.

"I want a leg, please." Justine bounced up and down in her seat. "And potatoes, please."

"Coming right up," Rafe said as he began to carve the chicken. "Who wants white meat?"

"I'd love some," Ellie said.

"Pop—" Rafe looked up "—what do you want?"

"I'll have that other leg," Emilio said.

As the family settled in their seats and the food was served, the conversation continued. The easy way in which they conversed surprised Jordan. Anyone with functioning vision could see this was a tight-knit group. These people genuinely cared about each other. She'd only ever experienced this one other time. Everything else she knew about families came from watching the occasional television show with a scripted family saying scripted, sappy things. The Ramirez family was different.

The talk at the table was mind-blowing on too many levels. Max and his brothers were particularly remarkable, acting like they didn't have a care in the world. When one topic petered out, they seamlessly moved on to another. Jordan learned that Ellie and her sister Claudia were planning a day-trip to New York City for a Broadway play. They quickly moved on to Ellie's three children, who Jordan learned owned a software company and frequently worked with Max and his brothers on new programs.

The fact that they were all acting normal, as if Archer hadn't hacked his way onto Max's computer and threatened his entire family and their business, seemed so incongruous to her that she didn't even notice she'd put food in her mouth. Mallory's words rang true. This family took time out of difficult situations to be normal. She didn't understand it, but she did try to relax into it. They were all pretending there wasn't a crisis brewing, and she wondered if that was what families did to protect each other. It was odd, for sure, but it was also oddly comforting. A normal evening with family. This was a new situation, and she decided that she might try to go with it instead of resisting it. This might be the only chance she'd get to be normal in all of existence.

"Would anyone like more chicken? There's plenty," Mallory said.

"I'll have another piece," Emilio said.

"I'm stuffed," Ellie said. "That was delicious."

"I'm glad you liked it," Mallory said, passing more chicken to her father-in-law.

"A toast to the chef," Zack said, raising his wineglass. A chorus of "To the chef" followed as everyone raised their glass.

"Mallory, you're not drinking," Zack said. Everyone at the table turned. Mallory was holding up a glass of water and smiling.

"That's the other bit of news," Rafe said. "We're expecting."

"¡Ay! Felicidades," Ellie cried, getting up from the table to hug and kiss Mallory and Rafe. She was followed by Emilio, Zack, and then Max. The sense of happiness around the table was palpable. It was something Jordan had never experienced, and for a moment, she, too, felt a new sensation of joy. She was genuinely happy for them.

"I did good, didn't I?" Justine smiled wide. "Mommy and Rafe said I had to keep it a secret, and I did." Justine looked to Rafe. "Did I do good?"

"You did great." He put her on his lap and kissed her forehead.

"I hope I get a baby brother. I really want a baby brother."

"It's too early to tell," Mallory said. "But we'll love the baby whether it's a boy or a girl." She looked over at Justine. "Right?"

Justine pursed her lips. "Well, okay."

"A grandchild is a precious thing," Emilio said. "I only wish your mother could have been here."

"I know, Pop. Me too," Rafe said.

The table grew quiet, and Jordan saw strain on Max's face. To some degree, she knew how he felt. Not having a mother sucked. But to have a mother and then lose her, she thought, somehow, that might be worse.

"Who wants dessert?" Mallory asked. "We have apple pie, and Ellie made a flan."

Justine's hand shot up in the air like a rocket. "I do. I do."

"Coming right up."

"I'll help you," Ellie said.

"We'll clear the table and get the dishes," Max said. Jordan began to rise. "You stay. We got this." He looked at his brothers.

Before she knew what was happening, the brothers cleared the table, and everyone disappeared into the kitchen, leaving her alone with the judge.

"You're a guest this first time, so you don't have to help clean up. And they treat me like I'm too old to help." Emilio chuckled. "I let them believe that, but who do they think washes the dishes in my house?"

Jordan nodded.

"So, I guess we can dance around the real issue as my sons did at dinner, or we can talk about the giant giraffe on the table."

Jordan raised an eyebrow.

"I'm a county judge, so I'm not able to say much, except I know you're working with Max on those money transfers. From what I can tell, my sons are concerned."

"How could you tell? From where I sat, it seemed like a happy family get-together."

"Ahhh, to an outsider, yes."

The word *outsider* stung. Maybe because she'd gotten comfortable with them. And loathe as she was to admit it, once or twice during dinner, she'd imagined being part of this family. She shook away the thought.

"I know my sons, and not everything is right. But I believe they are working on a solution with your help." He paused. "I see how Max looks at you. He trusts you. And if he trusts you, then I do, too."

Jordan didn't get a chance to respond. The rest of the family filed back into the dining room with dessert. A pang of what she could only describe as sadness bloomed from inside her. Was she falling for Max? And if she were, after seeing this family and their tight bonds tonight, maybe the fair thing to do was leave. They didn't deserve the kind of trouble she had following her.

When dessert was finished, Emilio said good night, and Mallory and Ellie went upstairs to get Justine bathed and ready for bed. Jordan found herself in the kitchen with Max and his brothers.

As Max put the last glass in the dishwasher, his phone chimed. He pulled it out of his back pocket and read the text. He looked at Jordan. "See now, this is starting to jack me up."

"What?" Zack asked.

Jordan and Rafe moved toward Max to see the message. She read the text.

STOP THE CODE.

"What's that all about?" Rafe asked.

"Max and I have been getting these strange texts. I got one right after I fled my apartment. It freaked me out, and I threw my phone away right before I got on a bus to come here. But this is like the fourth one for you, right, Max?"

He nodded. "They're anonymous. I have no idea who

the hell is sending them. But now I'm thinking they're all somehow connected to Archer."

"Wait a sec," Jordan said. "We should have thought of this yesterday."

Max frowned. "Thought of what?"

"You're cybersecurity experts. You must have a software program that extracts the metadata from texts and emails."

"Man—" Max shook his head "—I don't know why I didn't think of that."

"We're all under a lot of pressure. Don't beat yourself up, bro. I have a laptop with the right software," Rafe said. "I'll get it."

Minutes later, Rafe returned and handed the laptop to Jordan. She placed it on the kitchen table and sat. Max and his brothers huddled around.

"Max, copy the text and email it to Rafe while I pull up the software." When the email arrived, Jordan took the time stamp and metadata from the text and ran it through the software program designed to extract detailed information. With her hacking ability and several more keystrokes, she determined where the text originated. She sat back and pursed her lips.

"What's the verdict?" Max asked.

"The text came from the cybercafe on West 12th Street in New York City."

"And that's significant because why?"

"Because that is the cybercafe I went to after I found the dead body in my bathtub."

Chapter 14

The road was dark, and Max's mind wandered as he drove. He mentally reviewed everything that had happened in the last forty-eight hours.

"You're awfully quiet over there. What are you thinking?" Jordan asked.

"I was thinking that was smooth maneuvering you did back there, finding out where the texts came from." Max didn't want to overwhelm her with all his thoughts, so he kept his answer short. "But we still don't know what they mean or who is sending them."

"I know. I'm chewing on that right now. My money's on Archer."

"You're probably right. But it still doesn't explain the significance of the messages."

"Yeah. Chewing on that, too."

They rode in silence for a few more minutes. "You know, you're good at this. How'd you decide on hacking as a profession anyway? I mean, is it something you always wanted to do?"

Several seconds passed before she answered. "It seemed like a perfect fit for me. I love computers, and the work is solitary, which is how I like it."

"I don't know about that. We seem to be working well

together." Apart from the fact that she was difficult, had an attitude, and carried a chip on her shoulder that weighed a good amount, he really liked her. She'd been able to hack through their impenetrable firewall undetected. That alone showed she was smart, capable, resourceful, and, if nothing else, persistent. For some inexplicable reason, they'd been thrown together, and while he'd resisted her at first, he now felt a pull toward her. In fact, he was attracted to her in every possible way.

"You think we work well together?"

He heard the doubt and cynicism in Jordan's voice.

"If it hasn't already occurred to you, let me break it down so you get it," Jordan said. "If we hadn't been forced into this situation, you and I would never have met. I would have gotten paid an obscene amount of money and moved on to my next job."

He could feel her eyes on him.

"And," she continued, "you would have gone on for the rest of your days believing Jordan Logan was a man."

Max laughed. "Yeah, well, I don't think that anymore."

"Whatever. The point is. I work alone. Always."

"Because of the foster homes?"

"Not really." Jordan looked out the window. "Maybe a little." She paused. "Maybe a lot. Anyway, I learned I could hack during my freshman year at MIT. And that I was good at it."

"Interesting. I didn't know hacking was an accredited subject."

"Ha! I wish. But no. I was assigned to a senior fellow working on a software program for the automotive industry. It had to do with electric cars. Out of a couple of hundred students who applied, five of us were selected. I thought it was a big deal, but working for Collin Tresel was the most infuriating experience of my life."

"How so?"

"Collin thought he was God's gift to the computer world and acted accordingly, like we were all supposed to genuflect whenever he came into the lab. The program he created wasn't working correctly, but he wouldn't let the five of us help figure out a solution. The whole purpose of the lab was to brainstorm. But collaboration wasn't in his vocabulary. He treated us like we had an infectious disease. We were basically allowed to work on nothing unless he told us what to do."

"I get the picture."

"Anyway, I thought I might have a solution to the problem, but I would have rather died than give him my ideas, because I knew he'd take the credit. The only way to see if it would work was to go into the lab after hours, hack into the program because he never gave us any passwords, put my solution in, and see if it worked. And that's exactly what I did. My program did work. I was happy about that. I never did share it with him. And it didn't matter because I was more excited about the fact that I got into his password-protected network undetected. I felt a secret thrill. I still do whenever I get past a wall."

"Fascinating beginnings, I mean—" Max abruptly slammed on the brake. They both lurched forward, and Max felt his seat belt cut into him. In the headlights, a deer stared back at them.

"Wow. That was close," Jordan said. "I didn't even see him."

Max didn't respond. His attention was on the car behind them. A tingling sensation crept down his back. He didn't like it. Max hit the car horn, letting out a short blast. The deer took off, and Max pushed down on the gas pedal. They were both jerked back into their seats. Max traveled faster to see if the car behind him also picked up speed.

"What's going on?"

Max's gaze went from the road to the rearview mirror. "We're going to take a little detour."

"But why?" Jordan turned her body to face him.

"There's a car that's been on our tail since I pulled out of Rafe's place. This road is rarely traveled. I think we're being followed. Could be I'm paranoid, but considering our recent track record, I don't think so." He pushed a little harder on the gas, and the BMW picked up speed. They were traveling in a forty-mile-an-hour zone, but the car's speedometer was inching its way up to sixty. The car behind kept pace.

Suddenly, twin high beams in the rearview mirror blinded Max. Another road appeared a short distance ahead. "Hang on." Max turned the wheel sharply to the left. The car skidded and swerved, fishtailing side to side several times as he struggled to gain control. He was leading their pursuer in a different direction, away from his house. They were now on a two-lane county road with a steep drop-off to the right.

"We need to call the police!" Jordan yelled.

Max didn't have a spare brain cell to respond. He was too busy using every ounce of his concentration to stay on the road and keep the car from rolling over. It took some maneuvering, but he was finally able to straighten it out. When he looked at the rearview mirror, the high beams were still focused on them.

"Grab my phone from my inside pocket. Call 911." Max barked the order, never taking his eyes from the road.

Jordan reached over to pull his mobile from his shirt pocket but was instantly thrown backward and then forward into the dashboard. "What the hell was that?"

"He's ramming us from behind."

"The phone fell under your seat, and I can't reach it!"

"Forget the damn phone and hold on."

Max pushed down harder on the accelerator. "There's a state trooper station at the Thruway entrance. That's where we're headed." The high beams behind him seemed to shift, and he squinted into the rearview mirror. "Damn!" He took a quick glance at Jordan.

She was staring straight ahead. One hand gripping the center console, the other white-knuckling the grab handle above the passenger door.

"Looks like whoever is behind us is trying to end-run us."

"What?"

Before he could answer, a dark SUV was racing along-side them. Max swung his attention back on the road in front of him and floored the gas pedal. The SUV kept pace and stayed neck and neck on the deserted road.

Max quickly glanced to his left just as the SUV slammed into them from the side, trying to push them off the road. The tires on the passenger side were now riding on a dirt shoulder overlooking a rocky drop down to a ravine. He could feel the car losing traction. Keeping a death grip on the wheel, he managed to right the car and gain level ground, but they were boxed in. Unless he got out of the trap, he was certain the car would roll down into the ravine.

On instinct, he slashed the wheel to the left, ramming

the SUV in the side. For a brief moment, Max had the advantage, pushed the speedometer toward one hundred, and inched ahead of the SUV. "See if you can get a look at the make of the car," he yelled.

Max was familiar with this county road. In ten miles, they'd hit the entrance to the state trooper station. That is if he could make it. The car took every rut in the road and then some as he sped forward. He was certain he'd left his transmission about five miles back. Whoever was following was now inches from his rear bumper.

Again, Max pressed down further on the gas pedal, and the speedometer hovered around one hundred and ten miles an hour. He'd never driven this fast, but then he'd never been in a car fighting for his life.

They were less than a mile from the entrance to the throughway when he saw the twinkle of lights up ahead. "Hang on!" Max took his foot off the gas, made a sharp left into the trooper station parking lot, and hit the brakes hard, the BMW spinning around twice before coming to a stop. The SUV screeched to a halt outside the lot. Max threw the car in Park and turned to get a look, but the SUV's windows were tinted, and he couldn't see who was driving. He was about to get out of the car when the SUV backed up and took off.

Max ran both hands through his hair. His heart thrummed. Adrenaline coursed through his veins. He turned to Jordan. "Are you okay?" His voice was low and urgent.

"Depends on your definition of okay." She released her grip on the grab handle. "We're alive. Great driving, by the way. But what in the hell was that?"

He heard the tremble in her voice. In the time he'd

known her, she'd shown no fear. This was different. Even he was rattled. Max unbuckled his seat belt and leaned toward her. His hand caressed the side of her face.

Jordan closed her eyes. Max took her face in both his hands. "Look at me." His voice barely above a whisper. Her gaze settled on him, and it pained him to see the fear in her eyes. He put his arms around her and held her. She stiffened, but he didn't let go. When her body finally relaxed into him, he held her tighter. There were no words he could think of to say. They'd almost been killed.

Jordan pulled away and looked him in the eyes. "Are you going in?" She glanced over at the trooper station.

"Go in and say what?" Max leaned back in his seat and rubbed a hand at the back of his neck. "I couldn't ID the make or model of the car. They had their high beams on the entire time." He let out a long, slow breath.

"You know what I think?" Jordan asked.

"Probably the same thing I'm thinking."

She nodded. "This was Archer's doing. It has to be. He sent someone to scare us. Because if he wanted us dead, I think whoever or whatever was in that car would have caught up to us and run us off the road."

Max's eyes widened. "You think that was only a warning?"

"Yeah. I think he wants to scare the crap out of us. He wants us to know he's watching—" Jordan stared out of the passenger window "—and he wants to make sure we don't go to the authorities."

Max put a hand on her thigh.

She turned to face him. "He needs to be stopped because he's capable of much, much more. Don't worry. I'm not going to do anything rash. But what I am going to do is use every bit of skill I have to destroy him."

Even in the dark, with only one streetlight to illuminate the inside of the car, Max could see the hatred and determination in her eyes. "Jordan. Don't make this personal."

"Don't make this personal? Are you for real? This is way past personal. I am on a vendetta. The man stole my identity. He is blackmailing your family. It doesn't get more personal." She scoffed. "You know, when I was still a minor, being shuttled from one crappy group foster home to the next, there wasn't a damn thing I could do about it." Jordan took in a breath. "Damnit!" She banged the passenger door with the side of her fist. "But no more. No. More. I'm not going to act like I don't have a choice."

"What exactly do you plan to do?"

"I have a funny feeling he may have people stationed outside your offices. Let's get to your house. I can figure out a way to work from there." Jordan turned away and looked out the passenger window.

Max had an overwhelming urge to protect her, although she seemed perfectly capable of taking care of herself. Maybe that was what drew him to her. She had a strength he admired. As much as he didn't want to admit it to himself, he had the kind of feeling for Jordan that he hadn't ever felt with any other woman.

"You going to start the car, or are you planning on camping here overnight?" Jordan asked, her voice nearly a snarl.

"Ah, there's the Jordan we've all come to know and love." Max let out a chuckle and, with it, experienced some relief that the tremble and fear in her voice were gone. She was back to being her sarcastic, caustic self. She was growing on him, for sure. He buckled up and put the car in drive.

Twenty minutes later, they arrived at his home. When they approached his front door, Max paused and grabbed Jordan's hand. "I've got the outside security cameras connected to my phone. I didn't get any alerts, but to be on the safe side, let me go first." Carefully, he put the key in the lock and turned it slowly. When he inched the door open, Buck came running and jumped on him, barking wildly. He danced around Max and then Jordan.

"I thought he was at your neighbor's?"

"He was. When we left Rafe's, I sent her a text to bring him back to the house. She has my emergency key. And I didn't want to take advantage of her time."

Jordan held on to his collar. "I think he probably needs to go out."

"Wait here, I'll get his leash and a flashlight. The last thing we need is for him to take off."

Within minutes, Max was back and hooked the leash to Buck's collar. "Let's head down to the lake. There's a clear path, no chance of getting hit with low-hanging branches or meeting up with some animal in the woods."

They walked in silence. The only sound was Buck panting heavily as he strained against the leash. "Easy, boy," Jordan said. "We'll get there." They reached the water's edge, and she let go of the leash. "Go on, boy, do your business."

Buck didn't go far, and Max watched Jordan watching Buck. "What are you thinking?"

"Thinking?" She turned to face him. "So many thoughts. But mostly, how to get out of this mess." She looked around. "Hey, where did he go? Buck? You there?" She stamped a foot. "Please don't make me chase you. Come on now. Buck!"

Within seconds, the sound of his paws in the silent night could be heard. "There you are. Did you finish?"

She crouched down. "Time to go back in." She hooked the leash onto his collar and stood. "We need to cut off the head of this thing. It's the only way."

"What do you have in mind?"

She stomped back toward the house, and Max hustled to catch up. "Hey, what's the plan?" He stepped onto the patio and opened the door.

"Not entirely sure yet, but it will require a fresh laptop and the ability to take my hacking skills to a new level."

"I'll get a laptop." Max walked toward his bedroom.

Jordan crouched down and gave Buck a good rub across his back before he went to the French doors and lay on the rug. She went into the kitchen area and poured herself a glass of water.

"Here you go." Max placed the "clean" laptop on the kitchen island. "Want something stronger?" He reached into a cupboard and pulled out a bottle of whiskey.

Jordan studied him over the rim of her glass and thought about it. As tempting as the offer was and as sexy as he looked, she couldn't go there. Her mind was too full of what needed to be done, and it wouldn't shut off. She shook her head. "I'm good."

She put down her glass and thought about what she needed to accomplish. She no longer just cared about getting her identity back. She also felt compelled to help Max's family. Until now, she'd never even thought about family.

Oh, sure, there were hundreds of times she wondered why her mother hadn't wanted her or why some family hadn't cared enough to adopt her. Being shuttled around, she'd adapted by forming a crusty seal no one could penetrate. But somehow, this family, these Ramirezes, had cracked something and gotten in. There wasn't any one thing she could point to. She hadn't even known these people for forty-eight hours. Yet, over dinner, she was instantly attracted to them and felt determined to help. "I need to stay sharp and make one last attempt to get into the mainframe."

Max poured himself a thimbleful of whiskey and downed it in one gulp. He put the glass down and looked at her. He moved in closer until they were inches apart. When his head bent toward her and his lips pressed against hers, Jordan was nearly lost. Or maybe she was simply lost in him. She'd been hoping he would kiss her. She parted her lips, and his tongue slipped in. He deepened the kiss, and her mind put on the brakes, like someone flicking on the lights in a darkened bedroom. *What are you doing?* She pulled back. Her gaze fell to the ground. "Sorry," she mumbled. "I… I… I have work to do." She grabbed the laptop and headed into the guest room, Buck fast on her heels.

Jordan took a five-minute cold shower and threw on a camisole and matching shorts from the items Mallory purchased for her. She dropped onto the bed and opened the laptop. She inserted the jump drive with the program she'd written *without* the added code Archer had sent. She prayed that by only uploading her version of the program onto the computer, there would be no way for Archer to trace her. Under normal circumstances, that would be the case, and she wouldn't have to worry. But these were far from normal times. It seemed Archer was capable of so much more than she could even have imagined.

Crossing the fingers on her left hand, she extracted her program and waited. It behaved as she'd programmed it. With a series of keystrokes, she worked to get into the back door of the Sintinex mainframe. An hour later, nothing she tried had worked. Archer had definitely made modifications to the firewall Max and his brothers had created. Loathe as she was to admit it, she wasn't going to be able to hack her way into the system. At least not remotely.

Jordan spent the next several hours investigating Sintinex and researching alternative ways to gain access into their system. When she finally had all the answers she could find, at least for now, she looked at the alarm clock on the nightstand. It was nearly five in the morning. She stretched, raising her arms over her head, and let out a long, loud yawn. She glanced over at Buck, who was sleeping in the corner, when she heard a noise. She stiffened and didn't move. All her senses were on high alert. The noise came again. She wasn't sure if she was hearing things or if she should wake Max. Her heart pounded like a jackhammer against her ribs, and she remained motionless with fear.

Minutes passed before she forced herself to get a grip. She looked around the room, not knowing what she was looking for, just anything that she might use as a weapon if she needed to defend herself. The only thing she could find was a decorative glass bowl filled with clear marbles. She thought this might knock someone out if she swung hard enough and hit at the right angle. She hoped Buck would stay asleep and not bark. If there was someone in the house, she didn't want them to know she was on to them. The noise stopped. What if they were right outside her door, waiting? Oh hell, she thought, and tiptoed to the dresser, silently picking up the glass bowl. With her pulse racing, she crept out of the room and into the darkened kitchen area. Her heart nearly stopped when she saw the silhouette of a large man standing at the kitchen island.

"Hey."

She almost threw the bowl before her brain caught up to the fact that it was Max's voice. "You scared the life out of me. I thought it was an intruder." She put the bowl down on the kitchen island.

"Sorry. I couldn't sleep."

"I never went to sleep, been working at it all this time." She sat on a stool and waited for her heart rate to slow.

"Did you make any progress?"

"As a matter of fact, I've got a plan."

"Really?"

"Yes. Finally. Something I think will work."

Max stepped closer. "Why do I get the strange sensation your plan may be on the far side of dangerous?"

"Let's say…it's challenging."

Max didn't respond, and she stared at him in the darkness until she could make out all his features. A lock of hair fell across his forehead, and without thinking, she brushed it aside. He took hold of her hand before she could pull it away and slowly kissed each knuckle. He wrapped his arms around her, and she felt desire in a way she never thought she could. He kissed her lightly on her forehead, her temple, and the side of her face. His gaze dropped to her mouth, and she felt a wave of heat building inside of her. His lips hovered over hers while his hands slid down her back and rested on her hips, pulling her in closer. When his mouth closed over hers and their tongues met, she pressed her body into him. She wrapped her arms around his neck, tilted her head back, and deepened the kiss. Her hands ran through his hair, and he lifted her up. She wrapped her legs around his waist. His body was muscular and strong, and he carried her into his bedroom.

He laid her on the bed, knelt over her, and stared into her

eyes. Her breath was heavy with anticipation. Slowly, he kissed her neck, lowering the straps of her camisole until her breasts were bared. She arched her back, and he closed his mouth over her breast. She gripped his back. It had been too long since she'd been with a man, and this felt so good.

Max put his hand between her legs, and she pushed against it, moving her hips rhythmically, nearly exploding with pleasure. She wanted him. "Now," she whispered and opened her eyes to see him staring, a sly smile crossing his lips.

"God, you're beautiful," he said. Then, with a relaxed slowness, he undressed her, taking all of her in. Max stood, never taking his eyes off her. He undressed, took a condom from the bedside table, and put it on. When he entered her, the pleasure was almost too much. They moved together at a slow, even pace, never taking their eyes off each other. It was almost too intimate for Jordan to bear, but she was helpless to look away.

No one had ever made her feel these many feelings. It was lustful and loving all at once. Max was taking his time to make sure she was satisfied, and as the sensation built inside her, she arched her back, closed her eyes, cried out, and climaxed.

Chapter 15

The early morning light filtered into the room. Jordan turned to face Max, but he wasn't there. She touched his pillow. It was cold. He must have gotten up early. She stretched and smiled. She hadn't felt this physically satisfied in, well, forever.

She squeezed her eyes shut. It was hard to believe how much had happened to her in the last three days. Now this? Her lips curled upward, and she sensed there was a goofy smile on her face. What was happening between her and Max? There was no way she could become involved in a relationship. *Shut up. This isn't a relationship. This was sex.* As much as she wanted to believe that, her heart was saying something different.

She curled onto her side and frowned. She wasn't the type to get long-term cozy with anyone. Besides, Max had a reputation. One only needed to check out his guest bathroom to know there was a revolving door of women. Honestly, she thought, they'd been through a lot and were simply blowing off steam.

In one smooth movement, she peeled the covers off, picked up her clothes, threw them on, and went to her room to take a shower. There was a lot to do today and much she had to explain to Max. After what she'd discovered last night, she had a definite plan, and she needed to put it into action this morning.

* * *

With her hair still wet, Jordan followed the scent of coffee into the kitchen area. She looked around but discovered she was alone in the house, and she figured Max had taken Buck for a walk. She poured herself a cup of coffee, and when the front door opened, Max walked in, Buck trotting close on his heels.

She smiled. "Oh, hey, boy." She scratched Buck behind the ear. "Good morning." She looked up at Max. "You went out early."

"I had to get my car towed." Max gave her a soft kiss on the mouth.

Surprised, Jordan stepped back. She wasn't accustomed to such intimacy. It confused her.

"Man, my car took a beating last night."

"Hard to believe that was less than twenty-four hours ago. Thinking about it makes me want to put my fist in Archer's face."

"Hey—" he stepped closer and placed his hand on her cheek "—we made it out of there alive. Until this nightmare is over, we're going to stay vigilant."

She stared into her cup. His closeness made her stomach drop. She could no longer deny that she was more than attracted to him. "Listen, we didn't get a chance to talk last night—"

"You mean at dawn when we had other things on our minds besides a conversation?" He gave her a knowing smile.

He was making it difficult for her to keep her distance, which was what she needed to do. Jordan felt her cheeks grow hot, and she wanted to smack herself for thinking about being with Max when their lives were quite literally in danger. *What was it about this guy?* She cleared her throat and put her cup down. "I found out a lot and came up with a plan. If we're going to get my identity back and keep your family safe, they're going to have to get involved."

Max tilted his head. "You mean more than they already are?"

Jordan nodded.

"Sounds scary."

"I know how protective you are of them. But I think what I have in mind will work. There are some things we'll need to handle first." Jordan was about to go into an explanation of what needed to occur when the doorbell rang. She gave Max a questioning look.

"That's Zack. I told him we had trouble last night. He's taking me to the car rental place over in Ravena."

"I thought fancy car places like BMW give you free loaners?"

He shook his head. "My car looks like it's been in a demolition derby. Nothing that happened to it is covered under the free loaner policy."

"Oh, I see."

"Anyway, after I pick up the rental, we're headed to Rafe's. They want the unabridged version of what went down last night. And we need to discuss how we get into the mainframe."

"I'll go get dressed. While we're all together, I can tell you what I found out and what I think our next steps should be."

An hour later, they arrived at Rafe's house and went straight to the backyard. Mallory was setting up coffee and cinnamon rolls on the picnic table. Jordan let Buck off the leash, and he instantly took off, sniffing each tree and marking his territory.

"Did *Tía* Ellie leave?" Max asked, straddling the picnic bench. Jordan sat next to him.

"Yes, this morning. And Justine's at school," Mallory said, pouring herself a cup of coffee.

"It's just us." Rafe reached for a roll. "We've been waiting for you to tell us what went down last night."

"Okay. But I'm going to give it to you straight up—nothing left out. So please wait until I'm done before you say anything or ask any questions."

Rafe and Zack looked at each other and then nodded.

Max paused, let out a breath, and then gave a blow-by-blow, cinematic description of what he and Jordan had experienced. When he was finished, his brothers and Mallory stared at him, shock etched on their faces.

"Son of a bitch!" Rafe pushed off the bench and paced around the table.

Zack let out a low whistle. "We need to go to the police. Enough is enough."

"That's not smart," Jordan said. "For one thing, the world thinks I'm Lauren Chambers, wanted for murder. And for another, we don't have enough hard evidence to go to the authorities, and it will only jack Archer up. If we make a move like that, there's no telling what he might do. He's already created enough havoc that our lives are beginning to look like the aftermath of a tornado. The only way out of this is by hacking into that mainframe and destroying the program. And so far, I haven't been able to get in remotely."

"But we created that firewall. And you've already gotten past it. I don't understand why you can't hack back in," Zack demanded.

Jordan gave him her death stare.

"Let's not gang up on her," Max said. "This is not Jordan's doing."

"Archer told us he made modifications. Well, those modifications prevent me from accessing the system remotely unless I have a whole lot of hours and four more weeks to devote to it. And we don't have that kind of time. But I'm pretty sure it can be accessed directly."

"Directly? What does that even mean?" Max stood.

"It means I need to be at a terminal that's directly connected to the mainframe."

"And how do you propose to do that?" Max let out a frustrated breath. "It's not like security at the Sintinex Corporation is going to sign you into the building and escort you right to it."

Jordan tilted her head and gave him a withering look. "I'm aware. And I have a plan. Let's all sit and take a breath while I explain."

Rafe walked around the table and sat next to Mallory. Max parked himself on the edge of the bench. "We're ready."

"So that we're all on the same page—" Jordan looked each one in the eye "—the program I created hacks into pretty much any system. If you combine it with Archer's snippet of code, it produces a worm that will take over an entire system."

"Yeah, yeah. We've established that," Rafe said.

"*Calmaté*, bro. Give her a chance." Max squeezed Jordan's thigh.

"Wait." Zack held up a hand. "You said before that there's much more at stake. What's the more?"

"I'm getting to that."

Mallory raised her hand. "Did you say take over an entire system?"

"I did. And it's scary. Without companies like RMZ Digital, we'd be living in a world of cyber outlaws," Jordan said. "We need cybersecurity. Not only to protect other companies but ordinary people. They need to know when they go to bed at night and wake up the next morning that their life savings will be where they left it and that it hasn't been hacked out of their bank accounts." Jordan clenched her fist. "I'm not being dramatic. But someone like Archer, with what he's created, could do that."

"He has to be stopped," Mallory said. Rafe wrapped an arm around her shoulders and pulled her in close.

"Yes. Because of what's at stake." Jordan climbed over the bench and stood at the head of the picnic table. "Let me spell it out for you. One—" she flicked out her thumb "—Sintinex can get into anyone's mainframe. That includes government agencies. Two—" she flicked out her index finger "—if that's not scary enough, once they're into an agency's mainframe, they can steal documents, create documents, manipulate documents, and use it all as leverage for extortion." Finally, she flicked out her middle finger. "And in case you weren't terrified enough, they would have the ability to halt all commercial shipments by ground, air, and sea. They could hold entire cities or even countries hostage. I mean, come on, with that kind of power, the possibilities are endless."

The silence was chilling. Jordan saw the recognition and the implications of what she'd said dawn on each of their faces—the fact that it wasn't just their lives at stake.

Max broke the silence. "You said you had a plan."

"Yeah."

"So, what's the first step?" Max asked.

"The family is going on a trip."

They stared at her with noncomprehension.

Mallory spoke first. "A trip where? Who's going on a trip?"

"All of you," Jordan scanned their faces. "Even your aunt Ellie and your father."

"¿Qué estás diciendo? Estás hablando loco," Zack spat out.

"I'm with Zack. Sorry, but that's crazy talk. How does going on a trip solve anything?" Max said.

Jordan blew a breath out through her nose. "Hear me out before you start calling me crazy." She gave Zack a pointed look. "You're all getting on a plane tomorrow for Puerto Rico."

Chapter 16

While the others lobbed a salvo of questions at Jordan until they were shouting over each other, Max remained silent, staring in disbelief.

"Listen. Please. Let me talk." Jordan's words could barely be heard over the other voices. She raised her hands in an effort to get them to calm down, but their shouts grew louder. She put her index finger and pinkie in her mouth and blew out a long, shrill whistle.

Buck, who'd been happily sleeping under the shade of a maple tree, began barking and ran to her. "It's okay, boy." Jordan crouched and rubbed his back until he calmed. When she looked up, she found everyone staring down at her. "Oh, good, you've stopped yelling. Are you ready to listen?" They remained quiet, although she detected one or two rude looks.

"This will be a two-pronged attack. In a couple of days, Archer will realize that the money has been moved, and knowing him, he'll take more drastic measures against this family."

"How can you be so sure?" Zack asked.

She stood, put a hand on her hip, and shifted her weight to one foot. "Stolen identity. Dead body in my bathtub.

An Indy 500 road race last night. Are you telling me that wasn't Archer?"

"Fair point," Rafe said.

"We are dealing with a lunatic whose sole reason for living right now is to gain enormous power. We need to be smart and take precautions." Jordan pointed to Rafe. "We can't afford to take any risks with your daughter, your wife, and the baby on the way."

Rafe moved closer to Mallory and nodded.

"Zack." Jordan pointed at him. "We need to keep your aunt and your father safe and make sure no one harms her or sullies his reputation."

Zack shifted in his seat and nodded.

"And Max, I don't need to remind you that RMZ has employees to protect. We need to keep Archer far away from them."

"I agree. Tell us how getting us out of the States helps."

Jordan raised a hand. "Track with me here. If you let me get through the plan and the reasons why, I think all your questions will be answered."

"The floor is all yours."

"Step one. Your father will supposedly get a call from his brother's wife with the news that Alfredo is gravely ill and was taken to the hospital. Emilio is urgently needed in case Alfredo doesn't recover. Your father—"

"Whoa. Whoa." Zack stood. "Are you for real?"

Jordan huffed out a breath. "You gonna let me finish, or are you going to keep objecting? Or maybe—" she crossed her arms over her chest and tilted her head to the side "—you have a better idea you'd like to share with the group?"

Zack stared at her for a moment longer before he sat and shook his head.

"Where was I? Oh, yeah. Your father will take family leave and have to clear his court docket and fly to the island of Vieques to see his brother—" she raised her hands to the side "—and if he's out of the country, he won't be able to hear the case against Davide Rustokov. That will make it impossible for the judge to be accused of taking bribes because he'll be nowhere near the case. The entire family will be going with Emilio because of the serious nature of Alfredo's illness. Not to mention, I think it will be safer to get the hell away."

Jordan marched on with her strategy despite the looks of skepticism. "I'm ready to hack into the Vieques hospital system and insert false admission records for Alfredo, should anyone want to dig deeper."

"This feels too elaborate," Rafe said.

"I worry it's not elaborate enough," Jordan said.

"I think we're missing one key element here," Max said. "Pop's too ethical. I don't think he'll go for this."

Rafe and Zack nodded their agreement.

"He's going to have to. And from the short time I spent with him last night, he strikes me as the kind of man who will do what it takes to protect his family." Jordan looked over at Mallory. "In particular, his future grandchild."

Jordan stuck her hands in her back pockets. "That's the first part of the two-pronged approach. Keeping you all safe until I'm able to ruin Archer and his plans. Because something much more pressing and terrifying is about to happen."

"*¡Ay, basta!* What more could there be?" Zack put his forehead in the palm of his hand.

The distressed looks on everyone's faces didn't go unnoticed, but there was no time to consult feelings. Jordan needed to press on. "Max, you know how much pressure Sintinex put on us for four straight weeks to get this project completed."

"I haven't forgotten."

"Turns out, the reason the deadline was so fierce was to ensure Archer would be ready for this weekend."

"What happens this weekend?"

"The annual transportation and infrastructure expo is happening in New York City at the Jacob Javits Center."

Max gasped. "Holy mother of…?"

"Exactly. Sintinex will be there selling its services to major corporations and government agencies. Each year, they provide attendees with Sintinex swag. It's always a silver thumb drive shaped like an airplane with their logo on it, providing attendees with samples of their latest offerings. You know, like faster shipment tracking, weather alerts for best shipping dates, and even more elaborate programs, like cost-cutting analytics that work in real time." She waved a hand. "It really doesn't matter what's on it. The point is, I think once a customer inserts the drive into one of their work computers, and they will, it's all over. A worm will infiltrate any system it's on, and Sintinex will have access to everything in that company's mainframe and anyone else they do business with. Lots of these companies work on big government contracts. You only need one email from an infected source and game over. This is how Archer will gain complete control of transportation, first in the United States, then globally."

"That is so demonic," Max said, eyes wide. "If what you're saying is true, and I don't doubt it, then that means we were only pawns in Archer's end game. All along, his goal was to gain access to corporate and government agencies' mainframes, and what? Destroy them? Hold them ransom? Disrupt the transportation system?"

"All of the above," Jordan said. "This is why I need to destroy the program before anyone gets a chance to download it."

"How do you plan on doing that if you can't get into the mainframe?" Max asked.

"I'm going to be at that convention. I'll be one of the vendors."

"Hold up," Zack said. "A convention like that would have locked up their vendors weeks ago."

Jordan placed her knuckles on the table and leaned forward. "You forget who you're dealing with. I'll handle that part. Don't give it another thought. The point is, I'll be on the convention floor. If this year is anything like the past five years, Sintinex will have a large booth with lots of displays and lots of computer stations. Those stations will be hooked up to the mainframe. All I need to do is figure out how to get onto one of those stations, and I'm in."

"Is that all?" Max gave her a pointed look.

"Have some faith. You know I'm good at what I do." She dropped down on the bench next to Max. "But listen, you all don't have to worry because you'll be in Puerto Rico."

"Oh, no. I'm going with you," Max said.

Jordan stared at him.

"Yeah. This is not a one-person job. We're in this together."

Jordan wondered if, because they'd become intimate, he now felt responsible for her. The last thing she wanted was for Max to do this out of a sense of obligation. The state had been obliged to take care of her for eighteen years. It had never felt good. That was not what she wanted from him. "Listen, Max, I don't need—"

"We're not arguing about this. Besides, where had you planned on staying once you got to the city?"

"I'm a big girl. I'll figure it out."

"I'm going with you, and we'll stay at my apartment in the city," Max said in a tone that expected no rebuke. "While Rafe, Zack, and Mallory are protecting the family in Puerto Rico, you and I are going to deal with Archer. And make no mistake, we're bringing him down."

"What about the business?" Rafe asked.

"Do you think you could run it remotely?" Jordan asked.

Rafe paused, then nodded. "We'll figure it out."

"But that's not the hurdle we need to be thinking about right now." Zack put his forearms on the picnic table and clasped his hands. "Who's going to tell Pop? 'Cause it sure as hell ain't gonna be me. He takes his cases very seriously. Walking away from this one isn't something he'll do easily."

"You have a point," Max agreed. "But, like Jordan said, we need to keep the family safe, and there is no telling what Archer will do next. Anyway, I'll tell him." He looked at Jordan. "I mean, together, we'll tell him."

"I'm sorry, but I have to ask," Mallory said. "Is there any other way that doesn't involve all of us traveling to Puerto Rico or you two getting so close to Sintinex? Anything?"

The table was quiet. Jordan saw hopeful faces looking back at her, expecting she'd give them a different way forward as if she hadn't thought of every single solitary possibility. What she'd come up with was a viable solution, but it wasn't without high risk. "If there were any other way, I promise you, I would have found it." She pressed her lips together. Waited to see if anyone had other thoughts. "Okay. If there are no more questions, I think our next stop is the home of Judge Emilio Ramirez."

Chapter 17

The judge lived on the outskirts of Hudson, New York, an idyllic town featuring boutique art galleries, antique shops, bookstores, coffee houses, and a well-known farmers market that ran every year from April through November.

Max had always enjoyed driving along the town's peaceful main street. But today, with the constant checking of his rear and side mirrors for anyone following them, the ride was anything but tranquil.

Buck slept in the back seat, Jordan jiggled her foot on the floorboard, and Max absently tapped the steering wheel with his fingers while he thought about how to approach his father. Jordan's plan to get the family out of the country made sense. They needed the judge to see it their way without feeling he would be compromising his judicial ethics.

Lost in thought, he continued tapping the steering wheel. Five days ago, his life was pretty perfect. Sure, it wasn't necessarily stress free. So what if he hadn't achieved all his goals? Five days ago, there was still time. He had a family he loved, he was working toward his future, and the business was gaining traction and attention. Then, out of nowhere, like the funnel of a twister dropping out of a cloud, his life had become unrecognizable. His family was literally running for their safety. All because he had signed a contract with a madman. Max shook his head and let out a sigh.

"You okay?"

"Yeah. Why?"

"Because if you tap that wheel any harder, it may fall right off the steering column."

Max flexed his fingers. "Sorry."

"What are you thinking?"

"How fast a life can change without warning or expectation."

"Tell me about it."

Max glanced at her. "I guess you've had a lot of that in your life."

"Too much." She let out a harsh laugh. "Silly me thought that moving to Brooklyn would be a step toward settling down. Having a real life. I guess maybe that's never going to happen for me. Because, well…" She turned to look out the passenger window. "Pretty town."

"Are you changing the subject?"

"Nah, just trying to stop my mind from spinning."

Max wondered if her tough exterior was cracking a little. In the last twenty-four hours, she'd barely slept. She had to be exhausted. But if they were going to beat Archer, he needed her. *He. Needed. Her.* That thought was truer than he'd ever imagined. Somehow, she'd worked her way into his heart like no one else ever had. Her toughness, her resilience, her cleverness, everything about her was attractive to him. He wanted to be there for her and with her. It shouldn't all be on her shoulders.

They stopped at a traffic light. Max turned to look at Jordan. Her brow was furrowed, and he wished he could wipe away her worries. "It's my turn. What are you thinking?"

"I was thinking about my one and only best friend, Becca."

"You had a best friend?"

"Shocker, I know."

"What made you think about her?"

"I'm not totally sure." Jordan clasped her hands on her lap. "Anyway, it didn't last."

"What happened?"

"I was twelve. We sat next to each other in homeroom. We clicked. I'd never had a friend before that. I didn't know what it was like to share secrets or look forward to seeing someone just because. I got invited to her house for dinner. She had a younger brother, a mother, and a father. The whole package. A real family. Her parents liked me, and pretty soon, I was having dinner with them once or twice a week and even had sleepovers."

"That must've been a nice change for you."

"It was terrific. But it also made the time I spent at the group home harder. I was mean to the other girls in the house because they weren't Becca and because I had to share a bathroom with six others. And because the dinners weren't what Mrs. Rice made. Hell, I complained about everything, to the point where the house manager stopped my visits to the Rices'."

"Harsh."

"And then some." Jordan's voice was ragged. "Without going into all the gory details, I was enraged that they'd taken away my privileges. I lashed out in so many ways. The next thing I knew, I was transferred to a different home."

"Just like that?"

"Yup, just like that."

Max glanced over. Her jaw was rigid, and he thought he saw tears in her eyes.

"You see," Jordan continued, "when you're a ward of the state, you have zero ability to decide your life or to really make any decisions. I think that was the turning point for me. I thought for sure Becca and her parents would save me. They didn't. That's when I knew I'd never have a family because no family ever really wanted me."

Max could not imagine a life like that.

"Working with you and your family is tricky for me." She glanced at him sideways. "I want to fully trust you. But something inside holds me back." She sniffed. "I thought you should know. I mean, since we're all working together."

He understood what she was saying and why she felt the way she did. But Max wanted her to know that she wasn't alone. "Jordan. I got you. You may not believe me. You may not trust me. You may not even need me. But. I got you."

More silence. Max didn't expect a response. He'd simply wanted her to know.

A couple of miles later, on the outskirts of Hudson, Max glanced at the clock on the dashboard. "Pop's probably going to ask why I'm driving this car. I think it's best if we don't mention what happened last night. I'll let him know mine's in the shop."

"But won't he ask why you're squished behind the wheel of a two-door subcompact instead of a BMW loaner?"

"I'll tell him they didn't have any. And… I…decided to rent this." Max felt his cheeks turn hot.

Jordan raised an eyebrow. "You're not very good at lying, are you?"

"Nope, not my style." Max slowed and turned onto a tree-lined lane. "We're almost there. Whatever you do, give him facts. No conjecture or suppositions. He's spent years on the bench and, before that, was a criminal prosecutor, and that makes him a careful listener."

"Are you trying to intimidate me?"

"Maybe a little."

"Good luck with that. Scarier people than you or your father have tried."

"I was afraid of that."

"What's that supposed to mean?"

Max thought for a minute. Between Jordan and his father, he wasn't sure who was more obstinate. It was a tough call. "Look, we're about to tell him to do something that may go against his moral code, and I think direct but sensitive is the right approach."

"Are you saying I can be abrasive?"

Max sighed. "What I mean is, if my father decides what you're saying doesn't make sense to him, he'll dig in his heels and will not, under any circumstances, go along with the plan."

"Ahhh. Got it."

"He deals with criminals every day. He knows what they're capable of. Stick to the facts. Keep all emotion out of it."

"I'm going to go out on a limb here and say that I think you're overthinking this. You do remember I spent some time with your father last night." Jordan turned to him. "Holy crap!"

"What? What?"

"Sorry, didn't mean to startle you. But I'm kinda shocked that the dinner was only last night. Man." She shook her head. "And it was only what—four days ago, Sam Morris was lying dead in my bathtub." She was quiet for a moment. "Damn. So much has happened." She stared straight at him. "The point I was trying to make is that when I met your father, he understood something was going on, and he said that he trusted his sons to handle it. What we're going to do is give him the rundown of the steps we're taking to handle it. I think that should be enough to satisfy him and get his agreement."

Max sucked in a breath. "I hope you're right because here we are." Max pulled in to an immaculate driveway, turned off the engine, and Buck sat up in the back seat and barked.

"Hang on, boy. I'll let you out." Jordan got out of the passenger seat, clipped the leash to Buck's collar, and pulled the front seat forward for him.

Max peeled himself out of his seat. His legs were a little stiff as he walked around the front.

"Not exactly your style, is it?" Jordan nodded toward the tiny rental.

"It wouldn't be my first choice."

"Snob," she said and winked.

The two-story clapboard house was painted a pale yellow. The wide wraparound porch featured a swing seat on one end and a couple of rockers on the other. Two round planters framed the pale blue front door.

"Is this where you grew up?"

"Uh-huh."

"Nice."

"Yeah, it was. My father refuses to sell it and get something more manageable. I don't blame him. Lots of memories here."

The front door swung open, and Emilio Ramirez stood waiting for them. Apart from the shock of white hair, Max knew he was the spitting image of his father, and he hoped he looked that good when he was in his sixties.

"Hello," Emilio said. "And this is Elliot." He pointed to his golden retriever, who immediately went to Buck. They circled and sniffed each other for several seconds. "It would appear they like each other."

"I think you're right," Jordan said.

"Now that everyone's acquainted, shall we?" The judge held out a hand, stepped aside, and let Jordan enter. Max followed, with both dogs trailing behind.

The bright, spacious living room had pale yellow walls featuring several large landscape paintings. Two oversize couches faced each other on either side of a large white brick fireplace. A large wood coffee table sat between the couches on a colorful area rug. The various side pieces, lamps, and corner reading chairs gave the room a cozy atmosphere.

Emilio waved an arm toward the couch. "Have a seat. What can I get you to drink? *¿Max, quieres una cerveza?*"

"Uh…yeah, why not. I'd love a beer." Max thought it might take the edge off. "That is, if you'll join me."

"*Claro que si.* Of course." Emilio looked at Jordan. "What can I get you?"

"Beer sounds good to me, too."

Max felt unsettled and walked to the picture window at the far end of the living room. The late afternoon sun shone bright. "Wow, Pop, the azaleas and lilacs look amazing. And are those rows of vegetables you planted?"

Emilio laughed. "Yes. Don't be so shocked. Your mother taught me a few things."

"She would be proud." Max smiled.

"Yeah, I think so. And I have time for it now. I took on fewer cases this year. Sort of easing into retirement."

"*No me diga.* You never told us. I thought you would work until they carried you off the bench."

"Things change. Why else would I be home at this hour?" He turned to Jordan. "My wife had a garden for years. After she passed, I didn't have the heart or the time to keep it up. But now I want to. It reminds me of her." He laughed. "I had to do a lot of research to learn what to plant, but I like research. That's the lawyer in me, and I found I like working in the dirt." He turned toward the window and put a hand at the base of his neck. "I think I may have gotten a little carried away."

"Maybe you did, Pop."

"Over there are the tomato beds." He pointed to the far corner of his one-acre plot. "In the middle, there, I planted rows of lettuce. On the other side, I've got beets, cucumbers, and peppers. You get the idea. I have what you could call a very large salad growing in my backyard." He smiled. "All right. Let me get those drinks." He stopped, turned, and gave them both a pointed look. "And then we'll talk about why you're both really here." Emilio headed for the kitchen.

"Nice place," Jordan said and sat on the couch. Elliot and Buck seemed to be content to lie in the corner by the cold fireplace. "Funny, if I had a house, this is exactly how I'd furnish it. I mean, that is if I were going to have my own home. This is what I'd always imagined."

"Really? I wouldn't have expected that."

"I love this country French look where nothing matches but still looks quietly elegant and cozy. I'd take this over your mid-century modern any day." She held up a hand.

"Sorry. No offense. But we don't have the same taste. We could never be an item."

Max tried to ignore her rebuke because he'd hoped she had feelings for him.

"It really is a perfect room," she said.

"All my mother's doing. She had a way with everything. Even with a full caseload at the law firm and her hands full with the three of us, she managed to make this beautiful home. She never missed a beat. Somehow, she was able to juggle it all. She was a remarkable woman."

"Ah, here we are." Emilio came in with a tray filled with three frosty bottles and glasses and set them out before Max and Jordan.

"Thanks, Pop."

There was silence while they each poured their beers.

Max picked up his glass and raised it. *"Salud."*

They clinked glasses, and each took a swallow.

"I know you didn't come here for a drink or to socialize. Something's on your mind, and it started yesterday with that money. Why don't you tell me what you can, and I'll stop you if it's something I shouldn't hear. *¿Intendes?"* Emilio narrowed his gaze in a subtle signal to Max that he would need to skirt around any illegalities or anything that would put the judge in a compromising position.

"I think I understand, Mr. Ramirez," Jordan said. "Do you have a personal computer in your home?"

The judge gave her a wary look.

Max knew that expression too well. It said, what in the world are you talking about? "Pop? Where's your laptop?"

"It's in my study." Emilio's tone was cautious. He pointed to his left.

"Can you get it?" Jordan asked.

Emilio didn't move.

"Pop, puedes confiar en ella."

Emilio gave Jordan a sideways glance.

"Judge, I understand Spanish. And Max is right. You can trust me."

The judge studied Jordan for a second and then stood. "I'll be right back."

Several minutes later, he returned and placed his laptop on the coffee table. Jordan and Max sat on the couch on either side of him.

"Can you pull up your bank account?" Jordan asked. "The one where the money was deposited."

Emilio did as she requested. Once the website loaded, he typed his username and password and then clicked the tab for his savings account. He looked at Jordan, eyes wide, brows raised. "What happened?"

"I moved some things," she said.

"Yesterday, there was a complete record of a quarter of a million dollars going in and out of this account. Today, there isn't a single trace of that transaction. What did you do?"

Jordan remained silent.

"Pop." Max shook his head. "Jordan wanted to show you so you could see with your own eyes. It's gone. Let's leave it at that."

"All right," Emilio said.

Jordan cleared her throat. "So, there is something that needs to happen. It turns out the person behind those money transfers isn't going to stop."

"Why is that?"

"Because I know too much about what he's planning to do, which will likely disrupt the entire transportation system as we know it."

Emilio put his beer on the table and sat forward. "Are you serious?"

"One hundred percent. He knows Max and I have proof of his criminal activities, and we were minutes away from turning him in to the authorities, and that's when he went after you."

"Why?"

"As a warning. His way of saying he's got the power and he has eyes everywhere. Without getting into too much detail, he wanted it to look like you took a bribe on an important case to get you disbarred."

"So you moved the money out?" Emilio asked.

Jordan nodded.

"Which case?"

Max hesitated. "You really want to know?"

Emilio stared at him, and Max saw the fury building in his eyes.

"Of course, I want to know. But…" Emilio paused. "Just tell me, is that the end of it?"

"Only if we can expose what he's trying to do and stop it. If we can't, he'll be able to move the money back into your account."

Emilio hung his head. "Is my family safe?"

"If you do what we say. We've arranged for you to leave for Puerto Rico for a few days."

Max waited for him to say something, and Emilio did open his mouth several times to speak, but no words came out.

Emilio stood and paced. His golden retriever, Elliot, followed in his footsteps, and Buck began to whine.

"Come here, boy." Jordan tapped the side of her leg several times. Buck padded over and sat by her knee. She put an arm around his neck and whispered in his ear, "It's okay. He's thinking."

Max knew his father was working out the sequence of events for himself and probably wondering if there was a way for him not to have to leave. It wasn't like Emilio Ramirez to run from a fight.

Minutes passed before he sat down on the couch opposite Jordan and Max, took a swallow of beer, and ran his hands through his thick white hair. "This is unbelievable." He let out a sigh of frustration. "In all the years I've worked in the law, no one has ever done anything so devious to me or my family. And I've put away a lot of bad people."

A lump formed in Max's throat. He'd never seen his father at a loss in any circumstance. Emilio Ramirez was a rock through the worst of times. When Rafe was in prison, when his wife of forty years died, he'd been stalwart. "Pop. Listen to Jordan. She's got a plan to make this go away."

"I'm all ears. *Dime*."

Jordan laid it all out. She explained that the family would go to the island of Vieques, off the eastern coast of Puerto Rico, to visit his allegedly sick brother. And while Emilio initially objected to the idea of saying his brother was ill, he couldn't come up with a better scenario. Jordan deliberately left out the falsifying of hospital records.

Although Max had an inkling that his father knew there was something more than they were saying, he was smart enough not to ask questions.

"We called your sister-in-law with a burner phone and gave her as much information as necessary. She'll phone you in about an hour and tell you the news. You're to play along and be appropriately concerned," Jordan said.

"Is that really necessary?" Emilio clenched his jaw.

"Yes. I'm afraid it is. We have no idea if anyone will be listening in on the call, and we need to be cautious and play it safe."

"Fine." Emilio's tone was curt. He stood and began pacing again. "Afterward, I'll call my clerk to let him know that I need a short leave of absence for a family emergency." He looked at Jordan. "Should I start making travel arrangements?"

"I'll handle all of that," Jordan said. "You'll get the tickets emailed later."

Max hadn't seen his father this furious in years. He texted Zack and Rafe to let them know they'd told their dad and asked Zack if he could check on him later that night.

"Jordan, we should go." Max stood. "Pop, we're heading out. There's still a lot we need to get done."

"I'm almost afraid to ask. But if you're not going with us, what will you two be doing?"

Max gave Jordan a cautious look. "There's some business in the city we need to take care of that we believe will end all of this." He walked toward the front door, and Jordan followed.

"Look, I appreciate what you're doing and the fact that you're protecting my reputation by not giving me too much information. But I know this has something to do with Archer Kelly, and that makes me nervous," Emilio said.

Max stopped and faced his father, shocked at the mention of Archer's name. "How did you know it was Archer?"

"Come on, now." Emilio shoved his hands in his pants pockets and rocked on his heels. "I was a criminal prosecutor. My entire life has been spent observing people." Emilio nodded at Jordan. "I spotted you at the diner the first day you arrived at Hollow Lake."

"Me?" Jordan put a hand on her chest.

"You were at the counter, nursing a cup of coffee that had long gone cold, looking around from under the bill of your cap. You nearly jumped each time the door opened."

"You are observant," Jordan said.

"I saw the news alert about Axis Industries and the follow-up interview with Archer Kelly and his technical advisor, Jordan Logan. But when you brought *this* Jordan to dinner at Rafe's—" he pointed again at her "—I knew something was wrong. Over the years, I'd heard of the meteoric rise of Archer Kelly, but to me, there were too many things he'd been involved with that didn't add up." Emilio exhaled. "For one thing, he went to court over intellectual property theft. When I looked up the case, there was a strong argument that he did indeed steal an idea for making steel faster and cheaper. But he got off on a legal technicality and reaped the rewards. There are several other lawsuits against him for intellectual property theft that he's managed to keep out of the media." His lips tightened in disapproval. "Then I remembered you had a big job with the Sintinex Corporation—"

"You remembered we were working for them?"

"You're my sons. I pay attention." He raised a brow. "When you mentioned going up against someone threatening the entire transportation system, I put two and three together and came up with five—Archer Kelly. And that scares me."

"*No te preocupes*, Pop."

"Don't worry? I'm your father. It's one of the job requirements." Emilio's eyes watered, and Max put his arms around him. They remained in an embrace for several seconds before Emilio stepped back and wiped at his eyes.

"I just thought of something," Max said. "We can't take Buck with us to the city."

Jordan nodded.

"Pop, can we leave him with you?"

Emilio turned to the fireplace. Both Buck and Elliot were sleeping side by side on the rug. "Look at that. Not a care in the world." Emilio lightly chuckled. "I'll arrange for my housekeeper, Ana, to stay here while I'm gone. She'll look after them. Now, both of you, go."

Jordan rested her hand on his forearm. "Thank you."

Emilio took hold of Jordan's hands. "Thank *you*. Please be safe. And take care of my son."

Jordan nodded and stepped back.

Emilio grabbed Max's hand. *"Vaya con Díos."*

"Thanks, Pop." Max began to pull away, but his father held his grip.

"You have feelings for this woman. *Es la verdad.*"

His father was right. It was the truth. He did have feelings for Jordan, and apparently, it showed. Max could feel the heat rise to his cheeks. He hadn't blushed a day in his life. But with Jordan, he was acting like a sixteen-year-old. If he didn't know it before, he knew it now. He was falling in love.

Chapter 18

"You hungry?" Max asked as he started the car.

"Starving," Jordan admitted. "But we don't have time to stop and eat. I've got to buy your family's plane tickets and get us set up for the convention."

"How 'bout I get us back to the office? You start working, and I'll get us some Chinese takeout."

"Yeah. That works. Make sure to get extra egg rolls." Jordan turned her gaze to Max, who wore an amused expression. "What? Why are you looking at me like that? I can't hack on an empty stomach."

"Extra eggs rolls. Got it."

She watched the road ahead and sighed, silently tapping her finger on her knee, itching to start.

Max turned the corner onto Main Street. They were one block from RMZ Digital. "Will there be a lot of people at the office?" Jordan asked.

"It's nearly seven o'clock. Most of the staff will have left by now. We'll work in my office with the privacy screen up just to be safe."

As they pulled into the parking lot at the back of the building, Jordan reached into her leather satchel and pulled out her ball cap and dark glasses. She didn't dare take any chances that someone would recognize her from the dozens of news alerts in the last couple of days.

The elevator door opened onto the second floor. They passed the empty reception desk and walked the corridor along the bullpen area. The place was fairly empty, with only a couple of techies sitting in their cubicles—headphones on and their eyes glued to their screens. A short man in a gray coverall wheeled a large trash can down the middle of the room, emptying wastepaper baskets.

Max waved to the custodian and then quickly ushered Jordan into his office, setting her up at his desk with a laptop.

She pulled up the airline's website. "I'm all set here. Anyone monitoring the company's IP address will know we're buying the tickets at the last minute."

"Let me get the corporate credit card for you." He reached into his back pocket, pulled the card from his wallet, and handed it to her. "Now I need to get in there," Max said, pointing to the built-in file cabinet on the far side of his desk.

"You mean the vault with all your secret information?" Jordan teased.

Max nodded. Jordan pushed back in her chair as far as she could, giving Max access. His arm brushed across her legs as he reached down, and much as she didn't want to admit it, she liked the feel of his touch.

Max squatted in front of his desk, punched in his code, and the hidden drawer slid open. He took out several index cards and handed them to her. "Here's everyone's full name, email address, and birthdate to make the airline reservations."

"You really are the executor for the entire family." She stared at him, knowing her expression emanated disbelief.

"I know you think I'm nuts. But I told you, no one is going to guess I'm old-school when it comes to storing valuable personal information. No one uses paper anymore. It's like I'm hiding everything in plain sight." Max pointed to his temple. "Admit it. It's clever. Right? I even have bank records in that drawer that don't exist anywhere else."

"Surely you could find a way to secure this information using modern technology. I mean, you've built impenetrable firewalls."

Max put his hands on his hips. "We're in this very situation because of that firewall." He leaned in close. "Turns out, it wasn't impenetrable. You broke through. And then, all hell broke loose."

He was so close Jordan's eyelids fluttered before she turned her gaze to the tips of his shoes. "Noted." She swiveled the chair around and placed her hands on the keyboard. "Much as I'd love to, I don't have time to argue with you about the merits of paper versus the cloud. We have work to do."

"If it makes you feel any better, my brothers think I'm crazy, too."

"Marginally." Jordan held up a hand, her forefinger and thumb an inch apart. "Makes me feel marginally better."

Max chuckled. "Do you need anything else to get started?"

"No. This will do it."

"Good. While you're doing that, I'll get us dinner. I won't be long."

"Finally. I'm so hungry." Jordan smirked. Then turned and went right to work purchasing the plane tickets directly from the airline's website using RMZ Digital's IP address. If Archer were tapped into their system, everything she was now doing on the computer would back up the story that a last-minute family emergency had the Ramirez clan on a flight out of Albany. She even purchased a ticket for Max. With the last seat assignment complete, she had the boarding passes sent via email to each family member.

With that done, it was time to create a VPN. The work she was about to do needed to be untraceable. The virtual private network would encrypt her internet traffic, making it difficult to trace anything back to RMZ, but she felt even that might not be enough. Not with Archer Kelly after them. One couldn't be too careful.

With a dozen more keystrokes, she created a multi-hop VPN so all traffic would route through multiple servers, making it that much more difficult for her to be traced. Finally, it was time to create a fake company that could then purchase a last-minute spot on the convention floor. She settled on the two of them being co-owners of a midsize trucking company looking to expand its business. Before she could begin the process, Max poked his head into the office with two large bags.

"Oh, that smells good."

"Come on." He winked. "The place is empty. Everyone's gone home. Let's eat in the back. We won't take long, but at least I can spread out the food."

"What all did you buy?"

"Stop talking and start walking and find out." Max turned on his heel and left.

"I'll be right there." Jordan was famished, but she stopped to turn off her Wi-Fi connection, close all the open tabs, and carefully erase her browsing history.

The smell of food led her straight past the ping-pong table, foosball, and arcade games to the luncheon area. A dozen brushed-metal round bistro tables, each with four chairs and a low-hanging pendant lamp, filled the space comfortably. Along the back wall, the counter was a deep mahogany with a brilliant shine. A white porcelain sink sat in the middle, and a large brass espresso machine nearly filled one entire side of the counter. The appliances were stainless steel. It was all super chic. "Nice break room."

"The people at this company work hard. Most times, they barely get out. The least we can do is give them some comforts."

Half a dozen white plastic takeout containers were spread out on the counter. Real plates, napkins, and chopsticks were placed at a corner table where Max sat.

"What did you order? The entire menu?"

"Pretty much. You said you were hungry."

She smiled. "You're crazy."

"I've been called that a time or two. Come on. Let's eat before it gets cold. I'm not a big fan of microwaved food."

Jordan grabbed a plate and filled it with fried rice, dumplings, chicken and broccoli, and two egg rolls.

"I think you might have missed the scallion pancakes."

"I'll get them on the second round." She sat, picked up her chopsticks, and dived in. Without speaking for a full ten minutes, Jordan ate, savoring each bite. This was the first meal she'd had all day, and she was ravenous. The way things were going, she didn't know when she'd get another chance to eat, so she planned on taking advantage of the generous spread Max had arranged. "This is delicious. Who knew you could get great Chinese food away from a metropolitan area."

"Hollow Lake isn't in the wilds, for goodness sakes."

Jordan gave a sheepish grin and got up for seconds.

Again, she piled her plate high and then sat. She exhaled, getting ready to dig in.

"Where do you put it all?"

"Fast metabolism," she said between bites.

"All right. Let's get to it. What's the plan?"

"You need to call your brothers. They're on the ten a.m. flight out of the Albany airport. They'll need to get there no later than eight thirty. I've arranged for a van to pick them up at seven thirty."

"Oof, that's early."

"We can't afford to mess around here. Their tickets and boarding passes were emailed to them."

"I'll send a group text and make sure they got their tickets and that we're all on the same page." Max took out his phone and began texting while Jordan continued to eat.

His phone chimed several times with the sound of incoming texts. Max took a minute and read what was on his phone. "Everyone answered, and it looks like we're all in sync."

"Great. Now that that's settled."

"Wait. Thanks for setting all that up."

"Sure. It wasn't anything."

"It was everything." He reached over and took her hand. "You were the one who figured out how to move the money. You were the one who thought to get my family out of here and keep them safe. I want you to know how grateful I am."

His sincerity threw Jordan off. She wasn't used to people appreciating her, and coming from Max, she had to admit it meant a lot. But it still made her uncomfortable. Again, too intimate. She pulled her hand away. "No problem." She cleared her throat. "Next item on the agenda. If you owned a midsize trucking company, what would you call it?"

Max turned his head and looked behind him. "Are you talking to me?"

"Yeah. Who else? You're the only one here."

"It was such a non sequitur."

Jordan huffed and raised a brow.

"Okay. Hang on. If I had a midsize trucking company, I'd call it Acme Deluxe."

Jordan burst out laughing. "That is lame."

"I gave you the first thing that popped into my head. Why do I need to name a trucking company, anyway?"

"Because you and I are co-owners of Acme Deluxe, and in two days, we'll be at the transportation convention drumming up business."

"How do you propose to do——" Max stopped himself and chuckled. "I won't insult you by asking how you plan on pulling that off. Because you are an internationally renowned hacker, and with everything you've been able to accomplish so far, I have a feeling you will somehow make this happen, too. But the bigger issue—is it legal?"

Jordan's smile turned into a pucker. "Look, Max, we've already been over this. I'm one of the good guys. I don't hack into places to cause disruption. It's unethical and wrong. I've only ever worked for businesses that needed me to solve a problem within their firm. And until I worked for Sintinex, that's what I did. I should have known that deal was too sweet to be on the up-and-up." She fiddled with her chopsticks. "Archer has forced my hand, and we have to stop him. That means we're going to have to cross a few gray lines—" she shrugged "—and I'm okay with that." She placed her chopsticks on the table with emphasis. "If you're going to have a problem with everything I do or question every action I take, then we aren't going to be able to work together. I bought you a ticket to Puerto Rico so it would look like all of you were out of town. You're welcome to use it if you think my actions will trample on your moral high ground."

Max raised his hands in a surrender motion. "You're right. He's already forced us to cross so many lines. We'll do whatever we have to. I'm all in. One hundred percent."

"Okay, good." She stood. "Let's clean this all up and get back to work."

"You go back. I'll take care of this. Be right there."

Jordan nodded and headed back to his office.

Her game plan needed to be simple. Arrive at the convention pretending to be one of the many exhibitors at the conference. At some point, she and Max would walk the floor and visit other exhibitors, checking out the supposed competition and various products for sale. It would include a stop at the Sintinex booth, where she hoped they would have several computers set up to show prospective buyers what Sintinex had to offer. From there, she'd have to somehow get access to one of them without being stopped, pray it was attached to their mainframe, and destroy the program. She hadn't figured out that little detail yet.

She dropped into Max's chair and got to work, creating a fake company, obtaining a last-minute entry into the convention as an exhibitor, securing signage for the booth, and mocking up fake IDs and driver's licenses for her and Max.

The hours flew by, but she managed to pull it off and was now in the copy room with Max, printing out fake driver's licenses.

"How did you even learn how to do this?" Max stared. The look he gave her wasn't kind. "I thought you said you only work as a white-hat hacker."

"Are we really doing this dance again? Didn't we go over this a few hours ago? Gosh, you are exhausting." Jordan snatched the licenses from the ID card printer. "I can still get you on that flight to Puerto Rico."

"No, no, no." Max waved his hands. "Sorry. Old habits. Always making sure I'm on the right side of the law. I guess I got overcautious after Rafe was arrested. I know what we need to do. No more questions. I promise."

Jordan pointed a finger at him. "Are you sure this time?"

"Yes."

"Then let's finish these IDs. We're going to need a laminator."

"There's one at the reception desk. Brittany uses it for all the office IDs. I'll be right back."

Moments later, with an exacto knife and the laminator, Jordan completed the job. She handed Max his ID for the convention and his new Indiana driver's license. "You're Jeff Riches, and I'm Amy Newell of Acme Deluxe."

Max held Jordan's license and stared at it. "As far as this looking like a legit license, it's flawless. But how is this going to work? You're not blond, and that's definitely not your nose." He then looked down at his license. "And me? This ain't me. I don't have a mustache and beard, and I'm not bald."

"Don't worry about what we look like in the photos. A package will be waiting for us at your apartment in the city tomorrow. It will have everything we need to turn us into Jeff Riches and Amy Newell. I didn't want to take any chances that we could be spotted for who we really are at the convention."

"Aren't you the clever one?" Max stepped closer. He stared for a moment, almost making Jordan feel uncomfortable. She tilted her head silently, asking the question What's wrong?

Max brushed a lock of hair off her face. "You're pretty remarkable."

Jordan glanced down, and Max lifted her chin, giving her no choice but to look him in the eye.

"Seriously. Most people would have crumbled under the pressure. But you...you keep working angles. Determined to get us to the finish line. And now we have everything we need to be vendors at the transportation convention and get into that mainframe. You are one remarkable woman." Max leaned forward. Their lips were inches apart.

Desire blossomed within her. She could no longer deny that this man made her feel things she'd never felt before. It confused her and exhilarated her. She wasn't going to kid herself. Her life was on the line, and regardless of how much attention to detail she'd put into the plan to destroy the program, it was still fifty-fifty that she'd make it out of this unscathed. Why not enjoy this thing between them? Even if it was temporary.

Max leaned in even closer, and they were practically breathing the same air. Her lips parted, and she could no longer control a rational thought. She wanted him to kiss her. When his lips touched hers, she closed her eyes and sighed. But within seconds, they both froze.

"That noise. That's the elevator," Max whispered.

"I heard it, too."

Jordan glanced at the digital clock on the copier. "It's four in the morning," she whispered. "Who could be coming here at this hour?"

Max put a finger to his lips. "Shhh." He motioned for her to help him gather up everything on the printer and table. Quietly, Jordan put their new IDs into a manila envelope from the stack on the table. She picked up the laptop, and they both remained motionless as the sound of heavy footsteps echoed down the corridor before coming to an abrupt stop.

"Wait here," Max whispered.

"Like hell," Jordan shot back.

Max leveled her with a glare, but Jordan didn't back down. He huffed out a breath and mouthed the word "Okay."

Max turned and stormed down the corridor, Jordan fast on his heels. She came to an abrupt stop behind him and realized they were at his office. He turned the knob and threw open the door.

"Brittany!" Max said. "What the hell?"

Chapter 19

"Geez, Max, you scared the crap out of me." Brittany jumped up out of Max's chair.

Max stepped into the room. "What are you doing here?"

"What am *I* doing here?" Brittany put a hand to her chest. "Don't stall."

"I… I… I," Brittany stuttered. "Are you serious?"

"Dead. Serious. Start talking. It's four in the morning, and you're in my office, going through things on my computer."

"Because *you* asked me to," Brittany snarled. "In what universe do you think I would leave my house before the crack of dawn to come to the office if you had not only called me but sent me a text telling me you were leaving for Puerto Rico first thing in the morning and it was urgent I remove the password protection."

Max couldn't decipher if what she was saying was true. Brittany had been with the firm for three years. They'd done a rigorous background check on her before they hired her. She'd been nothing but a terrific employee. She was more than a receptionist; the place didn't run without her, and she was handsomely paid for it. "Explain. Please. Because I didn't call you, and I didn't text you."

Brittany bent down.

"Whoa. What are you doing?" Max took a step forward.

She held up her hands as if she'd been caught. "I'm reaching for my purse. Sheesh, you try and do a favor and end up getting indicted." She retrieved her purse, took out her phone, and held it out to Max. "Take it. Go ahead."

Max reached for the phone.

She stared at him hard. "The code is 1509."

Max pressed the numbers on the screen.

"Now go to my voice mail and play the message that's listed as coming from you."

Max looked down, and under his contact information, there was a voice mail that looked to have come in at 3:15 a.m. He pressed the speaker icon and then Play.

"Hey, Brittany. It's me, Max. Sorry, really sorry to bother you at his unholy hour, but I need a big favor. The family's leaving for Puerto Rico in the morning, and I need you to go to the office and remove the password for the remote login so we can all access the system while we're away."

Max looked up. He couldn't believe what he'd heard.

"When my phone rang, I was sound asleep and woke right when the call went to voice mail. When I played the message, I had the same look of disbelief on my face, knowing you guys would never want me to do that. But then I started getting the texts—" she pointed to the phone "—take a look."

With Jordan standing next to him, he scrolled through the messages.

Max: Did you get my message?

Brittany: Yes. You sure you want me to do this? It makes no sense.

Max: Yeah, it will make it easier for all of us to work while we're down there.

Brittany: Are you sure???

Max: I would do it, but car in shop. And Rafe and Zack are asleep. Really appreciate it.

Brittany: This doesn't seem right. Call me.

Max: Just do it!

Max dropped into a chair. "That voice message sounds exactly like me."

"Sure does," Brittany agreed.

"And those texts look like they came from my number." He shifted in his seat and removed his phone from his back pocket. "Here." He handed Brittany his phone. "No texts from me to you." He watched her face as she scrolled through his outgoing messages.

"Then who contacted me?"

"Archer Kelly," Jordan said. "He's using AI. Looks like he wanted access to RMZ's system but knew we hadn't uploaded the worm program, and it would take too long to hack past your double firewall—so he tried this. Clever." She lifted one shoulder. "You gotta give him that."

"Fiendish is more like it."

"At least now we know he's monitoring traffic in and out of the office. He knew the family was going to Puerto Rico. Good thing I bought a dummy ticket for you."

"What's going on?" Brittany asked, her voice shaky.

"We've got a little problem, and it's better if I don't say

too much. But I do need you to do something now." Max leaned forward with his forearms on his knees and scrubbed his face with his hands. "We're going to close the office for a couple of days."

"Close? But why?"

"Please trust me. After what happened to you, I think it's for the best. Can you send a company-wide email that we're updating security? Everyone is to take the next three days off with pay."

"But it's the weekend."

Max gave her a look. "You and I know how many of our people work on the weekend. I don't want anyone back in the office until Tuesday. Not until we sort this out. I don't think we'll need to call any of our clients for now. If we still have a problem on Monday, I'll think of something for us to tell them."

"Got it."

"Jordan, you come with me. I need to check the cloud and make sure everything is backed up as of one hour ago. I don't trust we're in the clear with Archer. It needs to be fast with no mistakes, and I could use a second set of eyes." He turned to Brittany. "You good over there?"

"Working on a mail merge right now."

"Thanks. Jordan, let's go."

By four thirty, they were back in Max's office. The email to the employees was sent. The system was checked and backed up.

"There's one more thing I need to do. Hang tight, be right back." Max entered the conference room and pressed the side panel on the left wall, revealing a safe. He pressed his thumb on the front panel, and the door swung open. Max pulled out two new phones. He closed the safe and the panel and walked back into his office.

"Here." He handed Brittany one of the phones.

"What's this for?"

"Clearly, your phone's being tracked. It's better if you have a new one until we can wipe your old phone."

"That's scary."

"I don't want you to be scared, but I need you to be cautious." Max paused. "Archer isn't after you. He used you to get to me and my brothers. I truly believe you are safe," Max said, "but I don't want to take any chances. This is happening because of our company. I know you didn't sign up for this cloak-and-dagger stuff—"

"Max, I trust you and your brothers. I just never thought Archer Kelly would be crazy." Brittany glanced out the window. "Looks like the sun will be up soon. Maybe I'll take a drive—visit my mother in Buffalo for a few days."

"Sounds like a smart move," Jordan offered. "Do you know the phone numbers of the people you'll need to reach, like your mother? Other close relatives? Max?"

"I'll put those numbers in this phone now."

Max glanced at the clock. He wanted to get to Rafe's house before they left for the airport, but he couldn't shake the feeling that they were still exposed. "Jordan. I don't think it was enough for us to back up the system. I'm going to shut the entire thing down. I don't want to give that creep, Archer, even an inch of opportunity to get into our system. And if it's off, there's no reason to bother Brittany any further."

"Makes good sense," Jordan said.

Max saw the look of relief on Brittany's face. "I'll be right back."

* * *

The sky glowed a fiery orange as the sun rose in the east. Max and Jordan walked Brittany to her car. "Pack a bag and go see your mom. If I need to contact you, I'll text you using my full name, Maximo. Any messages you get from Max, you'll know it's not me."

Brittany nodded, slid into the driver's seat, and closed the door.

Max tapped the roof, signaling for her to get going.

Max and Jordan arrived at Rafe's an hour before their airport departure. Max rang the doorbell and walked in, not waiting for anyone to open the door. "Hello. We're here!"

"Back in the kitchen," Rafe called out.

Justine came running to greet them. "Uncle Max. Guess what?"

He picked her up and twirled her around.

"Wait," she giggled. "I have to tell you something." Justine put her arms around his neck. "We're taking a trip. On an airplane. Have you ever been on an airplane?"

Max smiled. Even in the most difficult of circumstances, Justine was always a bright spot. He was thankful every day that Rafe had gotten back together with Mallory, and she'd brought this precious bundle of joy into their lives. "Yes, I have taken a few trips by plane. Come on. Let's see what everyone else is doing."

"Bor-ing." She rolled her eyes. "All they do is talk, talk, talk."

Max turned to Jordan. "Come on. Let's see if there's coffee. I could use a cup. You?"

Jordan nodded. "A pot is more like it."

Max found everyone crowded into the kitchen. Rafe was at the sink, loading the dishwasher.

"*Sobrino*, I'm glad you came," *Tía* Ellie said.

"I wouldn't let you leave without saying goodbye." He put Justine down and bent to kiss his aunt and his father. "Hey, Pop, how you doing?"

"Fine, son."

"Hey, Jordan. Want some coffee?" Mallory asked.

"Love some."

"How 'bout some breakfast?" Rafe offered.

"Thanks," Jordan said. "But you all have to leave soon."

"Yeah, don't worry about us," Max said.

"We have time." Mallory pulled out a chair. "Sit. I'll make it."

"Uncle Max, look what I'm taking with me." Justine held up a coloring book of flowers.

Max smiled. "Which one's your favorite?"

"I love tulips." She flipped open the pages. "See. I'm going to color this one red."

"Jordan, how would you like your eggs?" Mallory placed butter in a pan on the stove.

"Uh. Simple. Scrambled, please."

"Max? How about you?"

"Hold the eggs. I need to speak with Rafe and Zack for a minute."

The room got quiet, and all eyes focused on him. "Nothing to worry about." Max stood and poured himself a cup of coffee.

Mallory cracked eggs into a bowl. "Okay then. Jordan, you eat, and the guys will have their little mini-conference."

"I'll check on Justine's travel bag," *Tía* Ellie said.

"Oh, that would be great. Thanks," Mallory said.

Max left the kitchen through the back door, stepped onto the porch, and waited for his brothers.

"What gives?" Zack asked, stepping onto the porch with Rafe close behind. "Everything okay?"

Max spent the next twenty minutes giving his brothers a rundown of what he and Jordan had accomplished during the night and what they planned over the next couple of days. He saw the relief on their faces and hated that he now had to tell them about the Brittany situation. He couldn't keep it from them. They weren't just his brothers. They were business partners. Max sucked in a breath and relayed the details about the fake voice mail and texts Archer had sent to Brittany and why he decided to close the office and shut down their system.

"Holy crap," Rafe said, punching one of the posts on the porch. "This man is unrelenting. He wants to destroy us."

Zack paced. "You know how long it will take us to get the system back up and running. It could be a week before we get everything back online. It could really hurt the business."

"That is not what we should be thinking about right now," Max said.

"He's right," Rafe agreed. "If he had left everything online, we would have been way more vulnerable to Archer, and who knows what havoc he could have wreaked." He looked at Max. "Bro, you gotta destroy that program. Jordan is right. It's our only hope."

"Is Jordan's plan solid?" Zack asked.

"I think so," Max said.

"You *think*? Bro, this is no time for uncertainties."

"Don't jump on him or Jordan," Rafe said. "They're

under a lot of pressure. So far, she's been solid. Let's keep our fingers crossed this plan of hers works."

"It's got to," Zack mumbled under his breath.

"Before I forget, I had to take phones from the safe," Max said. "I thought it best if me and Brittany had new, clean mobiles."

Zack fist-bumped Max. "Smart thinking."

"Take out your phones. You're going to need my new number."

Max tapped his to each of theirs, transferring contact information.

The screen door squeaked open, and Mallory stuck her head out. "Hey, let's wrap this up. The van will be here any minute."

"We're coming," Rafe said, and Mallory went back inside. "Listen, Max. Watch your back." He pulled Max in for a hug. "And don't take any stupid chances," he whispered in his ear.

Max gave a tired smile and stepped back. "No stupid chances. Promise."

"That goes for me, too." Zack embraced Max, then patted him on the back.

"Okay, you guys, let's get you off."

They entered the empty kitchen and headed for the front entryway, where the rest of the family was gathering with their bags.

Max stepped forward and hugged his father. "Try and enjoy yourself and have a vacation."

Emilio shook his head. "Whatever it is you two are doing, be careful."

For a moment, no one said anything, and then Emilio reached out to hug Jordan. "Take care of my son."

"I will."

"The van is here," Mallory announced. "Let's hit it." She grabbed Justine's hand and headed out the door. The rest of the family followed, each one carrying a suitcase.

Rafe stopped and looked at Max. "Keep us posted. Even sending a text to let us know you're still alive will go a long way to putting us at ease."

"Will do." Max and Jordan watched as they piled into the van and waved them off. He was silent for several seconds, then said to Jordan, "So, now it begins."

Chapter 20

The two-and-a-half-hour drive from Hollow Lake to New York City was quiet. Jordan was too exhausted and freaked out to have a conversation. What would be the point? They both knew what needed to be done. The thought that she might fail in destroying Archer's program and getting her identity back nagged at her the entire ride.

When they turned onto Route 17 and the Manhattan skyline appeared in the distance, Jordan clenched her fists. Her heart raced with the speed of someone just completing a sprint, not someone who'd been sitting in the passenger seat of a car for over two hours. Go time was approaching.

She closed her eyes, trying to center herself. If she was going to pull this off, she needed to keep her wits about her. The fact that she still hadn't totally worked out how to get onto a Sintinex computer terminal once they were in the convention center kept her on edge.

"You okay over there? For the past half hour, you've been dancing in your seat."

Jordan looked down. Without realizing it, her leg was jiggling nonstop.

"You nervous?"

Jordan looked out the window.

"Talk to me."

She turned to him. "I've been thinking about how I'm going to get onto one of the computers at the Sintinex booth."

"Once we see the layout of the convention floor, I think we'll be able to see what we need to do."

"I sure as hell hope so."

An alert sounded on Max's phone. "Can you see what that's about?"

Jordan picked up his phone and stared at the screen. "It looks like there's an alert from the cameras outside your house."

"Seriously?" Max moved into the right lane. "Shoot, there's nowhere to pull over. Press the icon to play the live feed video."

Jordan hit the live feed icon, and her eyes widened. "Holy crap. There's someone on your porch. They're looking in the front window."

"What? What do they look like?"

"I can't tell. I think it's a guy wearing a hoodie. His face is hidden. What should I do?" Her words came out in a rush.

"Look in my contacts and dial the sheriff's office."

Jordan scrolled through his contacts, pressed the number and the speaker icon, and, with a shaky hand, held the phone up to Max.

A deep baritone voice came through the speaker. "This is Sheriff Wilkins."

"Sheriff, it's Max Ramirez. I'm out of town but got an alert from my security system. There's someone prowling around my house. Looks like they're trying to get in."

"I'll send one of my deputies over right away," the sheriff said with no preamble.

"Appreciate it."

The call ended, and Jordan put the phone back in the console. Her heart raced. "Shouldn't we turn around?"

Max didn't say anything for several seconds before he hit the steering wheel with the palm of his hand. "No. Let the sheriff's office handle it. We stick to the plan. I'll bet money it's someone Archer sent. Remember, he thinks I'm in Puerto Rico." Max paused. "Damn. Maybe he sent someone after you."

"You think?"

"With that lowlife sleazeball degenerate, anything's possible." Again, he banged the steering wheel with the palm of his hand. "Let's forget about it. The authorities will handle it. We cannot be distracted." He reached over and took hold of her hand. "For now, we're safe. What we have to do is more important." He glanced at her. "This time, we just may be a couple of steps ahead of him."

"Let's hope."

"What time are we allowed on the convention floor to set up our booth for Acme Deluxe?" Max asked.

Jordan glanced at the clock on the dashboard. "The materials for the booth are scheduled to be delivered to the Javits Center by one this afternoon. The people I hired to put up the booth will be there at one thirty."

"That gives us a couple of hours."

"Yeah. We have enough time to stop at your apartment first and change. Then we can hit the convention floor."

"I still can't get over how fast you were able to get a fake logo and signage made for the booth," Max said.

"Don't get too excited. Your credit card took a big whack with the rush charges."

"It will all be worth it when Archer is finally stopped." Max deftly maneuvered the car through traffic as they drove down the West Side Highway toward Battery Park. "My place isn't too much farther."

Jordan stared at him. Even though she was the one who'd come up with this idea, she hoped she was up to the challenge. Stopping Archer was a tall task. Whether she wanted to admit it or not, having Max at her side boosted her confidence. He had a way about him, and she was beginning to rely on his steadiness. For her, that was a first. The thought made her feel a little uncomfortable, and she shifted in her seat. She had to remind herself that they were thrown together out of necessity, and once this was over, there would be no reason for them to stay together.

When they reached the southern tip of Manhattan, Max pulled up to a sleek glass high-rise that reflected the pale blue sky and wispy white clouds. Along the side entrance was a private underground garage for the building's tenants. "We're here." Max punched in a code, and the aluminum door rolled up. He drove in and parked in a spot marked with the number five. "We'll be able to go in and out of the building without anyone noticing."

"How's that?"

Max pointed to the dark corner of the garage. "There's the elevator. It requires the same passcode that gets you into the garage. It'll take us right to the floor of my apartment."

"Clever."

"Secure," Max countered.

"What's the code?"

"5980."

"Got it. Let's do this." Jordan opened the passenger door, grabbed her bag, and briskly walked toward the elevator.

With only two apartments per floor, Max's was nearly as big as his home in Hollow Lake. The decor was also mid-century modern, with low, sleek lines. The colors ranged from pale blue to dove gray. The wood features were blond, and the fixtures were a polished silver. The expansive windows looked out over the Hudson River. The unobstructed view from the fortieth floor also featured a sweeping sky that seemed to flow into the apartment and become another element of the decor. It was peaceful, and her shoulders relaxed. "This is nice."

"Thanks. When I worked on Wall Street, I spent a lot of time here and only went to my house on Hollow Lake on the weekends. Now it's the reverse."

The house phone rang, and Max stepped into the kitchen to answer it.

While he was on the phone, Jordan looked around. Most of his apartment was on one floor with a kitchen, dining room, two bedrooms, and a bathroom. She looked at the staircase leading to the second floor of the duplex and thought that was probably where the primary bedroom was located. She picked up her bag and placed it in one of the bedrooms on the main floor. They had a lot of work ahead of them, and she had to concentrate. Getting any more involved with Max would only interfere with that.

"Hey, Jordan. Where'd you go?" Max called out.

"Back here."

Moments later, Max was in the doorway to the guest bedroom. "There you are."

She turned and thought she detected a look of disappointment on his face. Inwardly, she sighed. It couldn't be helped. They needed to keep their distance.

"The packages arrived, and the doorman is bringing them up on a trolley. What all did you order?"

"You'll see."

Several minutes later, the doorbell rang, and Max rushed to the front door with Jordan behind him. He checked the peephole and then opened the door. A trolley with at least a dozen boxes was wheeled into the foyer.

"Where would you like these, Mr. Ramirez?"

Max pursed his lips. "Uh…how about unloading them here? Thanks, Fred."

When the doorman left, Max scanned the pile. "What *is* all this?"

"Like I said. You'll see." She grabbed her leather satchel and pulled out the large manila envelope with their fake IDs, paperwork for the convention, and the printed receipts of what she'd ordered on Max's credit card.

"Before you open the boxes, let me check that everything I ordered is here." Methodically, she matched each box to its receipt, separating them into two piles as she went. "Okay. It's all here." She pointed to a stack of five boxes on her left. "Those are yours. There are clothes for today and business clothes for tomorrow. There's a briefcase, business cards, some facial hair, and a wig."

"Wait. Did you say *wig*?"

"Yes. Your photo ID shows you're bald on top."

"What are these other boxes?" Max pointed to another pile.

"They're my getup."

"I can hardly wait to see."

His sarcastic tone didn't go unnoticed, and she gave him a look. "For today, we'll go with business casual. We'll head to the convention center and make sure our booth is being put up. Then, we need to scout the Sintinex exhibit. Who knows, maybe we'll get lucky—" she crossed her fingers

"—and I'll be able to jump on one of their computers today. It would save us all a lot of time and anxiety."

"I like your thinking."

"I'll be ready in half an hour." Jordan headed to the bedroom in the back.

She had no trouble putting on the wig or the blue contact lenses. But the costume nose was trickier. Her first attempt left an obvious line around the outside of the fake nose. She tried blending the edges with makeup, and when that didn't work, she became frustrated, ripping the wig off and then the nose.

She crossed her arms over her chest and huffed. Sweat gathered on her scalp and above her lip. "Man, it's hot in here," she muttered. She picked up the paper instructions and read them one more time. "This shouldn't be that hard."

"Jordan, are you back here? Are you ready?"

She heard him knock on the bedroom door.

"In here, in the bathroom."

"Okay, I'll wait for you in the living room."

"No! Come back here. I need help."

Max entered the bathroom and stepped behind her. "You're not even halfway ready."

Jordan looked up and froze, her fight-or-flight instinct kicking in before she realized the reflection in the mirror was Max. She cracked up and couldn't stop. She laughed so hard she bent over and held her stomach.

"What is so hilarious?"

She looked at him and held up a hand. "Please...don't talk... I can't." She was literally in stitches.

Max leaned against the wall by the vanity. "I'll wait right here until you calm yourself."

Through tears of laughter, she stared at him and couldn't

believe how different he looked. The beard and mustache did hide his incredibly sexy, chiseled features. The top of his head, without hair, would take some getting used to. It had the effect of making her focus on his eyes. He still had those warm, deep brown eyes.

"Come on, Jordan. Get a grip. It was you who designed me this way."

Still howling, she straightened and managed to get out one coherent sentence. "I had to. Archer knows what the real you looks like."

"Fine. But enough about me. What about you? What's taking you so long?"

She heard the note of impatience in his voice. "Don't start. I've been trying to get this nose on for the last thirty minutes. The first time, it fell right off. The next time, it was crooked, and just now, the edges were visible. It looked like I had a disease, and my skin was falling off."

Max laughed, deep and loud.

"This is not funny. There are no real instructions. It simply says, put the glue on your face, let it get tacky, and then press the nose on."

"So, what's the problem?" Max grabbed the paper instructions from the vanity. Jordan watched his eyes travel over the page. "You're right. The instructions make it seem very simple."

"Exactly," Jordan smirked. "That's what I said. If you've got your phone, let's pull up a YouTube video. There's got to be one."

Max took his phone out of his pocket, and Jordan stepped beside him, her head leaning in to see the phone screen. He typed the query into the search bar, and up popped over a dozen videos.

"Try that one." Jordan pointed to a man holding up a fake nose. The caption read *Halloween Fun*.

Together, they watched a makeup artist apply the nose. It seemed as simple and straightforward as the instructions she already had. Why hadn't she been able to do it? She was frustrated. If she was nervous to the point that she couldn't perform this simple task, what would happen with the added pressure of trying to get into the Sintinex mainframe undetected? The idea made her stomach queasy.

"I think it might be easier if I do it for you." Max stepped back, faced her, and lifted her chin with his hand. "It's okay to be nervous. I'd be shocked if you weren't. What we're doing is all kinds of crazy. But I know it's our only alternative, and I believe in you."

Jordan looked straight into his eyes, and Max bent down and brushed her lips with his, and she giggled. "Sorry." She pulled away, covered her mouth, and snickered. "Looking at you. It's an adjustment. And then the feel of that beard and mustache. Weird. That's all I can say."

Max rolled his eyes. "I've been laughed at enough for one day. Let's get this nose on and get out of here."

Within ten minutes, the nose was in place and appeared flawless. They were both completely transformed. To avoid questions from the doorman, they took the elevator to the garage and exited through a rarely used side door. "This door needs the passcode to get in and out," Max said, punching in the numbers as they exited. "I booked an Uber. It's one block that way." They took off heading north.

The glass and steel structure of the Jacob Javits Center spanned six city blocks. The sedan pulled up behind other Ubers and yellow taxis. Jordan opened her compact mirror and checked the placement of her wig and nose before exiting.

"You look gorgeous," Max said.

Jordan smirked. "Flattery will get you nowhere. Let's just do this."

Together, they entered the Javits Center, joining a queue behind other vendors working their way through security for an ID and bag check.

At the security station, the line split into two. Jordan nudged Max to move to the right, where a boyish, red-headed guard seemed less threatening than the one on the left, who looked like he was moonlighting from his day job as a CIA interrogator. Military crew cut, thick biceps, and a stone face that would crack if it smiled.

Jordan tried to slow her breathing as they approached the head of the line. Max grabbed her hand and squeezed. Unlike every other high-stress time in her life, she wasn't alone in this. Max was with her, and that knowledge calmed her.

The stout, red-headed security guard scrutinized their registration papers and compared them to their photo IDs. She thought he was lingering over their paperwork longer than necessary. Had she chosen the wrong line?

"Acme Deluxe?" the security guard asked.

"Yes," Max said.

"Where you located?"

"As the registration form indicates—" Jordan pointed to the paper in his hands "—Terra Haute, Indiana." She smiled.

"Well, that's a real coincidence because that's where I went to school."

"ISU?" Jordan asked.

"That's right."

"What was your major?"

"Criminology. I'm at NYU now getting my law degree."

Jordan gave him a wide smile. "Good for you. Your parents must be proud."

"Yes, ma'am."

Max cleared his throat and looked at people waiting in line behind them.

"Oops. Sorry," the security guard said. "It's amazing the people you meet in New York." He handed them their IDs and registration forms. "Floor maps are behind me. Have a great convention."

"Thanks," Jordan said. "Good luck in law school."

"What in the heck is ISU?" Max whispered.

"Indiana State University." Jordan looked up at Max and acted as if they were engaged in the most interesting of conversations. "When I picked Terra Haute as our place of business, I did some research into the area, in case anyone asked." She pointed to a high table to the left of the entrance. "Over there. Maps. Let's find our spot and how far away from Sintinex we are."

Max grabbed a fold-out map and pinpointed their location. "Looks like we're on the main floor. That's good."

"Yeah, but look." Jordan used her forefinger to draw an imaginary line between their assigned spot labeled G12 and where Sintinex would be at G89.

"That's a trek."

"With the last-minute registration, I took what I could get."

"We'll make it work. Let's go find our booth."

The main floor of the convention center covered over seven hundred thousand square feet. Hundreds of people were putting up booths of various sizes. They ranged from a single table with PVC piping and simple draping to elaborate arrangements with jumbo television monitors, interactive displays, large module panels, touchscreen kiosks, and video walls.

Holding the map, Max took the lead. "This way." They walked with a determined step toward the far end of the convention hall.

To her surprise, the four people she'd hired at the last minute and at great expense were nearly finished with the booth. The simple black-and-white logo of a ten-wheeler over an American flag did the job. All the booths in this section were of similar size, about ten by ten. With PVC piping, they had white vinyl drapes on the back against the wall and on either side of their allotted space.

Jordan hadn't bothered to print brochures. In fact, she hadn't planned to man the booth at all. The sole purpose of having a fake company at this convention was to give her the ability to scope out Sintinex's booth and computer layout before it opened to the public. She hoped there would be enough access to their set up that she'd devise a way to get into their mainframe.

"Ms. Newell?" A tall, rail-thin man with a long nose gave her a nod.

It took a moment for Jordan to respond, not yet used to being called by her new alias. "Yes?"

"I'm Ralph. We're from Marketing Express."

"Nice to meet you." Jordan pointed to Max. "This is my business partner, Jeff Riches."

Ralph nodded in Max's direction. "How does it look?" He pointed to the booth behind them.

"Looks terrific. Thanks."

"We didn't see any boxes with brochures or flyers,"

Ralph said. "I had one of my guys check at the shipping entrance, and they said nothing came in for you. Did you bring them with you? Or if you have the tracking number, I can hunt it down and get your stuff here before this opens up tomorrow."

Max stepped forward. "That won't be necessary. Thanks. We have someone from our office coming tomorrow, bright and early, with everything we need. You did a great job. And I think you're done." Max stuck out his hand.

Ralph extended his hand, and they shook. "Well. Okay. If that's all you need. I guess we're done." He searched his pockets. "I have a receipt somewhere." He looked around. "What did I do with it?"

"No need," Jordan rushed to say. "I printed it last night."

"All right then. We'll be back in two days to take it all down."

"Thank you," Jordan said, plastering on a smile. Her foot tapped anxiously as if it had a mind of its own as she watched the four men methodically pack their tools, pick up their shoulder bags and backpacks, and finally head toward the escalator. She turned to Max. "I thought they'd never leave."

Max checked his watch. "Let's go scope out the Sintinex booth."

Together, they casually walked through the various alleyways with booth after booth in various stages of assembly, feigning interest. They passed exhibits two and three times the size of Acme Deluxe, while others were only a table and two chairs.

When they'd walked the length of two city blocks, they stopped in their tracks. Ten feet ahead of them was the Sintinex booth. While it was still in the throes of being assembled, it was incredibly impressive. "It's ginormous," Jordan said.

"And then some." Max shook his head in obvious awe. "That's got to be at least forty by forty."

"It makes the two exhibits on either side look puny."

Sintinex seemed to be the largest exhibit at the convention. It stretched across a prime section of the convention floor, nestled against one of the towering walls. A crew of five people hung a deep blue satin curtain on PVC piping that would cover what appeared to be a back alley of sorts. The front and sides of the exhibit were open, inviting attendees to roam the space. While the booth was still very much in the process of being set up, several components were already in place. A twenty-foot screen hung from the rafters, playing glossy film clips of beautiful people enjoying the goods and services Sintinex transports throughout the world. Big, bold signage was everywhere. A person would have to be visually impaired not to know this was Sintinex. Jordan counted a dozen kiosks with desktop computers being assembled.

Jordan nudged Max with her elbow. "I have to believe those are connected to the mainframe," she whispered.

A woman in jeans, a T-shirt, and sneakers lifted a piece of the curtain covering the back wall to make room for a large box being delivered.

Max grabbed her arm. "Are you seeing what I'm seeing?" he said under his breath. "Take a good look at that woman," Max urged.

"Why? Do we kno—holy crap. That's Lauren Chambers."

Before they could move, Archer Kelly burst from behind the curtain and came stomping toward them.

Chapter 21

Max took Jordan's elbow. "Come on, let's go."

With an annoyed look, Jordan pulled back.

"What are you doing?" he barked in a whisper. "Move!"

"This is my one chance to see the layout before this exhibit is packed with people tomorrow. I need to see how to get onto one of those computers." Jordan's tone was low and urgent.

"We're taking a chance being this close."

"Max, no one will recognize us. I don't even recognize us. Pull out your phone. I'll talk, and you pretend to take notes."

While Max did as Jordan instructed, he snuck a sideways glance at Archer, who stood four feet away, facing the Sintinex exhibit. The purple veins at his temples seemed to pulse as he barked orders to the setup crew. Archer was shorter than Max had imagined.

"Damn it!" Archer yelled.

The sheer volume of his voice made Max stare. He wasn't the only one. The dozen or so people working stopped to look at him, waiting for his next words, but Archer was silent. With his weight on one leg and his index finger pressed to his lips, he appeared to be studying the booth. He walked the length of the exhibit once, then twice. Stopped again and pursed his lips.

Archer's outburst was sudden and harsh. "What in the hell? I wanted four panels of digital displays! Are you all brain-dead? The new software is the most important announcement we've ever made, and you're all too stupid to get it right. Come on, people." He clapped his hands several times. "Wake up! That's why we're here. Where are the panels? Jordan, get over here!"

At the mention of her name, Jordan stepped in Archer's direction. If Max hadn't grabbed her by the belt loop of her jeans, she probably would've been by his side instead of the imposter walking toward him, Lauren Chambers.

"None of this is right," Archer told Lauren/Jordan.

For several more minutes, Archer reamed out most of his staff, berating them for everything he perceived as wrong with the displays, from the logo's font size to the brightness of the images on the large monitor. He paced the length of the booth, spewing a string of curses. He kicked a box over, tools spilling all over the floor, then commanded they be cleaned up immediately. The setup crew of over a dozen people scurried around, trying to keep up with his demands. "Jordan!" Archer screamed. "Coffee. Let's go. When I get back, this all better be right." Archer stormed off with Lauren/Jordan close behind.

"He's a regular charmer," Jordan muttered. "Max, give me your phone."

"Why?"

Jordan snatched it from his hands, faced the booth, and began taking photos.

"Are you crazy?"

"Nope." Jordan looked up at him and smiled. "Making

memories," she said out loud. "This is my first convention, and I want to capture everything." Those words were spoken even louder.

Before Max could stop her, Jordan turned and walked briskly through the exhibit, taking photos as she passed the setup crew cleaning the wreckage Archer had created, acting like she was one of them.

To Max's horror, Jordan lifted the drape against the back wall and disappeared. Everyone seemed to be too busy to notice her. Max realized she was investigating their options for getting into the mainframe, but that didn't stop him from nearly experiencing heart failure. He took several steps toward the back wall but quickly decided his best bet was not to go after her—instead, he opted to stay where he was and keep an eye out for Archer.

As Max paced, his gaze locked onto the large clock hanging in the corner. The second hand went around several times. He continued to pace. More minutes passed. His palms became sweaty. He had no idea what was taking her so long. She'd been gone for over fifteen minutes.

Max's heart rate ticked up another notch when he spied a man with white hair walking down the aisle amidst a crowd of other vendors. It was Archer on his way back. Max's gaze shot to the back wall of the exhibit. "Jordan, where the hell are you?" he muttered under his breath. He looked again and spotted Archer closing in. He was about to go back behind the curtain and grab Jordan when, from behind, he felt a tap on his shoulder and nearly jumped out of his skin. He turned to find Jordan. "Where did you come from? I've been watching that back curtain."

"I took the long way around the back and came out through another exhibit."

"We gotta go." He grabbed her arm. "Don't look back—Archer's headed this way." The two of them practically sprinted in the opposite direction and made a beeline up the escalators, across the lobby, through the revolving doors, and onto the street.

Max expected to see a line of yellow taxis at the curb but found none. "Phone." Max held out his hand to Jordan while simultaneously checking the doors behind him.

"Here." Jordan handed him his phone. She, too, looked behind them. "We're in the clear. Remember, we're unrecognizable."

"Keep an eye out just in case. I'll get us an Uber."

While they waited, Jordan tapped her foot nervously against the pavement and glanced around.

"What did you find out?"

"It's all in the photos. I'll show you when we get to the apartment. But the short story is there's a large system in the back, and from what I could tell, it's connected directly to the Sintinex mainframe. I only had a few minutes to check it out before I was stopped by security guards."

Max raised a brow. "Security guards?"

"Yes. As in two, and they were private security. They both wore suits and had bulges under their jackets."

"Guns?"

"That's my guess."

"Damn. Hold on. That's our car."

A black sedan pulled up. Max held the car door open, and Jordan slid in.

Max got in, closed the car door, moved close to Jordan, and held her hand. "Looks like we have some planning to do."

Jordan looked straight ahead and nodded.

"Between the two of us, we'll figure this out." He rubbed his thumb over her knuckles. "Don't be nervous."

"Nervous?" Jordan motioned toward the driver and whispered, "I'm terrified. There's so much riding on tomorrow—like the fate of global transport." She closed her eyes and slumped against the back of the seat. "Not to mention, none of this would be happening to you or your family if I hadn't stalked you and insisted you help me."

Max leaned close and whispered in her ear, "Listen, Jordan. Archer was after RMZ, anyway. Maybe we'll find out why, but that doesn't matter now. We will stop him. We're in this together."

The car stopped a block from the side entrance to Max's building. When they got out, Jordan ripped off her wig.

"Are you nuts? What are you doing?"

Jordan looked around. "This cheap wig itches like crazy. I couldn't take one more second. Besides, no one is looking at me."

"Come on. Hurry." Max took hold of her hand and picked up the pace. Within seconds, they were at the side entrance to the garage. Max quickly punched in the code and ushered Jordan inside. Before the door closed, someone grabbed Max by the shoulder. With a speed he didn't know he possessed, Max turned and grabbed the man's arm, spun him around, and, with the assailant's back against his chest, wrapped his arm around the man's throat.

The man struggled to get away. "Stop. Please."

Max didn't recognize the voice of the strangled plea. "Who are you?" Max said through gritted teeth.

The man's hands grabbed at Max's forearms as he tried to get free, but Max tightened his grip.

Jordan took a step toward them.

"Stay back," Max yelled.

"Stop! You're choking him. It's Sam. Sam Morris."

Max wasn't sure he'd heard right, but seeing the concerned look on Jordan's face, he loosened his hold.

"It's Sam Morris," Jordan repeated.

"Sam's dead," Max yelled, still holding on to the assailant.

"She's telling the truth," came the strangled voice. "I'm Sam Morris."

Max released his hold, and the man nearly fell to the floor. Jordan rushed to him, and with Max's help, they propped him up.

Sam Morris rubbed at his throat. "I… I…didn't expect that." His voice was a hoarse whisper. He looked up at Max and blinked several times.

One of the lights in the elevator alcove was out, but through the dimness, Max could now clearly see it was Sam. "Man, I'm sorry. You snuck up on me, and I reacted."

Still trying to catch his breath, Sam nodded. "It's okay."

"How did you even recognize us?" Jordan asked. "And how are you still alive?"

Sam bent to pick up his eyeglasses, which fell during the scuffle. "Your hair gave you away. I'll tell you everything. But it's not safe for us to be standing here." He looked at Max. "Can we go up to your apartment? I'll explain everything then."

Max didn't move. He was too shocked by this latest turn of events.

"Max?" Jordan said. "Can we go up, please?" Her gaze darted around the garage.

He nodded and punched in the elevator passcode. "Let's go."

When they crossed the threshold into his apartment, Max ripped off his wig and began pulling at the beard and mustache in agitation. He almost couldn't believe Sam was alive. "How is this possible? The news reports were...well... they were definitive."

Sam rubbed at his throat. "It's a long story."

"That means we've got a lot to discuss," Max said, scratching at his scalp.

"I'm being accused of murdering you," Jordan said.

"I know. And I'll tell you everything. But I'm here because we have to stop Archer."

Hearing Sam say those words was oddly reassuring, but Max didn't totally drop his guard. There was plenty Sam needed to explain, and he wanted answers.

"Do you think I could have some water?" Sam continued to rub at his throat.

Max nodded curtly and headed into the kitchen, his mind buzzing with this new revelation. He decided to hold off on any judgment until he got satisfactory answers from the newly alive Sam. He grabbed a bottle of water from the fridge and handed it to him. "Catch your breath. I'm going to get out of this." He pulled on his beard. "I'll only be a few minutes, then you can tell us everything."

"I'm going to take this off, too." Jordan waved a hand across her face and headed toward the bedroom she'd used earlier.

It didn't take long for Max to shower and change. His hair was still wet when he entered the living room and found Sam sitting on the couch, still rubbing at his throat. He was short and thin, and Max knew he'd unintentionally hurt him. "Again, sorry. I didn't know it was you."

"Don't apologize. I came from behind in a dark alcove.

I see exactly how it might have appeared to you." Sam put up a hand. "But I'm okay. Really."

Jordan walked back into the living room wearing a loose T-shirt and sweatpants. Sam stood—a surprised look on his face. "There you are."

She plopped onto the sofa, crossing one leg underneath her. "Sam, you have no idea how relieved I am that you're alive."

Sam gave a tired smile. "Me, too."

Max sat back and sized him up. He didn't look too worse for wear, considering he was supposedly dead these last four days. Even though Max had lots of questions, he found he was reservedly optimistic about Sam's miraculous resurrection. Because if anyone knew how to get into the Sintinex mainframe, it would be their former chief technology officer.

Before starting his inquisition, Max wanted to put Sam at ease and get to the truth of what was a very bizarre turn of events. "So, there's a lot to catch up on and for us to do," Max said. "Why don't I order sandwiches from the deli around the corner? I know Jordan's got to be hungry."

She made a face at Max then glanced at Sam. "I'm perpetually hungry. Especially when I'm stressed."

They told Max what they wanted, and he placed the order on his DoorDash.

While they waited for dinner to arrive, Max decided to jump right in. "So, where've you been while we all thought you were dead?"

"I've been in hiding," Sam said, casting his eyes downward. "I guess I should start at the beginning."

"Good idea," Jordan said.

Sam took a swallow of water. "For a few months, I knew

something was going on at Sintinex. Things weren't above board."

"How so?" Max asked.

"Uh…a lot of things." Sam put his elbows on his knees and placed his hands on either side of his face. For several seconds, he stared off in an apparent attempt to collect his thoughts before he spoke again. "You know, at first, I thought I was being paranoid. Then I figured, well, maybe I shouldn't be territorial and give others a chance to shine. After all, I was the CTO. The top of the food chain in the tech department at Sintinex. I told myself not to stress about it." He pushed his crooked glasses farther up the bridge of his nose. "But no matter how hard I tried to ignore what was going on, my instincts told me something was off." For the next twenty minutes, Sam went on to tell them, in more detail, about the last four weeks he'd spent at Sintinex and the secret meetings and emails he hadn't been part of.

The house phone buzzed, and Max stood. "Hold that thought. It's probably the food."

When Max returned with the sandwiches, they settled in the dining room, and he urged Sam to continue with his story.

"Like I was saying. There were new projects at the company I wasn't involved in, and I couldn't take it anymore. I knew something was wrong. I started staying late and arriving at the office well before anyone else. In those few hours, I was able to piece together what Archer was doing. At first, I thought it was clever." He pointed at Max, then Jordan. "He had you two working at opposite ends. One of you creating a foolproof firewall, the other a program that could crack it. Without knowing it, you gave Archer the ability to protect himself with a firewall no one else would be able to hack their way through, but also a program that breaks into every other company's system."

"But now we can't get through the firewall we created. We have no idea what he did, but we're definitely locked out of Sintinex." Max eyed Sam cautiously. He wasn't sure what disturbed him most, that Archer's motives were devious and destructive or that Sam knew about them and didn't stop it.

"So," Sam continued, "before you think I was in on this, let me explain."

"Good, because that's exactly what I thought," Jordan said.

"The moment I found out what Archer was up to—I knew it had to be stopped. But I couldn't march into his office and insist he put an end to it. He'd either deny it or, worse, figure out a way to get rid of me altogether." He shook his head. "I didn't think he'd harm me. But Archer has enough power in the industry and government circles to completely discredit me so that no one would believe me if I blew the whistle on his plans."

"That was a big weight to carry," Jordan said.

Sam became quiet and seemed to stare off.

"What are you thinking?" Max asked.

"If I'd said something, even if he discredited me, maybe we wouldn't be in this situation. Maybe Leon wouldn't have had to die."

"Who's Leon?" Jordan asked.

Sam exhaled. "He worked for me in my department. He was new, young, and super talented. Archer took him under his wing and had Leon create that snippet of code that, attached to the program you created, would worm its way into any system and take over."

"Did he know what he was creating?" Max asked.

"Not at first. I think Leon felt special that the head of the company was taking an interest in him and recognized his genius. He probably thought this would be a rocket ride to the top." He turned to Jordan. "Remember when I texted you not to add the snippet of code Archer sent you?"

"Yes. Of course."

"Right after I sent you that message, I texted Leon to meet me at a coffee shop near Central Park. When I got there, the place was packed. I had no idea so many people stopped for coffee in the middle of the afternoon. So we went for a walk in the park. I explained to Leon what the purpose of his code was and that, combined with the code you created, it would be dangerous in anyone's hands and that he needed to alter it so it wouldn't work."

"Why not just change it yourself?" Max asked.

"Digital fingerprint," Jordan answered.

Sam nodded. "That's right. I needed his digital fingerprint on the change so Archer wouldn't notice."

"But eventually, he would have noticed when it didn't work," Max said.

"Yeah, but it would have taken him some time to figure it out. Enough time to go to my friend and mentor at the Federal Trade Commission in Washington and have Sintinex investigated."

"So that's why you were meeting me and then going to DC?" Jordan asked.

"Yeah. But obviously, I never went. While I was walking with Leon, he was shot."

"What? And you left him there?" Jordan asked, a horrified look on her face.

"I knew that bullet was meant for me. Leon and I

are similar in height and build. We were both carrying backpacks—"

"Hang on." Max held up a hand. "Where in the park were you? Weren't there people around? Didn't anyone notice he was shot?"

"We were by the skating rink, and we walked under the footbridge. There wasn't much light under there, and that's when he was shot. I'm sure the sniper thought it was me. It was all a horrific coincidence." Sam looked down and shook his head. "There was mass confusion. People were running. I knew Leon was dead. Half his head was blown off. It took a split second for me to decide to grab his wallet and put mine in his jacket. In my gut, I knew Archer was behind this, and I wanted him to think I was dead." Sam let out a long, slow breath. "I ran with the crowd as an ambulance came speeding by on the path. I stepped into the bushes and watched two men get out, put Leon on a stretcher, and drive off."

"Just like that?"

"Surprised the hell out of me because not more than two minutes had passed between the time Leon was shot and when the ambulance arrived." Sam rubbed at his throat. "I didn't wait around to find out what was going on. I got the hell out of there." He looked up at Jordan. "My gut told me I had to warn you because this all started with the program you wrote. I hopped on the subway and got to your place. I knocked on your door, but there was no answer. I decided to wait."

"What time was that?" Jordan asked.

"I... I...can't remember. Maybe three, four o'clock. But that's not what's important. A white van pulled up to your apartment. Two men got out carrying a big black bag. The kind you see corpses wrapped up in. They each held one end of the bag."

Jordan held a hand to her mouth.

"I put my head down, acted like I was leaving, and watched as they walked into your building. I knew it was Leon they were carrying, and Archer was going to pin his death on you."

"But my furniture. What happened to all my things?"

"About ten minutes later, the white van was still parked outside, and a moving van drove up. Three burly men got out, walked into the building, and came out a few minutes later, hauling furniture. At first, I thought someone was moving out of the building. But then the two guys from the van began helping them, and I knew it had to be your apartment they were emptying." Sam pressed his lips together and rubbed his forehead with the palm of his hand.

"I'm the one who followed you to the cybercafe. I didn't approach you because…well…look what happened to Leon. But I wanted to warn you, so I sent you the text to trust no one. And when you threw your phone away, I sent texts to Max."

"They were so cryptic we had no idea what they meant," Max said.

"I didn't know if Archer had access to your phones. I was afraid to say more. Enough time had passed, and I thought it might be safer to talk in person, so I went to your house this morning. But you'd already left."

"I called the sheriff on you."

"I saw them coming and ran."

The pieces were finally beginning to come together for Max. Sam had been trying to steer them in the right direction with the text messages, but that still didn't answer who had tried to run them off the road the other night. Maybe they'd never know, but if he had to put money on it, his coin was on someone Archer hired.

"How did you know we'd be here, at Max's apartment?" Jordan asked.

"When you weren't home, I guessed you might be at the convention." Sam leaned forward. "I hacked into the transportation convention website. I saw a new entry as of early this morning. Acme Deluxe. When I traced it back, not only did the company not exist, but the IP address was bouncing all over the place." He gave Jordan a pointed look. "That was some very slick re-routing you did. Incredibly sophisticated. I knew it must be you. I checked a few more things and found that Max had an apartment, so I drove down."

"Impressive sleuthing," Jordan said.

"Yeah, but Leon would be alive now if I'd confronted Archer sooner."

"Oh, man." Max rubbed the back of his neck. "It wasn't your fault."

"Hell it wasn't. If I hadn't asked Leon to meet me—"

Jordan reached over and touched his forearm. "Don't do that to yourself. Archer is evil. If none of us had met Archer, we'd all be in a better place. But we cannot change what's already happened. We can only stop the program from getting out. Are you here to help us do that?"

Sam looked Jordan in the eye. "That depends."

Chapter 22

"What do you mean, that depends?" Jordan snarled. "That was so not the answer I was expecting."

"Sorry." Sam waved his hand. "That came out wrong."

"Then make it right," Max said.

"It depends on if the two of you are willing to skirt the law."

"What do you think Max and I have been doing?"

"Again, sorry. I've never been in this situation, and it's been a long four days."

"Tell me about it," Jordan huffed.

"I want to bring Archer down as much as you do. I have an idea, but it's not legal, and it's dangerous. I was a little skeptical about involving you after what happened to Leon."

"Stop trying to protect us. Max and I are neck-deep in danger at this point. Let's get this thing over and done with and try and get our lives back."

"Yeah. Okay. Let's do this," Sam said.

"I took photos of the Sintinex setup. They're on Max's phone."

"We haven't had a chance to look at them yet. Jordan managed to sneak behind the back drape and photograph the main system that the computers on the floor are connected to."

Sam held out a hand. "Let me see."

Max handed over the phone. Jordan stood behind Sam as he scrolled through the photos. He stopped at the shot of the main system. With his thumb and forefinger, he enlarged it, turned the phone sideways, and zoomed in even closer. He inspected several more photos, enlarging them for a closer view. When he was done, Sam put the phone down and looked up at Jordan. "Is this everything?"

Jordan nodded.

"This is *my* setup."

"Your setup?" Jordan went back to her seat. "What are you saying?"

"They're using my design." He shook his head. "I don't mean the design of the exhibit, but I designed the technical aspects, you know, how the computers are connected to the main system, how each computer on the exhibit floor takes in a prospective client's information and stores it, how the computers talk to one another."

Jordan leaned forward. "Are you saying Archer is using the same tech specs this year?"

"That's what it looks like. Every year we are at the convention, businesses of all sizes and government agency reps flock to our booth because we offer the most advanced software in transportation."

"Oh, my goodness." Jordan stood and paced the length of the table. "Why hadn't I thought of this before?"

"What?" Max asked.

"When Sam mentioned advanced software for transportation, a light bulb went off. All this time, I thought Sintinex would offer their usual swag, and participants would get a sampling of the products on a drive. And that drive would contain the worm. But I bet Archer can't take the chance that they won't insert the drive into their computers or, worse, toss it in the trash with all the other convention swag."

"Where you going with this?"

"When we were at the exhibit, Archer was bitching about the panels not being correct. Max, do you recall what was on one of those panels?"

"Uh, I was a little too busy trying not to be discovered to pay attention."

"There was a panel on cybersecurity."

"Your point is?"

"Pull up the Sintinex website on your phone. I have a hunch."

Max hesitated.

"Just do it. And tell me what you see."

Max studied his phone's screen for a few seconds. "Jeez. I don't believe this. Sintinex is offering a free giveaway at their booth tomorrow at noon."

Sam frowned. "What's the giveaway?"

Max sighed. "The world's first impenetrable firewall."

Jordan snapped her fingers. "That's his plan. That's how he ensures there's massive distribution of the worm."

"Because what company or agency doesn't want to be free from cyberattacks," Max said.

"Yeah." Jordan sat. "And since he's got a quote, unquote, 'stellar reputation' in the business…well, I don't need to say anymore. No one would suspect."

"No one," Max reiterated. His throat felt dry, and he took a swig of water. He knew most people couldn't resist anything free. Without a doubt, Sintinex would have all the major corporations in attendance and the government agency reps lined up to get their hands on an impenetrable firewall. And there wasn't any question Archer would be on the exhibit floor hawking the hell out of it. "Damn, this is bad."

"There is one bright light in all this," Sam said.

Jordan looked skeptical. "What could that possibly be?"

"We have until noon tomorrow." Sam leaned forward. "If Archer's kept everything the same as my setup, the computers in the exhibit will be connected to the mainframe, but each computer will have a unique password. Here's where it gets tricky—there will be several hired security guards stationed around the exhibit to make sure only employees touch the computers."

"Jordan saw two this afternoon. How did you know about the security guards?"

"It's what he had last year. I can't imagine with what he's planning, he won't have the same conditions in place. I remember sending an email saying I thought hired security was overkill. And getting a terse response saying our equipment was valuable. And that was that."

"If you need a password to get onto a computer to access the mainframe, and if there's all this security, what's the solution?" Jordan asked.

Sam smiled. "It's something I've been thinking about over the last several days. But it wasn't something I could pull off on my own—" he pointed at Jordan "—because it needs a stealth hacker."

"I'm all in," Jordan said.

"First, I will give Max a mobile phone with a special chip inside. That chip will be able to record the password."

"Huh?" Jordan said. "How is that possible?"

"It's a new technology I've been working on."

"New? Should I be concerned?" Jordan asked.

Sam shrugged. "It hasn't been tried in a situation like this, but the beta testing has had one-hundred-percent positive results."

"Sam!" Jordan slapped a hand on the table. "You want us to use something that has only been beta tested?"

"Wait," Sam said. "Hear me out. It's not as flimsy as all that."

"I'm listening," Jordan said and sat back in her chair.

"As a rep from Acme Deluxe, Max will ask for a demo. When the demonstrator logs in with their username and password, Max will have his phone next to the computer, and it will record what's being entered. You'll be sitting in the tech lounge, and Max will text you the recorded info. Once you enter the information on your laptop, you'll have almost instant access to the mainframe."

"That's if everything goes perfectly," Jordan said. "What if I don't have instant access?"

"Don't worry. You will. But that doesn't mean there's a clear path to the program once you're inside. You'll probably have to code your way through to get to the heart of the program and destroy it."

Jordan didn't want to be skeptical, but this scheme made her nervous. It wasn't as if they had another option. She had to hope it went off without a hitch.

They reviewed the plan several times, discussing various what-if scenarios until they could think of no more potential mishaps. Jordan stretched her legs out and her arms over her head. It felt like a million o'clock, but it was only half past nine. "I'm exhausted. I don't know about you two, but I need some sleep."

"I've got an extra bedroom," Max said to Sam.

"No. Thanks. I need to get to that all-night printer uptown and make my fake IDs. I have no idea who may or may not be tracking me, and I can't take the chance of bringing them back to your doorstep. I've already been here long enough. Let's not take any more chances. We'll meet in the morning at the Javits Center. There's a Starbucks kiosk on the main floor in the east wing. Wait for me at one of the round table tops."

"I know where that is," Jordan said. "I saw it this morning. Eight thirty?"

"See you then."

They said their goodbyes, and Max locked the door behind Sam and turned to Jordan. "You okay?"

"That was some story." She rubbed her arms with her hands as if warding off a chill. "You realize we're not only going to have to destroy the program, but also I need evidence that will somehow nail Archer."

"I'm right there with you."

Jordan pressed her lips together. "Well, it won't do either of us any good if I don't get some sleep. I need to be on my game tomorrow. I'll get a drink of water and then head off to bed."

Max followed her into the kitchen. "I'm not sure I can sleep."

Jordan grabbed a bottle of water from the fridge, and when she turned, Max was right there—no space between them. In one smooth movement, he framed her face with his hands. Her heart skittered, and for one fleeting moment, she wished there could be a future with him and his loud, butting-into-everyone's-business family. But she knew that wasn't possible. It was the kind of life she could never have.

He angled his head and came closer. When his lips were inches from hers, the room tilted. Or was that her imagination? *Oooooo, steady girlfriend. This is all about the heat of the moment. Max isn't a forever kind of guy. And you have issues.*

As his arms wrapped around her, she felt something that could only be described as a sense of belonging. He was going to kiss her, and she wanted to give in to it. To him. Their gazes locked. He slid his arms down her waist, and his mouth gently settled over hers. His breath was warm, and he tasted sweet.

She eased her hands over his shoulder and pulled him closer, deepening the kiss. Their tongues collided, and butterflies danced in her stomach.

When their lips parted, he gave her a questioning look. Jordan understood he was giving her the opportunity to stop now, but that was not what she wanted. She reached to him and kissed him hard.

Max carried her up the stairs and into his bedroom. Gently laid her on the bed. He hovered above her, one knee on the bed, one foot on the floor, as he gently lifted her T-shirt. Jordan was braless, and Max smiled at her. "You're beautiful."

She felt the heat rise to her cheeks, and she wanted to cross her arms over her chest. But there was no time. He took her nipple into his mouth, and she lost all sense of inhibition, arched her back, and moaned. His hot breath and tongue sucked and licked until every nerve ending was on fire. "Max," she whispered his name. But he didn't stop, moving onto the other breast, caressing and sucking with his mouth and tongue, while his hand moved between her thighs, at first gently stroking. She moved her hips, pressing against his hand until her breath came out in quick gasps, a wave building up inside of her until it was released in one long orgasm.

Max kissed her lips, his gaze never leaving her. He stood, reached for a condom, and slowly removed his clothes. He was gorgeous. He kissed her slow and deep. She was lost to him in so many ways, body and soul. Her hands wrapped around his neck as she pulled him closer. "Please. Don't make me wait anymore."

Max entered her slowly, and she gasped. He filled her, and she arched her back and closed her eyes. She was wet and slick, and she couldn't get enough of him.

He moved in and out, not rushing, until she raised her hips to meet his, matching him stroke for stroke. Within minutes, the intensity of the wave inside her built to a crescendo, and once again, she found herself in one long satisfying release. Max only moments behind.

Now they lay spent. His arm draped across her waist. His nose nuzzled in her neck.

"Jordan, you're amazing."

She didn't know what to say. It had never been in her nature to have after-sex cuddling, let alone talk about feelings. She wasn't sure how to handle this because, contrary to what she'd experienced in the past, she liked lying here in his arms, enjoying the moment, not thinking about all that they'd been through and all they had yet to get through. She sighed. "You're not so bad yourself."

Max laughed. "No. I didn't mean in bed. Although you are pretty spectacular."

Jordan gazed up at the ceiling, wondering what she was doing here.

"I mean, in life." Max continued. "All that you've had to overcome. You're smart, thoughtful, quick on your feet, gorgeous, sexy, and when you're not pissed off at the world, you're damn good company."

Jordan let out a one-syllable laugh. "You're easy on the eyes."

"That's all I get?"

She looked away. "I'm not great with affection."

"For now."

She reached over and kissed him on the shoulder, then his neck. Soft kisses around his jaw until she fully claimed his mouth. Then she straddled him, and they made love once more.

The alarm went off at six, and Max turned to find Jordan wasn't next to him. He stretched and closed his eyes. A smile that he couldn't help crossed his face. Making love with her had been exceptional, but that didn't completely describe what he was feeling. In fact, he'd never reacted this way with any other woman. A yearning to be with her. To spend time with her. To have her in his life. Max shook his head. This was a first.

He closed his eyes, remembering what they were here to do and wishing it was over so they could be free of the threat of Archer. Free to live normally without looking over their shoulders. He wanted to work on the next steps with Jordan. He wasn't sure what a life with her would look like, but he wanted to find out.

Jordan now stood at the bedroom door in a T-shirt and nothing else. Her beautiful auburn hair was loose and framed her face. She was gorgeous. Her green eyes vibrant in the sunshine that poured into the room. When she smiled at him, a warm tingling sensation flowed through him, and his desire for her flared.

"I made coffee. You didn't have any cream. You'll have

to deal with black." She handed him a mug and sat beside him with her legs folded under her.

"Good morning." He reached over and put a hand on her bare thigh. "You ready for today?"

"As ready as I'll ever be."

Max's cell phone rang, and he reached over to the dresser. "It's Zack. I better take this."

"You want me to leave?"

"No. Stay." He swiped open his phone. "Hey, bro. How is everyone?" Max put the phone on speaker. "I'm here with Jordan."

Jordan looked surprised, as though she hadn't expected to be part of the conversation.

"Hey, Jordan," Zack said.

"Hi. How's the family doing?" she asked.

"We're trying to enjoy the time visiting, but we're all more than a little on edge waiting to hear what's happening up there."

"We had some good luck yesterday," Max said.

"Oh, yeah, what?"

"I'd rather we didn't talk about it over the phone."

"I understand. Listen, Max. Don't worry about us. This shouldn't be all on you and Jordan. Whatever happens, we'll get through this. Remember, this family always survives."

"Thanks, bro. Love you, and give my love to everyone."

"Will do. You two stay safe."

The call ended, and Max smiled at Jordan. "What's the matter? Looks like a shadow crossed your face."

"It's nothing." She picked at the imaginary lint on the duvet cover and lifted one shoulder. "A little anxious. Lots to do." She stood. "I'm going to take a shower. Time to get ready."

* * *

Jordan let the hot water run over her head as tears flowed down her face. What had she done? She'd fallen for this guy and his family. This was never supposed to happen. She'd been a reject all her life. Her mother discarded her. No one wanted to adopt her. She'd been shuttled from one group home to another. She was bad news. Now, she'd brought harm to Max and his family. They didn't deserve bad things to happen to them. And it was all her fault.

She pressed her forehead against the tiled wall, took a deep breath, turned off the shower, and grabbed a towel. As she dried off, she tried to center herself. The priority was stopping Archer. After that, painful as it would be, she had to disappear from Max's life. If she'd learned anything over the years, it was that she didn't deserve to be loved. Eventually, Max would tire of her, and she'd end up disappointed. That notion surprised her. She'd never really cared for anyone. What she felt for Max seemed to have come out of nowhere. How had she developed these feelings so quickly?

Jordan stared at herself in the mirror. Leaving Max would be hard, but she had to do it for his own good. She closed her eyes, inhaled deeply, and relaxed her grip on the edge of the sink. When her heartbeat slowed to some semblance of normal, she opened her eyes. "Who are you kidding? When you leave, you'll be devastated." Well, too bad, she thought. She'd never been able to have what she wanted in life—why would this time be any different?

By seven fifteen, Jordan was dressed in her wig, contacts, and nose prosthetic and ready, staring at a cloudless sky from the living room windows. When Max entered, she turned to face him, and he laughed.

"What's so funny?"

"You look so different," Max said, pointing at her.

Jordan realized he was trying to keep the situation light and played along. "Yeah." She turned in profile. "This is my better side."

"Definitely better." Max chuckled and checked his phone. "I called an Uber, and it'll be here in a few minutes. Let's head out."

They took the elevator to the garage. Max put in the code to the side door. When they were outside, they headed one block south to wait for their ride.

Once they were in the back seat of the Uber, Max put his hand over hers. She pulled away, inching closer to the door, and stared out the window. It took all her willpower not to turn to him.

"Don't be nervous. We got this," Max said.

"Hmmm." Jordan let him think she pulled away because of nerves, but that wasn't the case. She'd pulled away because they didn't have a future, and that saddened her. She forced herself to think of the task ahead because feeling sorry for herself wasn't a luxury she could afford. Instead, she focused on destroying Archer and imagined him being arrested. The idea brought a sly smile to her face. This was what she needed to concentrate on.

The Uber pulled up to the convention center. Jordan turned to Max. "Showtime."

Chapter 23

They headed for the convention center doors on 11th Avenue, leaving behind the blare of car horns, clogged rush-hour traffic, exhaust fumes leaking from buses, and pedestrians trying to hail cabs. Once inside, Max and Jordan stopped at Starbucks, got two coffees, and waited at a high-top table in the lobby.

"What's keeping him?" Jordan said, trying to keep the worry from her voice and her expression neutral.

Max checked the time on his phone. "It's only just eight thirty. Let's give him a couple of minutes." His gaze spanned the four entrance points across the large hall that led onto the convention floor proper. Lines were already forming, waiting to get past the security checkpoint.

Several more minutes passed, and now Max was beginning to feel anxious. Had something happened to Sam? Had Archer hurt him? Max's gaze darted toward the entrance again, hoping Sam would push through the revolving doors at any moment.

"Max. Stop. Look at me," Jordan said. "You don't want to attract attention. Let's give it another five minutes before we panic."

Max nodded.

And so, they waited.

Max tapped his foot and drummed his fingers on his coffee cup. He checked the time on his phone again. The Impenetrable Wall giveaway was scheduled for noon, and they didn't have the luxury of running late. His worry level was all the way at a ten. "I'm going to go outside and check."

Jordan put a hand on his forearm. "Hang tight. He'll be here."

"But what if something—"

"Sorry I'm late," Sam said, stepping up to their table wearing a baseball cap pushed halfway down his forehead.

Max didn't turn to face him but caught him in his peripheral vision. He kept his body positioned straight ahead and spoke in a way that suggested he was directing his comments to Jordan. "You had us worried. It's almost nine."

Sam acted as if he were a perfect stranger simply sharing a table because the lobby was already crowded with convention goers. "Ran into some problems with software."

The thought alarmed Max. "Is it working now?"

"All set." Sam nodded, patting his back pockets, searching for something.

Max semi-relaxed his shoulders.

Sam pulled a phone from his back pocket and slid it across the table toward Max. He removed the backpack from his shoulder, left it on the table, and walked toward a very long queue to order a cup of coffee.

As they had planned the night before, Max put the phone in his jacket pocket while Jordan grabbed the backpack holding a laptop. Max waited for her to leave. She walked to the left entrance of the exhibition hall.

Max headed toward the main entrance. He flashed his badge and walked past security. Taking his time, he stopped at a few booths, grabbed several business cards, and generally appeared to be someone who'd come to the convention to learn about all the new products available for the transportation industry.

By the time he worked his way to the large Sintinex exhibit, a sizable crowd was already milling around, with several people receiving personal demonstrations of the company's products. Max acted like an interested prospective customer, stopping in front of one of the display panels and pretending to watch a video on innovations. He checked the time on his phone. It would be fifteen minutes before Jordan was completely set up and he could make his move. Feigning interest, he stepped toward the next video panel when he heard a man say, "I've been hearing so much about this impenetrable firewall you're giving away. Is it really all you claim it is?"

"Hello, Senator. So nice to see you. Yes, our firewall is everything we say it is."

"I'm wondering if you might give me a demo. I'll have my aide come by at noon to pick up one of the free copies you're offering."

Max recognized the second voice as belonging to Lauren Chambers, the woman masquerading as Jordan Logan. But he had no idea which senator she was speaking with, and he didn't dare turn around and stare.

This wasn't good. Archer would have instant access to government files.

"Excuse me, Senator."

"What is it, Henry?"

"There seems to be some sort of dead zone here. There's no reception, and I can't make those calls. I'll go back to the lobby and see if I can't get a cell signal."

"All right, I'll be there shortly."

After overhearing the conversation between the senator and his aide, Max checked his cell phone. Sure enough, he had no signal. He wiped perspiration from his hand against his pants. If there was no cell service, how was he supposed to get the password transferred to his phone? Silently, Max groaned. They didn't have any more minutes to spare.

A twenty-something, dark-haired kid with a Sintinex lanyard around his neck walked toward him. "Can I show you our new products?"

It was too soon. Max wasn't ready. "I'm very interested. Unfortunately, I'm meeting a friend right now. I'll come back. What's your name?"

"I'm Gabriel Liston. Here's my card."

Max took the card, looked at it, put it in his pocket, then smiled. "Thanks." He headed for the tech lounge several aisles away from Sintinex's exhibit.

The convention had three lounge areas where exhibitors could get a coffee, plug in their devices, and use the Wi-Fi. He spotted Jordan immediately sitting at one of the consoles and sat next to her.

Without looking at her, he continued to speak into his phone, pretending to have a conversation with someone on the other end but actually addressing Jordan.

"What the hell are you doing over here?" Jordan hissed, staring straight at her laptop screen.

"Seems the Sintinex booth is located in a dead zone, and I can't get any cell service."

"Seriously?"

"Dead serious. I'm not sure what the—"

"Excuse me."

They looked up to see Sam wearing a different baseball cap with the Javits Center logo. He was dressed in dark gray coveralls with an embroidered logo on the left chest. Around his neck hung a lanyard with his photo ID, which identified him as Joe Hunt, and underneath, it read Electrician. He wheeled a black two-tier cart with various tools, plugs, and electrical cords.

Sam bent in front of their console, pulled out a plug, and began replacing wires as he spoke. "We have a slight change in plans. I couldn't get to the—"

"Hey, you!" A large, burly man wearing the same outfit as Sam walked over. "Who are you?" he said. The embroidered logo indicated his name was Jerome.

Sam cocked his head, straightened, grabbed his photo ID, and thrust it at Jerome. "I'm Joe. With electrical." His antagonistic tone matched his accuser's.

"Really? 'Cause I'm head of electrical, and I don't know any Joe."

Max looked around and tried to think of something that would create a diversion—anything to give Sam a chance to get away. He spied a half-full cup of coffee and was about to reach over and spill it on the wires when Sam pulled out some paperwork from the back pocket of his coveralls.

"Here's my work order."

Jerome pulled a pair of reading glasses from inside his coveralls, opened the work order, and read through it.

Max remained ready to knock over the coffee if this little ruse went off the rails.

"Says here, you're a contract worker."

"That's right."

"Mitchell contracted you?"

"Yup, Mitchell Deere."

"You here for the two days of this convention?"

"That's right."

"What ya doing over here with these wires?"

"Got a complaint." Sam held out a frayed wire. "See. Just replacing it."

Jerome took a look. "Okay. When you're done with that, we got some replacement fuses in the back by G3. Meet me there in twenty."

Sam nodded. Jerome looked him up and down before he turned and walked away.

Once again, Sam bent down and pretended to be fixing a wire.

Jordan blew out a breath. "Damn. That was close."

"How did you manage to get a convention center ID—" Max stopped himself. "Never mind. We got other problems. No cell service over there."

"Uh. Yup. That's why I'm here. Spotted that two minutes after I arrived and had to do some fast dancing." Sam stood and looked through some things in his cart. He pulled out what looked like a flip phone and slid it onto the console in front of Max.

"What am I supposed to do with this?"

"It's old-school for sure, but it will work," Sam said.

"I don't understand," Jordan said. "I thought Max was using his cell phone to pick up the password into the mainframe?"

"I don't have a lot of time to explain, but Sintinex is using some sort of jamming signal. Archer isn't taking any chances. So I had to do some last-minute maneuvering."

"How do you even have one of those?" Jordan asked.

"Always carry one. They can't be traced. This phone will pick up the password."

"Sam, this is barely out of beta testing, and it's never been tested on a flip," Jordan hissed.

"We don't have another alternative. Let's do this." Max stood. "I'll meet you all back here in thirty minutes."

Without giving Jordan a chance to object, Max strode quickly through the aisles, heading straight for the Sintinex exhibit. There was no time to waste, not with the exhibit as popular as it was and already hosting a United States senator.

He crossed the imaginary threshold onto the carpeted area of the Sintinex booth. Glancing around, he searched for the kid who had given him his card.

A security guard built like someone who spent hours in the gym approached him. "Looking for someone?"

"Yes. Uh…" He glanced at the card. "Gabriel Liston?"

The guard nodded and pointed to a computer terminal on the other side of the exhibit.

"Thanks." Max walked toward Gabriel. "Hey. I'm back."

"Hello," Gabriel said. "I didn't get your name."

"Jeff. Jeff Riches. Acme Deluxe."

"Ah." Gabriel nodded. "Where you located?"

"Uh…our headquarters are in Terra Haute, Indiana." Max quickly ran a fake scenario in his mind to seem legit. "We mainly service the Midwestern states. But…uh…we're opening up more in the South." His heart was beginning to race, and he gave himself a mental warning to slow it down. "And…yeah…by the end of the year, we'll have an office in San Diego."

"Sounds like a lot going on. I think you'd be very interested in our real-time tracking program. With all those locations, I imagine weather could also be a problem, and we have a program for that as well…"

Max barely listened as Gabriel droned on, extolling the advantages of using a Sintinex program. The palm holding the flip phone was becoming sweaty, and time was running out. He wanted this kid to cut to the chase and put his password in.

"I believe our 'super-suite' of transport programs could boost your productivity and sales," Gabriel continued. "Let me show you."

Finally. Max took a step closer to the computer.

Gabriel put his ID against a scanner, and the computer screen came to life.

Max put his flip phone on the table, covering it with his hand. Gabriel blocked his view and entered his username and password. Max prayed the phone captured what it needed. When Gabriel pulled up the program, Max said, "Hey. Is that the time? I didn't realize it was so late." He looked around. "I need to make a quick call. But there doesn't seem to be any cell service here."

"I've been hearing that all morning. Our head of IT is trying to find out what the problem is."

"I'll be right back." Max stepped far enough away from the booth until he was sure he had cell service. He opened the flip phone and smiled. The password was on the small monochrome screen. Using his own mobile phone, he texted Jordan with the password. Pocketing both phones, he turned to find Gabriel standing there. "If you're ready, I'd like to show you the demo."

For a moment, Max hesitated but then thought better of it. Maybe he was being paranoid, but he thought it best to stay for the demonstration and not raise any suspicions. In about five minutes, he'd politely excuse himself.

Max tried to concentrate, but he didn't have a single spare unit of attention because he was fully focused on Jordan, wondering if she was okay. From the corner of his eye, he caught sight of the same broad-shoulders-and-no-neck guard who had been staring at him earlier. He now seemed to have locked his gaze on Max.

When the text came in from Max, Jordan keyed the password into the Sintinex mainframe. *ComeonComeon-Comeon.* Her mind buzzed, waiting for the swirling ball to let her know if she was in or not. She tapped her foot for what seemed like minutes, but in reality, only a few seconds had passed. Jordan glanced around while waiting. Suddenly, the screen turned black, and code began to march across the screen. She was in. She studied the code as it revealed itself line by line, ending with a text prompt. Jordan knew there would be several more before accessing the target program. She typed in the answer to the first prompt and waited as several more lines of text scrolled horizontally, ending in a second prompt. Once again, she typed in a response. When the third prompt appeared, Jordan glanced at the time in the corner of the laptop screen. *Come on. I don't have all day.* She looked back at the text and saw something she'd never seen before. Jordan squinted at the screen. *What is this?* She entered a few more commands and realized she was looking at a second firewall. Something that would have gone unnoticed yet would have kept most hackers out. "Clever," she said under her breath. She would have loved to analyze it, but there wasn't any time. Her fingers danced over the keyboard, and after several prompts and commands, a dozen lines of text scrolled across the screen. "About time." She was in the program. "I finally got you, and I'm going to—"

The feel of metal against her rib cage wasn't as terrifying as the warm breath at her ear. "Get up and don't make a scene. There's a silencer on this gun, and I will not hesitate for a minute to pull the trigger. I'll be gone before they know you are dead."

An icy chill ran down her back, and for an instant, she thought she could run into the crowd, but realized she was virtually boxed in. On her other side stood a very tall, very wide man in a dark gray suit—clearly one of Archer's men.

"I said get up."

Jordan stood, and Archer put one arm around her shoulder while the gun in his other hand pressed against her ribs. "You thought you were so clever. You and your silly disguise. But you're not smart enough to fool me."

Jordan flinched when he jabbed the gun further into her side. "Keep your eyes straight ahead and keep moving."

"Where are we going?" Jordan tried to make her voice sound normal and not show any fear.

"You'll see."

The security guard led the way, Archer and Jordan following close behind until they reached the Sintinex booth. She spotted Max and tried to pull away, but Archer jerked her back so hard her knees buckled. "Say one word, and I'll shoot that kid talking to Max. Don't test me."

Jordan looked down to see him pointing the gun in the direction of the young man talking to Max. There wasn't a doubt that he'd pull the trigger.

Another security guard, well over six feet, with muscles that bulged through his suit jacket, walked over to Max and put his arm around Max's shoulder.

"What's happening?" Jordan's voice was panicked.

"None of your concern. I can still shoot that kid. Now move!" Archer pulled her toward the back curtain while the guard held it open. Backstage, behind the curtain, past the bank of Sintinex computers and hard drives were the outer edges of the convention floor. A catwalk loomed high overhead. Above that were the famed Javits Center glass panels with their hallmark steel frames. The guard opened a door with a red-and-white sign that said KEEP OUT, and Archer pushed Jordan inside onto the landing of a steel staircase with a flimsy railing. She took a quick look around. It appeared they were in some sort of electrical room. The noise was deafening.

"Get moving," Archer screamed to be heard over the blasts of air compressors and the hum of electricity.

She looked down the steep staircase and then at the heavy machinery in the large room and hesitated.

Archer nudged her with the gun at her back. Jordan stalled for time by taking each step slowly, hoping someone would come and get her out of what appeared to be a hopeless situation.

When she reached the bottom of the stairs, she turned to face Archer.

"Take that ridiculous disguise off. I want to know who I'm going to kill."

Jordan didn't move. If he was going to kill her anyway, she had no intention of helping him do it. Archer stepped forward, snatched the wig off her head, and threw it to the ground. "Either you take off that ridiculous nose, or I will."

The idea of him touching her again nauseated her, so she took it off. "Tell me one thing, Archer. Why me?"

He laughed. "Because you were the best. And I needed the best hacker in the world."

"Then why choose RMZ Digital?"

"I didn't choose them."

Jordan didn't understand.

"I chose Max. His family and their company were a bonus."

She frowned. Still not getting it.

"Twelve years ago, I needed funding to start my transport company. Max Ramirez was the quantitative analyst at the bank where I sought a loan. Turns out he was a straight arrow. Wouldn't take a chance on me, all because I had some, shall we say, previous questionable dealings. His veto cost me my business and soured my reputation on the Street. No one would touch me." He laughed. "I vowed to get him back. And I did."

"I don't believe you. Max never met you before."

Archer let out a maniacal laugh. "Oh, you stupid, stupid people. So easily fooled. I got some face work done, changed my name, and created Sintinex. I showed him, didn't I? My company got so big and so important that *he* went after securing business from *me*. Ironic. Don't you think? I saw my opportunity to take over the transportation industry and ruin him at the same time. Win. Win." Archer's laugh turned into a sneer. "Now turn around."

A movement from the stairs made Jordan and Archer look up. Max leaped from the staircase and tackled him. They rolled to the ground, but Archer held on to the gun. Max straddled Archer's back, grabbed his hand, and pounded it on the floor until the gun flew away.

Archer raised his head and slammed it back into Max's face. Max lost his hold and fell to the side. Archer scrambled to his feet.

"Jordan, grab the gun," Max shouted.

Archer brutally kicked Max in the ribs.

Jordan ran toward the gun. Before she could put her fingers on it, Archer yanked her back by her hair. She tried pulling away, but he jerked harder. It felt like her scalp would be pulled off. She reached behind her to loosen his grip when she was suddenly knocked forward.

Max had tackled Archer and threw him to the floor. Archer rolled, grabbed a metal broom, and jumped to his feet. Jordan looked around for the gun while Max and Archer circled each other. Archer jabbed at Max, who sidestepped each of Archer's thrusts.

"Jordan," Max yelled without taking his gaze off Archer. "Get to the mainframe before his security shuts us out. Then get help."

Jordan sprinted for the stairs. Archer swiped at her with the broom handle, and she stumbled. He took hold of her foot, and she grabbed on to the stair railing. She looked back, resisting his pull. She saw Max come from behind Archer, punch him in the back, and kick his legs out from under him. Max grabbed him by the shirt, lifted him to his feet, and landed several blows to his face.

Jordan fled up the stairs.

The moment she was out the door and backstage behind the Sintinex exhibit, she spied a fire alarm on the wall and thought this was a way to save Max. She pulled the lever. Instantly, the alarm sounded and lights flashed. Dozens of people began yelling and running backstage toward the exit doors. Within moments, a man wearing a fire marshal hat ran toward her with police officers behind him. Jordan screamed, "There's a man down there with a gun threatening my partner! He needs help." She pointed to the door.

The police officers drew their weapons and headed that way.

Knowing Max would be helped, she made for the exhibit floor but stopped when she saw Sam a few feet away. She was about to call his name but stopped short when one of the Sintinex security guards approached Sam and handed him a gun. Seconds later, Lauren Chambers appeared. Jordan hid behind a wide pole and watched Lauren and Sam kiss like lovers. Lauren handed him a hard drive the size of a small purse. Sam exited through a door that led to the street, and Lauren walked in the opposite direction.

Stunned, Jordan could barely believe what she'd witnessed. Whatever that was, she'd worry about it later.

Jordan slipped onto the exhibit floor, where pandemonium reigned, with lights flashing, the siren blaring, and everyone running for the exits. The Sintinex personnel seemed to have fled. She chose one of their computers, entered the username and password from before, and was instantly and directly connected to the mainframe. No prompts necessary. She quickly searched for the program but couldn't find the file. She checked the file extension, and nothing came up. She checked possible paths, but again, nothing. She looked in different directories in the system. The program wasn't there. *What the hell is this?* It made no sense. Before Archer grabbed her at gunpoint, she'd been staring at the program, and now it seemed to be gone. Her fingers flew over the keyboard, and she attempted to enter the mainframe's attic—hoping the program was backed up. But it was empty.

Jordan didn't understand what was happening. On impulse, she typed her name into the computer, and nothing came up. She typed in Lauren Chambers, but again, nothing. She stared in disbelief at that screen. The program was somehow missing, and any chance of getting back her own identity was gone.

Terrified, she ran backstage.

"Ma'am, you can't be here," a baby-faced police officer said.

"It's okay. She's with me."

Jordan fell into Max's arms. "You're safe. Thank goodness."

"It was close."

Jordan put her arms around his neck and stared into his eyes. She'd never been so happy to see someone. "Where's Archer?"

Max broke the gaze and nodded to his right, where several police officers surrounded a hand-cuffed, bloody Archer Kelly, who began screaming obscenities.

Jordan sneered his way. "He's going down. Finally."

As they began to escort Archer out of the building, he turned his vitriol on Max and Jordan. "I'll get you both. You'll be sorry you ever messed with me. You have no idea what you've done…" He screamed until he was on the other side of the exit door and could no longer be heard.

"He's gone. He won't be able to hurt us again." Max pulled her in close and wrapped his arms around her. "Did you erase the program?"

Jordan shook her head.

Max pulled away and held her at arm's length. "Did you say no?"

"I'm afraid so. I couldn't find it. The program is gone."

Epilogue

This was paradise. The sound of the waves lapping against the sand and the scent of the salty air made Jordan smile. She'd never been to Puerto Rico, and this was the beginning of a week-long dream vacation.

"Who wants another piña colada?" Zack called out.

"I'd love a virgin one," Mallory said.

"I'd like a piña colada with some party spirit, please," *Tía* Ellie said.

Jordan looked around the picnic table at all the smiling faces. She and Max had arrived last night, and the family had been overcome with joy when they heard Archer's plan had been stopped, Jordan had gotten her identity back, and the Ramirez family wouldn't be hearing from Archer Kelly ever again.

Picnicking on the beach was the family's way of celebrating, and Jordan couldn't imagine anything more perfect.

"I still don't understand this Sam Morris fellow. He was in on it the whole time?" Emilio asked.

"Surprised the heck out of us," Max said.

Jordan nodded. "It was diabolical."

"None of it makes any sense," Rafe added.

"Sam hired me. He insisted on meeting me in person,"

Jordan explained. "He became my sole contact at Sintinex so I would trust him. And I did. What I didn't know was that he was working alongside Archer the entire time. Somewhere along the way, he fell in love with Lauren Chambers, and together, he and Lauren thought they could be more powerful than Archer by stealing the program and selling it to the highest bidder."

"If they were working with Archer, why didn't *they* steal it? Why involve you and Max?" Mallory asked.

"Because Archer is insane and doesn't trust anyone. And to ensure he was the only one to control the program, a few days before the convention, he created a unique firewall around it to prevent anyone from stealing it," Jordan said. "The only way in was to hack through, and Sam needed our help. He recruited me and Max by pretending he would help us."

"The other part of his plan," Max said, "was to tell Archer we'd be there, and this would be the perfect time to fulfill his vendetta against me and take out Jordan at the same time."

"Diabolical with a capital *D*," Zack said. "Whew!"

"Yeah," Jordan said, "Sam was as big a dirt ball as Archer. While I was hacking into the program on the convention floor, Sam told Archer where to find me and Max. In the meantime, Sam was stationed backstage at one of the servers with Lauren. Once I'd hacked in, the firewall was down, allowing them instant access to the program. They copied the program onto a hard drive along with any and all evidence of my identity. They had what they needed at that point, so they erased everything from Sintinex's mainframe."

Max nodded. "Yeah. They already had a buyer for the

program. And they kept the information on Jordan's true identity as insurance."

"This is more convoluted than any telenovela I've ever watched," Zack said.

"In hindsight, Sam's story was so contrived, I can't believe I fell for it." Max tsked. "I can't believe we trusted that guy."

Jordan patted his hand. "I fell for it, too. And I don't trust anyone."

"You're both safe. And that's all that matters," Emilio said. "And the criminals are where they belong."

"I have to admit, I smiled for hours after I was told the FBI picked up Sam and Lauren at the airport." Max scoffed. "They were headed to Fiji."

"Don't suppose they'll be seeing any sand where they're going," Rafe said.

"And Archer may never get out of prison. His acts were treasonous. The government won't go easy on him," Jordan said.

"All that's over," Emilio said, smiling. "And the good news is, we've welcomed Jordan into the fold."

"Hear! Hear!" Rafe said and raised his glass.

"Woof, woof," Buck barked, and everyone laughed.

Jordan smiled. As grateful as she was to be an accepted part of this family, all the attention was still more than she could handle. She turned to Max and said in a soft voice, "Want to show me some of your famous Puerto Rican beaches?"

He kissed her. "You bet. *Vamanos*."

Max, Jordan, and Buck excused themselves and walked along the shoreline. He put his arm around her.

"You know I've never been to the ocean," Jordan said, gazing out over the blue water. "This really is paradise."

Max stepped back and looked at her. "I… I don't even know how to respond to that."

"No response necessary. Thanks for bringing me."

"I'm glad you're here." He kissed her lightly. "But I'm wondering if *you're* happy to be here. I mean, since last night, my family hasn't left you alone. Questions, talking, more questions. And, of course, feeding you as if you'd been starved for a year."

Jordan laughed. "Yeah. You're right. It's a lot. But you know what?"

He looked at her. "What?"

"When Archer had me trapped, I thought for sure I'd taken my last breath which sucked because for the first time in my life, I had something to live for—" Jordan turned to him "—awww what's that look?"

"What look?"

"That mushy sentimental look that's taking over your face."

"No look." Max straightened. "I'm listening. Go ahead."

"While we were busy trying to save your family and humanity from a global blackout—it seems I might have lost some of my defenses."

"Did you now?"

"Is that smugness I detect?"

"Not smugness. Interest. Keep going."

"What I'm trying to say, and clearly not doing a great job of, is that your family, and you, yes, especially you, have gotten to me in a way no one else has. And while I thought I could just walk away… I can't."

"So what are you saying?"

Jordan rolled her eyes. "You're gonna make me spell it out, aren't you."

Max nodded.

"I want us to be together."

"And?"

Jordan huffed out a breath. "All right. I love you. Happy?"

Max smiled and put his arm around her shoulder.

They walked along the beach for a stretch in silence.

"You have no response?" Jordan asked.

Max looked straight ahead and spoke. "You know, a week ago, I never could have imagined being with someone forever. Now... I don't think forever is going to be long enough."

He turned to face her, wrapped her in his arms, and held on tight. "I love you, Jordan Logan. Now and always."

* * * * *

Get up to 4 Free Books!

**We'll send you 2 free books from each series you try
PLUS a free Mystery Gift.**

FREE Value Over **$25**

Both the **Harlequin Intrigue®** and **Harlequin® Romantic Suspense** series
feature compelling novels filled with heart-racing action-packed romance
that will keep you on the edge of your seat.